D0817473

BOOK 2 OF THE MOURNING DOVE MYSTERIES

DEATH
OPENS A
WINDOW

MIKEL J. WILSON

This book is a work of fiction. The characters, incidents and dialogue are drawn from the author's imagination and are not to be construed as real. Any resemblance to actual events or persons, living or dead, is entirely coincidental.

MOURNING DOVE MYSTERIES: DEATH OPENS A WINDOW

Copyright ©2018 by Mikel J. Wilson.

All rights reserved.

No part of this book may be used or reproduced in any manner whatsoever without written permission except in the case of brief quotations embodied in critical articles and reviews.

Cover design by Damonza.com.

Author portrait by Dave Meyer at DaveMeyerDesign.com.
Hair by Adrian Mayorga at thecountryclubbarbers.com.

Mikel J. Wilson
555 W. Country Club Lane, C-222
Escondido, CA 92026

MIKELJWILSON.com

Paperback ISBN: 978-1-947392-38-0
Hardcover ISBN: 978-1-947392-39-7

First Edition, October 2018

Printed in the United States of America through Acorn Publishing at AcornPublishingLLC.com.

Dedicated to my BSM.

CHAPTER 1

AT THIRTY-TWO STORIES, the Godfrey Tower jutted from the Knoxville skyline like a shark fin in the Tennessee River. Unseen through the frameless exterior walls of silvery, reflective glass, a young woman on the twenty-ninth floor sat with a phone held to her ear, pretending to be on a business call as she stared out the floor-to-ceiling window behind her desk. While her colleagues busied themselves on phones or computers at the dozens of cubicles throughout the large, open office space, Angie was not contributing to the organization's productivity.

If she had looked down and across the street, the attractive brunette would've seen the unremarkable roof of the area's next-tallest building fourteen floors below her. Instead she focused on the unobstructed view of downtown and the hazy, snow-peaked mountains beyond. She imagined herself hiking below the snow-line with her new lumbersexual boyfriend and lying with him on a blanket before a tantric campfire. Angie could almost hear the crackling wood, until she realized the sound was coming from behind her.

She turned her chair around to see her boss tapping her desk with his pen. The hoary goat of a man stared her down, his pinched eyes straining to scold her through spotted glasses. "You're having a rather one-sided conversation."

Angie held up a silencing finger to her boss and made up something to say to her imaginary caller. "Thank you so much for your feedback, Mr. Watkins. We always appreciate hearing about good customer service, and I'll be sure to pass along your kudos. Okay. Take care now." She hung up the phone and greeted her boss with a smile. "I'm sorry, but I didn't hear what you said." She mimed a talking mouth with her hand. "He was talking my ear off."

Mr. Ramsey, however, did not return her smile. In fact, a look of horror sprinted across his face as something behind her snatched his attention. Before Angie could turn around to see what it was, she heard a great shattering, followed by the pelting of glass on her back and right cheek.

A dark-haired man in a brown suit flew through the window headfirst and thudded faceup onto the floor beside her. The impact against the man's back shoved the air from his lungs. He gurgled as he struggled to regain his breath – although no one could hear it over the screams of Angie and several of her co-workers. Shards of glass protruded from his head and neck, one at the base of an erratic fountain of blood that sprang from his carotid artery.

Angie, now shocked into silence, tore her eyes from the dying man and toward the broken window through which she had daydreamed just a moment earlier. Oblivious to the blood trickling from the small cuts on her own face, she took a step toward the large hole the man's body had punched into the glass wall. She poked her head outside and looked all around.

Her boss grabbed her and pulled her away from the precarious opening. "Angie, what are you doing? It's not safe!"

The young woman turned a confused face to him. "Where did he come from?"

This is a mistake. Wearing a gray suit with a paisley tie, Emory Rome fidgeted in an ill-padded chair inside the waiting room of the Law Offices of Neal and Reinhardt. *What the hell am I doing here?*

For the third or maybe fourth time, his eyes wandered around the room's cheap décor of dusty fake plants and scratched veneer furniture, seeking anything of interest. Of the half-dozen others waiting to be called, not one warranted more than a passing glance – not the bleary-eyed, fortyish man with the flask bulge in his jacket who was clutching the arms of his chair as if it were an amusement park ride; not the red-headed woman in flats with a smudge of white chalk on the elbow of her green sweater; and not the cross-legged woman in the tailored power suit who was trying to capture his attention with over-mascaraed eyes.

If I go through with it, that's it. I'm exposed.

Emory's gaze leapfrogged over the flirty-eyed woman to settle on the wall-mounted television. The breaking news story of a mysterious death at an office building held his attention for a few seconds, but it was on a local morning news program he never watched because one of the anchors irritated him.

I can't let her get away with it.

He retrieved a pill bottle from the inside pocket of his jacket and opened it. *One left.* He popped the pill into his mouth and forced it down with a swig of water from the bottle at his side.

The angular jawline and high cheekbones of the handsome twenty-three-year-old framed sunken cheeks that gave him the appearance of gritting his teeth, even when he wasn't. For the record, he was at the moment. He glanced at the ten-dollar clock on the wall. *I'm definitely going to be late. Screw it! I can't do this.* Emory ejected himself from the chair and headed for the exit.

"Mr. Rome? Emory Rome?"

He looked over his shoulder to the woman behind the desk, her long dark hair streaked by premature white. Seeing her scan the waiting room for acknowledgement, he hesitated but reversed his course. "I'm Emory."

The receptionist directed him down a short hall to an open door, through which he saw a robust man with sparse black hair sitting behind a desk and writing at a furious pace on a document clipped inside a folder. Perhaps sensing Emory's eyes upon him, the lawyer looked up, dropped his pen and rose to greet him. "Come on in." He shook Emory's hand. "Nathan Neal."

"Emory Rome."

Nathan waved to two shiny silver chairs facing his tidy desk. "Please sit down." He returned to the other side of the desk and fell back into his overstuffed chair. "You want to talk about suing your former employer for wrongful termination, correct?"

Emory removed the wool satchel strapped over his shoulder and placed it on the floor beside the chair. "Yes sir."

"Explain."

"Up until a month ago, I was a special agent with the Tennessee Bureau of Investigation."

"That's where I know you from! You're the guy responsible for that huge drug bust. What was the name of that kingpin?"

"Lonnie Hexum."

The lawyer slapped his hands together. "That's right! You're the one who busted him, right?"

Emory's face flushed. "Yes."

The lawyer grinned as if he had met a movie star. "Wasn't that one of the largest drug busts ever?"

Emory waved his hand in front of him. "No, just in the Southeast."

"Just in the..." Nathan interrupted himself with a belly laugh. "It was enough to get you all over the news! So the TBI let you go?"

Emory retrieved a document from his satchel and handed it to Nathan. "My termination papers. I served with distinction for almost two years, and I was officially released over a false allegation."

"Which was?"

"Eve Bachman, the special agent in charge, accused me of lying on a report."

"Did you?"

"No! During the course of my last investigation, I was drugged. Bachman asserted that I consumed the drug willingly."

The attorney pointed to both of them. "Just between you and me."

"I didn't take it knowingly or by choice! She was just using that as an opportunity to get rid of me."

"Okay, before we get deep into the details, tell me what you want. Are you looking for a financial settlement? Reinstatement? Revenge?"

"Mr. Neal, I loved my job. It's who I am, and it was taken from me."

"So reinstatement. We should also seek compensatory damages, just to get their attention."

"I don't care about the money."

"But they will." Nathan plopped his forearms onto his desk and scooched his body forward. "So what's the real reason your boss wanted you gone?"

Emory looked to the variegated carpet at his feet and sighed, uncertain how to phrase the answer. His eyes returned to the lawyer, and he took a deep breath.

Inside Mourning Dove Investigations, Jeff Woodard pushed open a hidden door and stepped into his office from the spiral staircase that connected to his apartment on the second floor. With walls adorned by wrought-iron sconces, gothic art and high bookshelves, the room would not have been out of place inside a 19th Century manse overlooking the foggy moors – except for one quirky feature. A smooth tree trunk was anchored to the floor behind the desk, and from it, two crooked branches extended to adjacent walls.

The tall private investigator glided over the exquisite map of the world painted on the floor toward an oil painting on the opposite wall. He pulled the frame down two inches, which triggered open a hidden door to the reception area – a similar room with its own artificial tree. Jeff brandished a perfect smile when he saw a beautiful young woman with ebony skin and short black hair sitting at the larger of the two desks in the room. "Good morning."

Virginia Kennon's eyes darted from her computer screen to the tan man with thick, wavy brown hair. "I know why you're smiling."

Jeff lowered his lips and raised an eyebrow. "I don't know what you're talking about." He put his hands on his hips and surveyed the room. "Does everything look okay?"

"He's seen the place before." Virginia petted the purring bobcat curled up on her desk. "You know, I don't think I've ever seen you nervous."

"And I'm not now. I'm anxious. There's a difference. This is a big deal for us." Jeff gave himself a glance in the antique mirror on the wall before focusing on his smirking partner. "For the business."

"Speaking of which, four potential clients called for appointments this morning." She retrieved four strips of blue sticky paper from her desk.

"Did you ask how they heard about us?"

"Of course, I did." Virginia walked from behind her desk to hand him the messages. "Three of them saw the new ad."

"Hot damn!" Jeff threw his arms around Virginia and swung her around. "It's already working! I told you it would bring in business. We're finally going to start making money."

"I hope you're right." Virginia returned to her chair.

"I am." Jeff glanced at the Lenzkirch clock on the wall. "Hey, where is our cash cow?"

Emory parked his white crossover on the street in Knoxville's Old City – an area that had served as the red light district a century earlier – and stared at the two-story, brown-brick building half a block away. His eyes moved to the one-story business with which it shared a party wall, and two items caught his attention. One was the colorful banner splayed across the front wall of the smaller building announcing a going-out-of-business sale for a comic book store. The other was a homeless man sitting on the sidewalk with a guitar in his lap.

What am I doing here? He closed his eyes for a few seconds before exiting the vehicle. *Let's get this over with.*

The morning sun did little to warm the mid-February air. Emory jammed his hands into the pockets of his black field jacket and squeezed his arms to his torso while his visible breath billowed to either side of his face. As he walked he heard an unrecognizable country song strumming from the strings of the homeless man's guitar. *He's young. Is he homeless or just a hipster?* Emory pulled out his wallet when he reached the singer in dingy clothes. "What's your name?"

Continuing to play, the man looked up with Prussian-blue eyes through drooping tousles of black hair. "Phineas."

"Phineas, I'm Emory. I'm going to give you two cards." He showed him a gift card he had received over the holidays for a restaurant chain. "This is to get you something to eat." He nodded toward the west. "I think there's one about three blocks from here." He dropped it into the hat and pulled out a business card. "This is the number to a woman who can help you get on your feet again. She's a social worker."

The homeless man stopped playing. "I don't need charity."

Emory tapped his foot on the sidewalk. "Then why the hat?"

"Getting paid for performing, I get to call myself a professional musician."

Emory placed the business card inside the hat. "In case you change your mind."

He continued to the brown-brick building, past a window with a painted sign that read, "Mourning Dove Investigations." He stepped up to the door and turned the brass knob.

Jeff's bright green eyes sparkled brighter when he saw Emory walk through the door, but he forced his face into a stern expression. He nodded toward the clock. "Late on your first day."

Virginia shot Jeff a dirty look. "You just got—"

"So why are you late?" Jeff crossed his arms as if expecting to be told a lie.

Emory hung his jacket on the vintage standing coat rack. "I had an appointment already scheduled. I told you that when I agreed to come on here, and I said I might be late."

"Still, not the best first impression."

"We had our first impression a month ago." Emory petted the bobcat. "Good morning, Bobbie."

The bobcat jumped from the desk to the artificial tree, climbing to the flap-covered opening that led to Jeff's upstairs apartment.

Jeff uncrossed his arms and circled Emory. "Speaking of impressions, you're representing Mourning Dove Investigations now."

"Yes. And?"

"We have a certain image to uphold." Jeff pointed his thumb to himself and Virginia, who rolled her eyes. "Now that we've made you a partner, you do too."

"What are you talking about?"

"Your clothes. You need to stop dressing like a government agent."

"Don't listen to him." Virginia came to Emory with a small box and hugged him. "Welcome aboard. This is for you."

"What is it?"

"Your new business cards." The phone on Virginia's desk rang. "I better get that."

"Thanks for the cards." Emory headed toward the door to Jeff's office. "So do I have a desk yet?"

Jeff blocked him. "Where are you going? This is your office."

"This is the reception area." Emory nodded to Virginia's desk. "Slash, Virginia's office."

Jeff placed his hands on Emory's shoulders and faced him toward the tiny desk in the corner by the tree trunk. "That's for you."

"That end table?"

"That's not an end table. It's a desk. Your desk."

Emory crept toward the desk and picked up the only object on it – a framed document. He glanced at the text and turned back to Jeff. "Is this a joke?"

"No, that's your PI license. It came yesterday, and I framed it for you."

"I'm not talking about that. I'm talking about the desk. My so-called office."

"Oh my god!" The two men's conversation was interrupted by an outburst from Virginia, whose phone conversation was taking a turn for the intense. "What happened?"

Jeff turned his attention back to his new business partner. "Look, I'm sorry, but it's not like we have unlimited space here."

"There's a lot more room in your office. We could fit another regular-sized desk in there and share—"

Jeff signaled him to stop. "Whoa! I don't share an office."

"What about when I have a client?"

"When *we* have a client, we'll meet in my office." He placed a hand on Emory's back. "Look, I know it's not ideal, but it's more than adequate. You just need to personalize it. Put a couple of pictures on your desk."

Emory returned the framed license to the desktop. "That should give me just enough room for my business cards."

Virginia hung up the phone. "Oh my god."

Jeff plopped his butt on her desk. "What is it?"

"That was Becky Melton."

"Who's Becky Melton?" asked Emory.

"Becky Melton," repeated Jeff. "You mean Becky Rand? Your homophobic best friend from high school?"

"She used to be Becky Rand. You know good and well she got married like four years ago. And she's not homophobic. She just didn't like you."

Emory stood and wagged his finger between his partners. "I thought you two were best friends since high school."

Virginia side-eyed her seated partner. "We ebb and flow."

Jeff crossed his arms. "Oh whatever."

"Becky married while I was in the Marines, and I've only seen her a couple of times since I got out. The last time was at a Fourth of July party."

"Enough backstory." Jeff slapped his thigh. "What were you oh-my-godding about?"

"Her husband died."

Emory was the first to offer condolences. "I'm so sorry."

"I have to go." Virginia rose from her chair and grabbed her purse.

Jeff pushed off the desk. "Why?"

"Because she's my friend, and she asked for me."

"I just mean you haven't seen her in almost seven months, and she calls you the morning her husband dies? Don't you find that odd?"

"No. I. Don't."

Emory asked, "How did he die?"

"He crashed through the twenty-ninth-story window in a building downtown."

"He jumped out a window?" asked Jeff.

"No. She said he crashed *into* the building." They don't know if it's an accident or suicide or what." Virginia headed for the door but stopped once her hand touched the knob. "Guys, we need to look into this for her."

Jeff clapped his hands together. "Did she want to hire us?"

"Not exactly."

"What does that mean?"

"Her husband worked for the TVA, and she works at a museum. They don't have any money, so I know she wouldn't even think to ask for our help."

Jeff shook his head. "Virginia, I'm really sorry about her loss, but we have paying clients asking for our services. You want us to put them on hold to investigate a case we won't get paid for and that we haven't even been asked to take?"

Virginia looked him in the eyes. "*I'm* asking you."

Jeff broke from her stare and grabbed Emory's arm. "This is a three-way partnership now, so we have a tiebreaker. Emory, do we take the nonpaying job that no one has asked us to take, or do we serve one of the potentially loyal and well-paying future clients begging for our help?"

Virginia rolled her eyes. "No one begged."

Jeff raised his index finger. "No trying to sway the jury."

"What do you think you were doing?"

Jeff waved off her protest and flashed a coercive smile. "Emory, the choice is yours."

CHAPTER 2

ONCE THE THREE partners of Mourning Dove Investigations stepped out of Emory's car, their heads turned toward the Godfrey Tower two blocks away. Rectangular with no slopes or balconies, the building reflected the late-morning sun on the side facing the street. Emory visored his eyes with his hand and pointed to a broken window on the twenty-ninth floor. "There it is."

Virginia responded, "I see it."

"Let's just get this over with," grumbled Jeff, glaring at Emory. "I still can't believe you sided with her."

"Aren't you the least bit curious how a man crashed through a window that high from the outside with no obvious way to get there?"

Jeff started walking down the sidewalk. "Moderately."

Emory nodded to the fifteen-story building across the street. "The nearest structure is too far away and too short for him to have come from there."

Virginia looked up and down the street. "No cranes either."

Emory followed his partners as he continued scanning the perimeter. "Virginia, how much do you know about Becky's husband?"

"I only saw him a couple of times. The first time I met him, I was surprised because he wasn't anyone I would picture with Becky. She always dated athletic guys, and Corey was more chess club than varsity. He was really cute but thin and no taller than me. Plus, he was like nine years older than her." Virginia smiled. "I remember he was also funny as hell. Everyone around him seemed to enjoy his company." She pointed to Jeff. "You two probably would've become friends if you had met."

Jeff shook his head. "Too much work. Two funny guys, always competing to top each other? I prefer spending time with someone like Emory."

The newbie PI huffed. "I do have a sense of humor, you know."

Jeff smirked. "Let's make finding it our next case."

Virginia slapped Jeff on the forearm as they passed a bus stop. "That's not nice."

From behind them Emory would've responded, but something else caught his attention – a picture of himself in a poster ad on the side of a bus stop. The header in the ad read, "Here to help you," and the text below it stated, "Mourning Dove Investigations welcomes TBI hero Emory Rome!" Beneath that was a list of investigative specialties, including murder, missing persons, fraud and blackmail.

Stunned into gawking stillness, Emory could feel his face flushing. "Oh my god."

His partners backtracked to see what had captured his attention, and Jeff grinned. "My ad!"

Emory poked the billboard. "You did this?"

"Me and Virginia. Surprise!"

"How could you feature me in an ad without asking me first? And where did you get that picture?"

Jeff smiled at the photo of Emory leaning against a tree wearing a brown leather jacket, a cowboy hat and a sexy look that, knowing Emory, was unintentional. "Your mom sent it to me."

"You and my mom correspond?"

"Just the once. I asked her for a photo, and she said this was her favorite."

"You could've asked me."

"Yes, and I'd still be waiting."

Virginia grabbed her phone from her purse and took a picture of Emory next to the ad. "What's your issue with it?"

Emory gestured toward the picture. "For one, I was eighteen when that picture was taken, and I look like a dork."

Jeff grimaced at him. "That was five years ago. You haven't changed that much. By the way, do you still have that outfit?"

"Of course not!"

"Too bad. It's hot."

Emory ignored his comment and returned his attention to Virginia. "Another reason is I don't think we should leverage my service with the TBI for profit."

She shook her head. "That part's not up for debate."

Jeff agreed. "Look, we granted you full partner status without any financial investment on your part. Your experience is your capital, and we need to exploit that."

Emory frowned at them both. "Fine. I guess one little ad isn't that big a deal." His remark elicited an unexpected laugh from Jeff, while Virginia turned her face away from him. "What? Jeff, what is it?"

"I used the reward money from the Algarotti case to launch an aggressive new ad campaign."

"When you say *aggressive*—"

"I mean we have ads going up all over Knoxville and online. You'll be even more famous than you were before, and that halo's going to spread to the agency."

Although delivered as good news, Jeff's words intensified the horror on Emory's face.

"I want Mourning Dove Investigations to be the biggest detective agency in Tennessee, but I don't just want to compete with other PIs. I want to compete with the police. With the TBI. Hell, the FBI maybe. I want us to solve cases before they do. To take the cases they can't, or won't, solve. To be the go-to agency for victims of crime. Sure, call the police first, but Mourning Dove Investigations is your second call. We'll be the first step in privatizing criminal investigations." Jeff placed an arm around Virginia and one around Emory. "Now let's go crack this pro bono puzzle, and maybe we can move on to a real case by lunch."

Virginia told him, "Jeff, do not make Becky feel like less of a client because she can't pay. I want you to treat this like any other case."

"You call it a case. I call it charity."

"I'm serious."

"Do you think her husband had life insurance?"

Virginia insisted as they entered the building, "We're not asking for money."

Moments later, when the elevator doors opened on the twenty-ninth floor, the trio of investigators could already see the scene of the potential crime through the paned-glass wall that separated the office space from the hallway. While police questioned employees and cataloged the arena, the body stiffened on the floor in the center of a yellow-taped perimeter that included the broken window.

The three were about to enter the office when a policewoman stopped them. "You can't come in here."

Virginia was the first to speak up. "Officer, we're looking for Becky Melton, the victim's wife."

The officer centered herself in the doorway. "Unless you were here at the time of the incident and haven't given your statement yet, you're not coming in."

"Emory!" A grinning police detective greeted him at the door. "I figured the TBI would be here once I found out the victim worked at the TVA."

Emory shook his hand. "Lester, how are you?"

"Excellent. Who are your friends?"

He froze for a second as he debated whether to admit he was no longer with the TBI. "My partners."

Lester squinted at them. "The TBI is doing threesomes now?"

Emory pointed to Jeff. "He's actually a trainee. Virginia here is my partner."

Jeff sneered at Emory, displaying his displeasure at the demotion. "I'm learning so much."

Virginia stepped in front of him to talk to Lester. "Is the victim's wife here?"

"Yeah, she insisted on coming down." The police detective pointed to a wooden door beyond a quadrant of cubicles. "We put her up in that office over there."

"I'll go talk to her."

"She's pretty messed up. We didn't want her to see the body, but it's hard to hide."

As Virginia walked away, Lester gave Emory a light punch on the shoulder. "So what happened to your other partner?"

"I needed a change."

"I hear that. Come on, let me show you the victim." Lester led them to the body, their path littered with papers blown from the desks by the steady wind whistling through the new opening. He lifted the yellow tape for them and stopped at the edge of a pool of blood that surrounded the victim's head like a sanguine aura. "His name is Corey Melton. Thirty-four, married, no kids. The man who witnessed it kept saying he just flew into the window. Out of nowhere."

"What time?" asked Emory.

"Eight-forty-five."

While Jeff inspected every inch of the body without touching it, Emory took notes and pictures of the victim with his phone. "He's a small guy. What, maybe five-foot-six?"

The detective nodded and continued debriefing them on all he knew. "He's the manager of generation resources for the TVA. He's in the corporate branch office on the fifth floor of this building."

Jeff pointed to Corey's palms. "His hands are red."

Lester laughed. "That's probably blood, trainee." He looked at Emory as if hoping he would join him in laughing at the obvious observation. Emory did but stopped when he saw Jeff glaring at him.

"I'm not talking about the blood." Jeff pointed to a rough red line across the width of both palms. "It looks like burns, like he held onto something hot."

Emory zoomed in on the hands and took pictures. "You're right." He headed to the broken window, followed by Jeff, and each took a position on either side of the hole. They stuck their heads out to look down, up and toward both sides. "Where did he come from?"

Although not close to the window, Lester took a step backwards. "Guys please. You're making me nervous."

The men stepped away from the window, and Emory's eyes ping-ponged between the body and the opening. "Any idea how he got here?"

"None whatsoever. Someone joked he was a human pumpkin."

Jeff shook his head. "I don't get it."

"You know, pumpkin chunkin' – like someone catapulted him up here." Lester mimed a catapult with his arms.

"What the hell are you doing here?!"

The three men turned toward the door to see the profane inquisitor, and Emory's shoulders slumped at the sight of his former TBI partner.

CHAPTER 3

VIRGINIA KNOCKED ON the office door but entered without waiting for an invitation. Becky Melton, her narrow back to the door and blonde curls resting on drooped shoulders, spoke in the monotone of someone teetering on exhaustion as she recounted the last time she saw her husband alive. "He had to be at work an hour earlier than me, so he was always up and dressed first. The last time I saw him was through the shower door. He liked watching me shower."

One of the officers in the cramped room moved to intercept Virginia. "Miss, you can't be in here."

"Virginia!" Becky's voice sparked to life, and she pushed herself out of the chair.

As the new widow ambled toward her, arms outstretched, tears ran from her blue eyes down the dried channels of previous flows. Virginia embraced her, allowing her a moment of emotional release. "I'm so sorry, Becky. Officers, could you give us a few minutes?"

The officers grimaced at each other but complied. The last one out the door gave her the "five minutes" sign before leaving them alone.

Virginia reiterated her condolences as she eased her embrace. "Can you tell me what happened?"

Becky lifted her puffy cheek from Virginia's breast and threw up her hands. "I don't know. He left for work, and about an hour later, the police called."

"Do you have any idea how he ended up on the outside of that window?"

"Corey's deathly afraid of heights. He always keeps the blinds closed in his office because he can't even look out a fifth-floor window without getting dizzy."

"Do the police have any ideas?"

"They're not coming right out and saying it, but I can tell they think he killed himself." Becky looked her friend in the eyes. "Virginia, there is absolutely no way Corey committed suicide. He wouldn't have done that."

Virginia placed an arm around her shoulders and assured her, "I'm going to find out what happened."

Becky's eyes popped wide open. "What do you mean?"

"I've already discussed it with my partners—"

Becky shook her head. "No. No, I can't afford to pay you."

"This one's on the house."

"I can't let you do that."

"We insist."

"*We?* Not just you?"

Virginia smiled at Becky's underestimation of her offer. "I don't do field work. I brought my friend Jeff Woodard. You remember him."

"That skinny preppy from high school who talked you into going into business with him?"

"He's not skinny anymore, and he's an excellent private investigator. Plus, we just took on a new partner who was with the TBI."

Wayne Buckwald's round, ruddy face expressed outrage, but his eyes gleamed with the excitement of a sadistic child shaking a jar of lightning bugs. He repeated his question, stressing every third word. "What the hell are you doing here?"

Emory could feel the heat emanating from his face as his brain scrambled for words to say. "Wayne... How are you?"

"Why are you two standing in my crime scene?"

Glancing at Wayne and Emory, Lester forced a laugh in an apparent attempt at easing the tension before the air snapped. "Were you two assigned to the same case? Clerical error?"

Wayne lifted the yellow tape and stepped within two feet of Emory. "He wasn't assigned to any case because he's no longer with the TBI."

Lester's rosacea-stained cheeks dropped. His eyes grew to circles of confusion. "I don't understand. Emory?"

Seconds of silence answered before Jeff spoke up for his tongue-tied partner. "We're private investigators working for the victim's wife."

The police detective inspected Emory's face. "Is this true?"

Emory forced his eyes from Wayne to Lester. "It's true."

Lester's face hardened. "You should've told me."

Emory opened his mouth to apologize, but Wayne interrupted. "I'll give you and the missus here three seconds to get out of here before I charge you with impersonating a state officer, tampering with a crime scene and interfering with an investigation."

Emory and Jeff looked at each other, and Wayne pointed at the exit. "Get!"

In silence, Emory slipped under the yellow tape, followed by Jeff.

"Oh Emory." Wayne grinned when the PIs turned around to face him again. "Before you leave, I want to introduce you to my new partner, Steve Linders."

Until Wayne pointed him out, Emory hadn't noticed anyone standing next to his former partner. A bear of a man with a shaved head and a sweet face half-framed by a thick but shaped beard, Steve smiled and nodded to him. "Nice to meet you."

"Don't be nice to them! Crime is shit, and PIs are the dung beetles. They wallow in it, and we clean it up." Wayne patted his new partner on the back. "Steve here is totally by-the-book. A real straight-shooter. Straight and narrow."

"Okay, Wayne, I get it. You can stop now."

Wayne laughed. "Oh, I ain't nowhere near ready to stop. You always hated PIs. Now look at you. You are what you hated. Pathetic."

Fists cocked, Jeff was about to lunge at Wayne, but Emory stopped him with a hand to the chest. "Let's go."

After several tense seconds, Jeff relaxed his hands. The two PIs withdrew from the crime scene and returned to the hallway.

Emory looked through the glass wall at the TBI special agents conversing with the police. "What about Virginia?"

Jeff shook his head. "She's just comforting a friend. She'll be fine. Hopefully, she can get some worthwhile information from her."

"Well, at least you got what you wanted." Emory stepped in front of the elevator and stared at it as if the door would open without pushing a button.

"What do you mean?"

"You don't even want to take this case."

"Are you kidding? Now I want it out of spite." Jeff jabbed the elevator button to go up. "We're going to solve it first so we can cram it down that smug asshole's throat."

"What are you doing?"

"Going to the roof before we're banned from there." Jeff glanced at his partner. "Hey, are you okay?"

"Yeah. Fine. I'm just not used to being kicked out of a crime scene."

"It's irritating, but this won't be the first time. You'll get used to it."

Emory growled, "I don't want to get used to it."

The elevator doors opened, and the PIs stepped inside. "Why is the TBI here anyway?"

Emory hit the button for the top floor. "Because the victim is an employee of the Tennessee Valley Authority. It's a federally owned corporation, so any potential felony that might be linked to it is investigated by the FBI. However, in recent years, the federal government has been pulling back on its oversight of the company, so the TBI has taken over investigations."

They exited the elevator on the top floor and climbed the single flight of stairs to the roof. To their good fortune, the police had not yet cordoned it off.

Emory took a moment to snap pictures of every feature of the rooftop – from the expansive seven-foot ventilation system at its center and the sole access point through which they had just come to the empty flagpole jutting upward forty feet near one edge and the most prominent feature – a huge billboard that bisected one corner of the roof. The far side of the billboard protruded beyond the vertical planes of the building, making the hair product ad splayed within its frame more visible to drivers heading downtown.

Emory followed Jeff toward the side with the broken window, scanning the silicone flooring along the way for any evidence. As they neared the edge of the building, he stumbled and fell onto the three-foot-high metal railing that bordered the roof.

Jeff grabbed him and pulled him back from the edge. "Are you okay?"

"I stepped on something." Emory glanced back for the culprit in his misstep, and he saw a translucent object in the path he had taken. "It's just a rock."

For extra security, Emory grabbed the barren flagpole positioned two feet from the railing before poking his head over again.

Jeff looked over as well and pointed to the broken window. "There it is."

"No protrusions in the wall. It's straight down to the sidewalk. How could he have fallen from here and then horizontally into that window?"

"Well, the wind certainly couldn't have pushed him into the building."

"No." Emory backed away from the railing. "Assuming Corey Melton did jump from here, he was maybe two feet from the building on the way down. He weighed about 140 pounds, and the glass curtain walls in this building are laminated and tempered, requiring more horizontal force to crack than could've been exerted by his body if he had encountered a strong gust on the way down. It would've taken a tornado to push him through the glass from that short of a distance."

Jeff thought for a moment. "What if he jumped out, away from the building? He could've been maybe six feet from the side on the way down, which would've given more time to build momentum if the wind pushed him into the window."

"The wind still would've had to be super-strong, faster than the rate he was falling. No, I don't see how he could've originated from here."

"Then how did he do it?"

Emory looked around before answering. "I don't know. Maybe the autopsy will tell us more. Until then, I suggest we proceed as if he were murdered while the trail's still hot. If it turns out he wasn't, nothing lost."

"Except our time, effort and money." Jeff pulled a vibrating phone from his pocket and answered. "Hi Virginia. You're on speakerphone."

Virginia spoke from the hallway near the elevator. "I'm going to drive Becky home in her car. Can I call you later to come pick me up?"

"Of course." A biting gust of wind flew into Jeff's unbuttoned pea coat, giving him the momentary appearance of hulking out. He clenched the lapels together. "What did you find out?"

Virginia saw Becky leaving the office and heading toward her. "I'll tell you later. What's that noise?"

"It's the wind. We're up on the roof looking for evidence that he jumped from here."

"There's no way."

"You never know. Some people are good at hiding depression."

Virginia held up an index finger to an approaching Becky and walked further away from her so she could talk about her husband. "It's not that. He had a major fear of heights. He would've never gone to the roof of a skyscraper."

"Then maybe someone forced him up here and pushed him off."

Emory shook his head and interrupted their conversation. "That still doesn't explain how he fell sideways into the glass wall."

Jeff grunted. "The truth is, we're at a loss, and that really pisses me off."

CHAPTER 4

"THEY'RE LEAVING." JEFF held the door open a crack to watch Wayne and his new partner leave the TVA office on the fifth floor and waited to hear the elevator doors close. "Okay, let's go."

Emory followed Jeff from the men's room. "How are we going to get them to talk to us?"

"What do you mean?"

"We can't make them answer our questions." Emory tsked, unaware of the tic he had picked up from his father.

Jeff tapped Emory's chest. "You know, that badge you wore was a crutch. In my years as a PI—"

"You've been a PI for two years."

"Thus the *s* on the end of *year*. As I was saying, on the cases I've investigated, I never had the luxury of government-backed coercion to get information from people."

"Then how do you make them talk?"

"I don't make them. I help them realize they want to tell me what they know."

Emory huffed. "From what I've seen of your interrogation technique, you just wing it."

Jeff continued walking. "Maybe it seems that way to the untrained eye."

As soon as he followed Jeff into the TVA office, Emory felt

the weight of the air. The layout was similar to the space where the victim had died twenty-four stories higher, but a thick miasma of grief flowed around the maze of desks, cubicles and occasional walled offices. The staff was segregated into bands of two or three or four, peppered with disbelievers, mourners and condolers. A few of them shot curious glances to the PIs walking past, but no one stopped to question them.

Jeff whispered to his partner, "Ever feel like you walked into the wrong funeral?"

The buzz of multiple conversations muzzled the ringing phones destined for voicemail until one voice rose to dominance. "People!" called a fortyish blond man near the door to one of the offices. "If I could have your attention!"

As members of the staff circled around the speaker, so did the PIs, and Emory moved close enough to see his badge. "Darren Gleeson, director of generation resources."

Jeff crossed his arms and covered his mouth. "Our victim was manager of generation resources."

"This is probably his boss."

"And the one we need to talk to."

Although accentuated with wrinkles that only deepened his handsomeness, Darren's face was nevertheless blank. "I know this has been a difficult morning." He faced the floor, as if looking for a dropped emotion. "Our team has been dealt a terrible blow. We're all grieving, but the best thing we can do is work through it. Our grief will still be with us at five o'clock." He waited for a moment before his staff's inaction seemed to prompt a statement of clarity. "Let's get back to work."

While the others sauntered to their desks, the PIs followed the tall man to his office. Jeff called out before he could shut the door. "Darren, could we have a word with you?"

Darren kept his hand on the knob. "Who are you?"

Although he hadn't moved to allow him entry, Jeff wormed

through the doorway. "We're private investigators, hired by Corey Melton's widow."

"Becky hired you?" Darren stepped aside to allow Emory inside. As he passed, Emory noticed the man's sturdy frame. "Yes."

Darren ushered them to the guest chairs before sitting at his desk. "How is she holding up?"

"Distraught, as you can imagine." Jeff shook his head. "Hearing that her husband's been murdered—"

"Murdered?" Darren's eyes widened at the word. "I just spoke to the TBI. They said it was suicide or an accident. I figured it couldn't be suicide, but murder?"

Why does he do that? With a side-glance toward Jeff, Emory offered a clarifying statement. "Murder is just another possibility. The truth is that we don't know for certain yet how he died."

Jeff scowled at him before turning his attention back to Darren. "But based on some clues we've already discovered, we're confident it was murder."

Emory's eyes followed the smell of the Starbucks coffee and wrapped sausage sandwich on the desk. "Oh, we apologize for interrupting your breakfast."

Darren shrugged it off. "I had to drop my car off at the shop, so I didn't have time to eat at home. I thought I'd be able to when I got in. Little did I know what I would be walking in to."

Emory asked, "Do you know if Corey had any enemies or someone who might've wished him harm?"

"Everyone here liked him. Of course, we sometimes upset people in our catchment area."

"What do you mean?" asked Jeff. "What was he working on?"

Darren leaned back, almost tapping the large window behind him with the top of his dark walnut chair. The sunlight darkened his features and silhouetted the back of the seat. "I don't know if I should be talking to you about official TVA business. Some of the information is sensitive, and you're ultimately civilians."

Jeff slapped his desk. "You know, Darren, your staff thinks you're an asshole."

"Jeff!" Emory blurted, appalled by his remark.

He wasn't the only one. Darren's face teetered between anger and shock. "Why do you say that?"

Jeff waved his arm toward the door. "They're out there devastated because someone they worked with and saw every day has suddenly died and under mysterious circumstances. Did you console them? No. You told them to get back to work."

"I'm trying to protect their jobs. We're working against a negative budget and a shrinking staff. Every department is having to meet higher productivity levels."

"How productive do you think they're going to be until they get closure for this tragedy? How many of them are wondering if his death was work-related and if they might be next?"

"Why would they think that?"

"We can't tell you that without knowing what he was working on." Jeff placed his forearms on the edge of Darren's desk. "We can help you, but you need to help us first."

Darren shook his head and pointed at them both. "Just do me a favor and get to the bottom of this quickly."

Emory wanted to smile at Jeff, but he remained stoic. *He did it. He got him to ask for our help.*

Darren pulled up a file on his laptop and turned the screen toward the PIs so they could see a rendering of windmills dotting a small mountainside. "Corey was working on a windfarm we're planning to build in Brume Wood."

Emory examined the rendering for a motive. "What's sensitive about a windfarm?"

"Do you know what we do here?" When Emory nodded, Darren got out of his chair and walked to a wall, where a large photo of a dam hung. "Franklin Roosevelt established the Tennessee Valley Authority in 1933 as part of his New Deal to pull America out of the Depression. It gave people in the country's most poverty-stricken region jobs, and it brought electricity to Appalachia. Damming rivers for hydropower, like the Norris Dam." He pointed at the picture. "Back then that was enough. It's not anymore."

Darren returned to his chair. "The TVA is deep in debt, and there are two primary reasons why. The number of customers in our service area has ballooned to nine million people, so we can no longer generate enough power to meet the demand. On top of that we've been mandated by Congress to increase the amount of electricity we get from green technology. To satisfy the demand and the mandate, we've had to import electricity from windfarms in other states. If the TVA is going to survive, we have to start producing our own green energy right here in Tennessee."

"What was Mr. Melton's role?" Emory held up his phone to take a picture of the rendering. "May I?"

Darren nodded his permission. "Corey was in charge of determining the optimal location for the windfarm and then securing the land for it."

Jeff asked, "When you say *secure*..."

"Once he decided on a suitable tract of land, he purchased the private properties within that tract."

Jeff opened his hands. "And if the owners didn't want to sell?"

"We use eminent domain to oblige compliance. The land—" Darren was interrupted by a knock on the door. "Come in." A slight, middle-aged man with half-moon glasses and dark, thinning hair entered. "Gentlemen, this is Frank Belcher. Frank, these are private investigators looking into Corey's death."

The man in the doorway pursed his face, deepening the lines of his forehead and the corners of his eyes. "Private investigators?"

"What do you need?" Darren scratched the edge of his contoured sideburns.

Frank retreated. "I'll come back."

"What is it, Frank?"

"I'm making copies of Corey's files for the TBI, but there's some sensitive information I'm not sure we should share."

"Give them what they want. It's the TBI for god's sake." As soon as Frank closed the door, Darren turned his attention back to the PIs. "I appointed Frank the interim manager this morning."

Emory tilted his head. "Replacing Mr. Melton? That was fast."

"The role is too important to leave vacant for even a day. I have people on my ass... Look, I really have a lot of work to get to."

Emory rose from his chair. "We understand. Could we have a look at Mr. Melton's office?"

"Why do you need to see his office?"

Jeff answered for him. "If it was suicide, maybe he left a note."

Darren tilted his head. "Two doors down on the right. Before you go, I want you to know that Corey wasn't just an employee. I considered him a friend. If someone did murder him, I want you to find out who."

Jeff followed his partner from the office and whispered, "I wonder how many of those property owners resisted their obliged compliance."

"We should find out." Emory pointed to a closed wooden door with Corey Melton's name on it.

Jeff twisted the knob and found Frank Belcher seated at the desk, pulling a flash drive from the computer. "Are we interrupting?"

Frank looked over his rims at them. "What are you doing here?"

Jeff answered, "Darren asked us to look around the office for any potential clues. Your turn."

Frank stood and held up the flash drive. "Corey's files for the TBI."

Jeff told him, "We're going to need a copy of those." When Frank's mouth opened in apparent protest, the PI added, "Darren's orders."

"I have another flash drive in my desk." With that, Frank left the investigators alone in the small office – about half the size of Darren Gleeson's.

"Close the door, and keep lookout," Jeff ordered before he hurried around the desk.

Even as he asked, "Why?" Emory shut the door to a crack just wide enough for one eye to see through.

"So I can look around for the 'suicide note.'" Jeff put air quotes around the last two words and began rummaging through the desk drawers.

"People who leave a suicide note tend to put it where it's easily found, not buried in a cluttered drawer."

"Man, you have a lot to learn about cover stories."

"We shouldn't be doing this without a warrant."

"We can't get warrants. Remember?"

"Which is why we shouldn't be doing this."

Jeff popped his head up from behind the desk. "Damn it, Emory! Throw away the rules from your last job. This is how we solve cases." He continued his search. "Besides, the boss gave us permission to look around."

"Then why am I on lookout?"

"To keep you occupied while I do the dirty work."

"You're ridiculous." Emory rolled his eyes and stepped away from the door. He scanned the room, taking a mental note of everything within the space – fluorescent overhead lighting, a large window behind the desk with the blinds closed, a chair behind the desk and one in front of it, generic artwork on the walls and a tall wooden bookcase against the wall at the side of the desk. Emory headed for the bookcase.

Jeff opened the last drawer. "I'm finding nothing. This guy had to have the most boring job ever, which means he had to be boring. I don't know why Virginia thinks he was funny."

Among the books, pictures and knickknacks on the shelves,

Emory found an item of interest. "What on Earth is that?" He pointed to an animal skeleton mounted on a piece of driftwood.

His hand still in the drawer, Jeff jerked his head back to see. "Are those real bones?"

Emory nodded. The exaggerated curvature of the skeleton's spine met a large skull with four primary fangs on one end and a long tail on the other. "I think it's a possum."

"I've heard of eating roadkill, but to put it on display? That's disgusting."

"I doubt this was roadkill. No broken bones."

"That's even worse. Whoa! Please tell me this guy didn't have any kids."

"What is it?"

From the drawer, Jeff pulled a crude eight-inch doll made from chicken bones and twine. "That possum is no longer the most disgusting thing in this room."

Emory took the doll and held it up to the possum skeleton. "Was this doll his amateurish attempt to do something like this?"

Closing the drawer, Jeff stood and inspected both sets of bones. "Well, that's a freaky aspiration. Seriously, who was this guy?"

CHAPTER 5

A FLAX-COLORED COMPACT pulled onto the cement driveway of a small blue-paneled house on a nondescript street. Virginia stepped out of the driver's seat and met Becky Melton on the other side. "Your car is making a funky noise, especially going uphill. I know it's a bad time to bring it up, but you need to get it checked out. I can do it if you'd like."

Becky waved off her concern and trudged up the walkway to the front door of her house. "It's been doing that since last week. The damn tire actually fell off when I went over a speed bump in the Walmart parking lot."

"You're lucky you weren't on the interstate."

"I know. The mechanic there said the car's fine though – no damage to the axle."

Virginia unlocked the door to Becky's house. "How could it just fall off?"

"Don't know."

Virginia helped her friend to the spinach-green futon in the living room. "Can I get you anything?"

Becky buried her fingers in her blonde locks. "You don't have to babysit me."

Virginia sat next to her. "I'm not leaving you alone."

"I won't be alone for long. Corey's parents are driving in from Memphis."

"Where are your parents?"

"Trying to catch a flight back from Cancun. They're on their second honeymoon." Becky's eyes dropped to the Berber carpet. "We never even took our first honeymoon. We were so broke." She allowed herself a gentle laugh. "Of course, not much has changed." She looked at Virginia. "You should get to work. I need you to prove Corey didn't commit suicide."

Virginia waited a second to respond. "Becky, forgive me for asking this, but are you sure he didn't?"

Becky jabbed the air between them with her index finger. "I know my husband. He had no reason to want to die!"

"Okay. I had to ask." Virginia texted Jeff to ask for a ride.

Becky heaved a great sigh. "How did he end up outside that window? He was so scared of heights. When we went to Gatlinburg last summer, I actually coaxed him into taking the Sky Lift. He panicked as soon as it took off. He kept his eyes closed the entire ride and sweated through his jacket by the time we reached the top. We had to Uber down the mountain. I felt so bad for making him do it, and he was completely embarrassed. That's what prompted him to try getting some help for it."

"He was seeing a therapist?"

Becky nodded. "He was seeing Randy Graham, a counselor at the Mountain Light Holistic Center."

"What's that?"

"It's kind of a New Age treatment spa. I go there for the yoga classes."

"I didn't know you did yoga."

Becky touched her waist. "I know I've gained some weight since I last saw you."

"That's not what I meant. I was just thinking we need to hang out more, and that's something we could do together. I go to this great temple not far from here."

Becky waved off the invitation. "I like where I go."

Virginia waited a few seconds for Becky to extend an invitation to her yoga class, but it didn't come. Her eyes wandered around the tidy and tiny living room, coming to rest on an item of interest perched on the coffee table. "Is that real?"

Becky followed Virginia's pointing finger to a skeleton of a bird mounted on an onyx base. "Unfortunately. Corey moonlighted as a bone taxidermist."

"I've never heard of that before." Virginia picked up the sculpture by the base to inspect it. From the ribcage extended wing bones that looked like handless arms, while the sternum protruded from the ribs like the business end of an axe. "Is this a hummingbird?"

"Gross, isn't it?"

"In a way it's actually kind of beautiful." Virginia touched the disproportionate skull and ran her finger over the long beak. "It looks like a baby dinosaur."

"We agreed Corey could keep one item out here, and I chose the smallest one he had." Becky nodded toward a white door. "He has to keep everything else in his workshop."

Virginia returned the sculpture to the coffee table. "He's talented."

"Yeah, of all the things to be talented at... At least, we were making some money off it. About four months ago, I got him signed up as a contractor at the natural history museum where I work, providing animal skeletons for display." Perhaps realizing that she was smiling, Becky pinched her lips together. "Listen to me talking like he's going to come walking through the front door any minute now."

Virginia wrapped an arm around her friend, who covered her crying eyes with her hand. The PI let a moment of silence pass before speaking. "Becky, if this wasn't an accident, do you have any idea who could want to hurt Corey?"

Becky shook her head. "Corey was a gentle man. No one had any bad feelings toward him, at least not personally."

"What do you mean?"

"His work put him at odds with some people – through no fault of his own. Corey moved up the ranks pretty quickly. He was such a hard worker, devoted to his job. Frank Belcher, his direct report, used to be Corey's boss, and he was none too happy when Corey was promoted over him."

"Did Corey say if he had threatened him?"

"No. No, not at all. Corey didn't even tell me any of that. He didn't like to bring work home with him. Darren, his boss, told me about the issue with Frank." Her head bobbed forward. "Whoa."

"Are you okay?"

"I took a sedative to calm me down, but it wasn't working, so I took another one before we left the building." Her head bobbed again. "Now it's hitting me."

Virginia jumped to her feet to help Becky to hers. "Let's get you to bed." She walked her to the bedroom and sat her on the edge of the double bed. "Do you need any help?"

"It's all right. I can undress myself." Becky began unbuttoning her blouse. "I'm just going to sleep."

"Can I get you anything?"

Now in a bra and panties, Becky slipped under the covers. "A glass of water?"

"I'll be right back." Virginia headed into the kitchen and filled a glass from the faucet. As she turned from the sink, a voice startled her and loosened her grip.

"Someone asked for a ride?"

"Jeff! You scared the hell out of me." Virginia's eyes dropped from her partner in the kitchen doorway to the shard-strewn puddle at her feet.

"Sorry about that."

"You could've knocked."

Jeff shrugged. "The door was unlocked."

Virginia retrieved another glass from the cupboard. "I'm getting this for Becky, and then we can go. Can you help me with the cleanup?"

"Sure thing."

While Jeff unspooled some paper towels, Virginia filled the new glass and left the kitchen. Before she reached the bedroom door, she heard the light vibrato of Becky's snoring. She slipped inside, placed the glass on the nightstand and exited, closing the door behind her.

When she returned to the kitchen, she saw wet paper towels over the broken glass but no Jeff. She walked through the living room to the front door and looked outside, but her partner wasn't there or inside his car. She turned around and scanned the living room. "Jeff?" she whispered without a response. Her eyes zoomed in on the open door to Corey's workroom.

She found Jeff inside wandering around the two metal work benches and four shelving units in the room. Scattered about on the various surfaces were dozens of animal skeletons – some mounted and others in pieces.

Virginia whispered, "Jeff, what are you doing?"

"Did you really think I'd pass up a snooping opportunity? This is our victim's house. It's our obligation to look around. And man, this guy was into some freaky shit." Jeff held up a mounted skeleton of a bobcat. "I didn't realize he made these. This is what Bobbie looks like underneath. I don't know, but I don't like thinking about her like this."

Virginia took the skeleton from him and returned it to the shelf. "It's not freaky. Well, not entirely. Corey sold these to the natural history museum for extra money."

"We saw a possum skeleton in his office and some voodoo-esque thing made of chicken bones. Must've been a prototype." Jeff closed in on a waist-high box covered in black cloth. "I wonder what this is."

"Don't touch it," ordered Virginia, but she was too late.

Jeff pinched the black fabric and lifted it from the box. Both PIs gasped and jerked back. Strung up inside the glass-topped wooden box was the half-decomposed body of a housecat. Crawling over and throughout the carcass were hundreds of brown bugs with pale, speckled bands around the middle third of their bodies.

Virginia pointed at the box. "Is that... Is that a tabby?"

"And this isn't freaky?" Jeff took a picture with his phone.

"Cover it back up. I'm going to check on Becky before we leave. And can you please clean up the glass in the kitchen?"

Virginia left the workroom for Becky's bedroom. She pushed open the door and saw her friend now sleeping on her side, facing the bathroom on the other side of the room. Virginia was about to close the door again when she noticed something purple covering the back of her friend's right shoulder. She stepped forward to examine it and gasped when she realized it was a large bruise in the shape of four fingers.

CHAPTER 6

SEATED AT HIS rickety rosewood desk, Emory Rome examined the contents of the flash drive Frank Belcher had given them during their visit to the TVA office. Plugged into his laptop, the files from Corey Melton's computer proved to be mind-numbing in their tedium. All except the one now on his screen, the only one that might have a bearing on Corey's death. Emory hit the *Print* button.

The printer hummed awake just before the front door to Mourning Dove Investigations slammed open. "This discussion is over!" insisted Virginia as she stormed to her desk.

"You're right," responded Jeff as he entered and closed the door. "We're not dropping the case, and that's that."

"Guys!" Emory jerked up from his chair, catching his desk before it tipped over. "What's going on?"

Virginia turned her attention to her computer and began typing. "I want us to drop the case."

"Why?" asked Emory.

Without looking up from her monitor, Virginia answered, "Because I don't care why Corey's dead now. He deserved to die."

"Where is this coming from?"

"She thinks Corey was beating Becky." Jeff sat on the edge of her desk, scooching the desktop organizer with his robust cheeks.

"Really?" Emory leaned against his flimsy desk, but it scooted away, forcing him to slam a hand against the wall to keep from falling back. "Did she tell you that?"

"No." Virginia pushed away from the computer. "When I put Becky to bed, I noticed a bruise on her shoulder. It was in the shape of someone's fingers."

Emory stepped closer to them. "Did she say Corey was responsible?"

"Who else would it be?"

"Well, if that's true, it gives her a motive for killing him."

Jeff shrugged, "Why the elaborate scheme to somehow make him crash into that high-rise? A spouse has an abundance of opportunity. She could've just poisoned him or offed him a hundred easier ways than that."

Virginia looked at Emory as if he had insulted her. "If you knew her, you'd know she's not a killer."

"Perhaps you know her too well to be objective."

Jeff stood and chopped the air with his right hand. "We're not quitting the case."

Virginia said, "You didn't even want to take it in the first place."

Jeff pointed at Emory with his eyes still on Virginia. "I'm not going to let his asshole ex-partner take this from us! This is our case!" The PI lowered his hand and his tone. "Look, you told your friend we were going to find out what happened to her husband. That doesn't change because the guy might've been a horrible person."

"Virginia, I have to agree with Jeff."

"Really?" asked Virginia. "I expected a moral decision from you."

While Jeff huffed in mock offense, Emory told her, "Give me a chance to explain where I'm coming from. First, you saw a bruise that may or may not have been caused by a hand. Second, you're assuming the bruise was caused by her husband, but for all we know she got in a tussle with someone over a parking spot. Third, unless it was self-defense, a murder victim's lack of morality does not absolve the actions of the killer. That person still needs to be brought to justice. Now my first two points can easily be addressed by simply asking Becky what happened. Hopefully, she'll give an explanation that doesn't point the finger at Corey so you'll feel better about continuing our investigation."

Virginia looked at both of them. "Fine. Maybe I am jumping to conclusions."

"Great." Jeff clapped his hands together. "Besides the creepy workroom—"

"What creepy workroom?" asked Emory.

"I'll fill you in later. Virginia, did you find out anything else about the victim? The dead victim?"

Virginia returned her attention to the computer and began typing. "She told me he was going to this holistic healing center to see a counselor about his acrophobia. Randy Graham."

"Randy-gram?" Jeff shot her a confused glance. "Is that when someone comes to your door and talks dirty to you?"

"That's who you should talk to. He's a counselor at the Mountain Light Holistic Center."

Emory tapped both names into his phone. "We can question him later." He pointed to the printer behind Virginia's desk. "I printed the names of the displaced land owners and the addresses their checks were sent to."

"Who?" Virginia grabbed the paper from the printer and handed it to Emory.

Jeff told her, "Corey Melton was developing a windfarm for the TVA, and he stole the land he needed from property owners who are all now potential suspects."

"He didn't steal the land." Emory scanned the printout. "Eminent domain is used by the government to acquire property when a court determines the public need for it outweighs the private owner's rights to keep it."

"I know what it is, but I don't agree with it. It's just not right.

Emory said, "It's necessary. Interstates were built on formerly private land. Homeowners had to be displaced to establish just about every national park."

Jeff crossed his arms, frowning at his new partner. "But the owners get no choice in the matter."

"Once approved for eminent domain, the land is condemned and the owners are compensated the fair-market value for it." Emory handed the printout to Jeff. "The TVA condemned thirteen separate pieces of property in Brume Wood for the windfarm."

"Brume Wood?" Virginia asked. "Where's that?"

"In the mountains about an hour east of here. Seven of those properties had houses on them. The rest were empty lots."

Jeff's eyes went from the printout to Emory. "How do you condemn an empty lot? Was it contaminated with something?"

"Condemning land is just a process for acquiring it. It doesn't mean it's unusable."

"And you said he didn't steal it." Jeff ripped the paper, taking seven names and handing the rest to Emory. "Let's split up."

Emory hurried up the walkway to a modern two-story condominium in the up-and-coming Oakwood section of Knoxville. He looked at the fourth name on his list, Mary Belle Hinter, and checked the address. *Unit C.* He knocked on the door of the ground-floor unit and waited. Nothing. He tried once more with the same result. Removing one of his new business cards from his wallet, he wrote a note on the back asking Ms. Hinter to call him before slipping the card into the crack of the doorway.

"Hey man, no soliciting," a voice scolded from behind.

Startled, Emory faced his misguided chider. "I'm not a solicitor. I'm leaving a message for Mary Belle Hinter."

A blond man approached on the walkway, rolling a metallic suitcase behind him. "What do you want with her?"

He looks like a surfer in a suit. "I'm sorry, but who are you?"

The young man stopped just shy of stepping on Emory's toes. "I'm her nephew, Luke Hinter. Grandnephew, actually. My grandmother was her sister. And who are you?"

"Emory Rome. I'm a special... private investigator. I need to ask her some questions about a man with whom she had a business dealing."

Luke laughed. "That sounds vague and nefarious. Who?"

"Corey Melton."

"How do I know that name?"

"He purchased her land for the TVA."

Luke daggered the air with his finger. "That's it! He's the reason she got dumped in my lap."

"What do you mean?"

"We moved away from that hillbilly town—"

"Brume Wood?"

"Yeah, when I was like three years old, so I don't remember ever seeing Aunt Mary Belle before I had to go up there and get her. The sheriff arrested her because she refused to leave her land after that Corey guy snaked it from her. I missed half a day's work."

"If you didn't know her that well, why did the sheriff call you?"

"Apparently, I'm her only living relative."

Emory nodded toward the door. "When will she be home?"

"Oh, she doesn't live here." Luke laughed. "Dude, I'm twenty-five. How am I supposed to get laid with a seventy-eight-year-old woman here? I got her set up at Willow Springs. It's an assisted-living home in Mechanicsville."

Emory couldn't keep a hint of disapproval from blipping across his face.

"Don't give me that look. It's a nice place. So what do you

43

Mikel J. Wilson

want to ask her about him? Is he in trouble or something? She won't have anything nice to say."

"He's actually dead."

"Dude! Really? What happened?"

"We're not sure yet."

"Huh," Luke grunted. "So I'm confused. Why do you want to talk to my aunt... Wait, you think my little old aunt killed him?"

"We're just checking out everyone who might've had any animosity toward Mr. Melton." Emory nodded toward Luke's suitcase. "Vacation?"

"What? No, this is some of my aunt's stuff. She can't keep everything in that small room they have her in, so I have to store it for her."

Emory looked over Luke's shoulder at the gold Hummer parked in front of the building – a car that wasn't there when he walked up. "Nice Hummer."

Luke beamed at Emory. "Sweet, isn't it?"

"Yes, it is. Looks brand new."

"Yeah, I just bought... Wait a second. You think I spent the money my aunt got for her land on my car."

"It crossed my mind."

"Just uncross it. I don't need to steal money. I make enough of my own." Luke pulled a business card from his wallet and handed it to Emory. The card identified him as an investment broker at local firm. "One of the last things my parents did before they died was convince me to stop studying rocks in favor of finance, so I could make some real money after college. My aunt's money is in an account that I have access to, but it's only so I can pay for Willow Springs."

Emory placed the card in his pocket and nodded. "All right. Well, thank you for your time."

As Emory headed back toward the street, Luke said something that made him spin around. "You know, maybe she did do it."

44

"Do what?"

"Kill that guy."

"Why do you say that?"

"I don't mean like she physically killed him." Luke's voice lost its careless tone. "My mom would tell me stories about Aunt Mary Belle. She's not normal, and she's not one you want to anger."

"What are you saying?"

"She has a way of… making things happen. The locals have a name for her. They call her the Crick Witch."

CHAPTER 7

JEFF PULLED INTO the parking lot of the Black Bear Motel, an inexpensive local chain that catered to road-weary passersby more than the reservations crowd. He gazed up at the sun, about two hours from dropping behind the mountains, and checked the time on his phone. "Peter, you're my last one today."

Before he was close enough to see the number on the door of room 107, he could hear the squeal of children's voices coming from inside. When he rapped on the door, a scrawny, pimple-faced fourteen-year-old boy answered. Behind him, he could see three other children playing among the rubble of a single room stuffed with enough clothing and boxed belongings to fill four rooms. "Hi. I'm looking for Peter West."

"That's my dad. He's working."

"Where does he work?"

"Cleeson's."

"The one in West Hills?"

"Yeah."

"Thanks for the info." Jeff was about to walk away, but his concern for the children nagged at him. "By the way, where's your mother?"

"Grocery store."

"Okay. Listen, don't open the door again. It's not safe."

The boy huffed at him. "You're not my daddy." He shut the door before Jeff could say another word.

"What a brat."

Emory tapped the bell on the counter in the lobby of Willow Springs – senior living spaces converted from a nineteenth century Italianate house. Sounds of a mountain forest from overhead speakers pacified the air, and silk flowers sprung from every available surface. *This place doesn't seem so bad. It's peaceful.*

A scream rippled through the tranquility. Emory leapt over the counter and pounded through the door behind it. His eyes darted about in search of danger, but all he found was a fiftyish woman clutching her chest with a horrified look. Before her was an open drawer. Inside was a chicken-bone doll with a bird's foot attached as if grabbing at the heart. The woman saw Emory and pointed frantically at the drawer. "Get it out of there! Get it out!"

That's odd. It looks kind of like the one from Corey's office. Emory threw the doll into a nearby wastebasket. "Are you okay?"

"I'm fine." The woman's breathing ticked down from asthmatic. "Okay, I'm fine now. Thank you." Her chest-clutching hand dropped to her side, revealing a company badge hanging from the collar of her purple polyester blouse. "Can I help you?"

Emory found himself staring at her swept-back, brittle hair – a patchwork of brown shades given a yellow luster from the fluorescent ceiling light. *She must color it herself.* He pulled his eyes away, glancing at the name on her badge before offering her a smile. "Hi Lucy. I'm here to see Mary Belle Hinter."

"Ms... Ms. Mary Belle?" Her hand returned to her chest. "Are you a relation?"

"I'm Emory Rome. I'm investigating the death of someone she knew."

"Oh good heavens. How awful." Lucy fanned herself with her hand. "She's on the veranda. The door down the hall to your right. You can't miss it."

"Thank you." Emory pointed toward the wastebasket. "By the way, how did that thing get in your drawer?"

The woman placed a hand over her heart. "I can't rightfully say. I imagine someone confiscated it from… one of our residents. We're a Christian establishment." Emory started toward the door when the woman stopped him. "Em'ry, you don't believe she had something to do with that death, do you?"

"No, I just need to talk to her."

Lucy pursed her lips. "Are you sure?"

That's an odd question.

Lucy continued, "I don't mean to speak ill of the misfortunate, but that woman is a hellion straight from the loins of the devil!"

"Thanks for the warning." Emory left Lucy to her shudders. *That's twice I've been warned about Mary Belle Hinter. Who is she?*

When Emory stepped onto the veranda, he was greeted by a stifling warmth, in spite of the weak winter sunlight slavering through the glass roof. *I wonder which one is her.* Among the tight scattering of more patio heaters than were necessary, he saw about two dozen elderly denizens – some sitting alone and others playing cards or board games. One small woman with wild silver hair, however, was kneeling in front of a tree and digging in the dirt with her hands, just beyond the veranda's wood-slat flooring. Emory smirked. *Lord, don't let it be the crazy one.*

A thin fortyish man in scrubs approached him. "Can I help you?"

"I'm looking for Mary Belle Hinter."

The man scanned the area before the tips of his mustache reached for his chin. "There she is digging at that tree again."

Emory's shoulders slumped. *Of course, it's her.*

The attendant hurried toward her. "Ms. Mary Belle, what have we said about messing with the foliage?"

Either she didn't hear him or she ignored him altogether because she broke off a small offshoot of the horse chestnut tree's root and pulled it from the ground.

"Don't put that in your mouth!"

Before the attendant could grab it, she sure enough stuffed the piece of root into her mouth and sucked on it as if it were hard candy.

The attendant threw his hands up in the air and turned to Emory. "She's all yours."

Emory nodded and extended a hand to the old woman. "Ms. Mary Belle, could I help you to your feet?"

She looked up at him and rasped through cracked lips, "If I'd a wanted on m' feet, I'd be on 'em."

"Fair enough." Emory crouched on the ground next to her. "Ms. Mary Belle, I need to talk to you about Corey Melton. Do you know who that is?"

"I know who he was." She looked at him with jaundiced eyes and pointed an arthritic finger at his face. "Who're you?"

"I'm Emory Rome." He handed her a business card. "I'm an investigator. You said you knew who Mr. Melton *was*. Why did you say that?"

The old woman buried Emory's card into one of the oversized pockets of her brown tattered cloak. "I ain't ne'er forget a name or face."

"No, why did you use the past tense?"

Ms. Mary Belle's lips curled toward her withered cheeks. "I know why you're here."

"And why's that?"

"You're askin' 'bout a feller I knew but for one reason. The curse musta met its intention."

Emory clenched his jaw. *Here we go.* "Curse?"

49

"The thief stole m' prop'ty! So I hexed 'im. Hexed 'im good."

Yep, she's crazy.

Ms. Mary Belle laughed so hard, the root fell from her mouth. "When God closes a door, Death opens a window."

"When did you last see him?"

"Ne'er did. Coward wrote me a letter! Sheriff done his dirty work. Cursed 'im too." Her last statement added a proud glimmer to her eyes. "He still wit' us?"

"As far as I know."

"Well, give it time. Give it time. Oh me…" Without warning, a flash flood of tears washed away Ms. Mary Belle's self-satisfaction.

Emory placed a hand on her shoulder. "Are you okay?"

"That prop'ty's been my family's for gen'rations. From when I came ta 'wareness as a girl, I knowed I was gonna die there." She looked over his shoulder as if she could see her erstwhile land from where she sat. "Summer's always m' fav'rite. Dancin' ina black willer seeds that're floatin' ina wind. Cooling off ina crick. Course, 'tweren't deep enough ta swim in, but it's fun all a same. Ne'er did learn ta swim. And the taste o' the sassafras trees." Her tongue poked through her gummy smile to lick her crackled lips. "You e'er had a place like that?"

Emory shrugged. "I can't say I have."

Ms. Mary Belle wiped her eyes and focused them on Emory. "So you fixin' ta 'rest me?"

"What? No, I'm not going to arrest you."

"Takin' pity ona ol' woman." She patted the back of his hand. "You're a good young'un."

"Thanks."

"Can you he'p me get m' prop'ty back?"

"Unfortunately, there's nothing I can do about that."

"Sweet sassafras, you an inves'gator! Inves'gate how ta git back what's mine."

"I'm sorry." Emory shook his head. "It's not that simple."

"I got money. I can pay."

"It's not that. It's just too late to do anything about it now. It's out of our hands."

"Our?" The old woman's pitiable fragility evaporated, leaving behind a desiccated grimace of anger. "You workin' wit' 'em! You all in cahoots!"

"No, I meant there's nothing you or I could do."

"Stealin' what's mine!" Ms. Mary Belle clawed at the back of his hand, drawing blood. As Emory recoiled from her, she sucked the tiny bits of his skin from her fingertips and then spit in his face. "I curse you! No moment's peace 'til your reckonin', whena cold handa death'll come a beckonin'!"

Emory jumped to his feet and backed away, almost tripping. He wiped the spit from his face and glared at her in disbelief.

Ms. Mary Belle screamed, "Git out!" followed by incomprehensible words.

Emory could feel his arm hair shrieking to attention as he retreated to his car.

CHAPTER 8

EMORY STEPPED ONTO the curb from the parking lot to Cleeson's department store. "It's getting dark. Why did you want to meet here?"

Jeff arose from the brushed steel bench in front of the store and grabbed him by the arm. "We need to debrief, and I have shopping to do. Two birds. What happened to your hand?"

Emory glanced down at the large bandage he had placed over the scratches from the Crick Witch. "Just a scratch."

Jeff gave his partner a side-glance. "What's wrong?"

"What do you mean?"

"You look worried."

Wide-eyed, Emory opened the door for Jeff. "No, I'm fine."

Jeff shrugged as he entered the store, followed by Emory. "So how's your first day as a private investigator been?"

"Challenging, if I'm being honest."

"Good. I promised you wouldn't be bored." While they walked, Jeff scanned the aisles as if he were looking for something specific but had no idea where it would be. "As soon as we get this freebie out of the way, our biggest challenge will be finding time to spend all the money we'll be making. The TBI angle is going to be our goldmine."

"On that subject, I need to talk to you about my meeting this morning."

"It's fine. Just don't be late again."

"That's not what I meant. I was meeting with a lawyer."

"A lawyer? What for?"

Emory took a deep breath and muttered, "I'm suing the TBI for wrongful termination."

Jeff now turned his full attention to his partner. "You can't do that!"

"I'm glad I can count on your support."

"I'm sorry, but leaving the TBI for the private sector so you can help more people is a much better story than being fired and taking the first job that came along."

"Story for who?"

"Anyone who asks. Look, a lawsuit – especially one like that – is bad for business. Just drop it." Emory went silent, prompting Jeff to change the subject to something happier. "I shouldn't be telling you this, but I'm working on a surprise for you."

"I think the billboard was all the surprise I can handle for one day."

"Don't worry. I'm not going to tell you what it is until I'm sure, but it's big!" Jeff returned to his search.

"What are you shopping for?"

"Clothes, probably."

"You don't know?"

"It'll come to me."

Emory smirked. "We're passing some clothes now. Are they ringing any bells?"

Jeff looked around the area before shaking his head. "Not sportswear."

"You're not even looking at the clothes."

"How did your interviews go?"

"I couldn't reach two of the people on my list." Emory nodded at the racks they were passing. "You realize we're in the kids' section now."

"I like my gym wear tight. Did you leave your card and a note?"

"Of course. Two others I interviewed weren't happy with the forced sale, but they seem to have moved on. No pun intended. One had inherited the land and wanted to sell it anyway, so he was happy."

"Two of mine already had their land up for sale. I had three who weren't home and two who were unhappy but not murderously so. Wait, I count only five on your end."

"The sixth one is an elderly woman." Emory sighed. "I'm not sure about her."

"Found it!" Jeff made a beeline for the nearest counter, which was in the women's clothing department.

"You need a dress?"

"Of course not. I need some new work clothes."

Emory waved in the direction from which they had just come. "Then why aren't we over there?"

"Do you see any salespeople there? I don't like waiting to be helped." Jeff approached the sales associate at the counter and didn't even wait for him to finish helping a customer. "Excuse me…" He nodded toward the associate's nametag. "Peter. Could you help us?"

The thirtyish man's lips curled toward disengaged eyes. "Sure." He bagged the customer's garment and handed it to her before asking Jeff, "Do you know her size?"

"Whose?"

"No ring, so I assume your girlfriend's. You want to buy her a dress?"

"I don't have a girlfriend. I was hoping you could help us in men's clothing."

With a thick, veiny hand, Peter picked up the phone on the counter. "I'll get someone to assist you."

"Can't you do it?"

Emory could feel warm air piping from the rattling vent above the counter. The same air buffeted the sales associate's hair, which was kempt but uneven, like a former crewcut overgrown from several missed visits to the barbershop.

"That's not my department. It's Martin's."

"You're a man, and you wear clothes. Any reason you can't help us with men's clothing?"

"As I said—"

"We'll be fast, and I swear we'll buy enough to make it worth your while."

Peter hung up the phone. "All right, but if Martin shows up, I'm going to have to turn you over to him."

"Understood." Jeff led them to a section with racks of clothes that could be considered club wear/progressive business wear. "I'm guessing I'm about a seventeen in the neck, and I'd say—"

"We shouldn't guess." Peter removed a cloth tape measure from his pocket. "Can I measure you?"

"That would be ideal. Where are you from, Peter?"

"Here." As the sales associate answered Jeff's questions, he measured the PI's neck, chest, arm length, waist and inseam. "Well, a little town east of here, up in the mountains."

"What did you do there?"

"Farmer. Didn't make much, but it was enough to provide for me and mine."

"So you're married?" As soon as he asked the question, Jeff turned away from Emory's sudden scowl.

"With four kids."

"Do you like working here now?"

Finished with the measurements, Peter stood and faced Jeff. "Sure. It's a great opportunity for me. What kind of clothes were you looking for?"

Jeff didn't answer his question, positing one of his own. "Would you mind terribly taking Emory's measurements as well?"

His sudden inclusion in the conversation caught Emory off guard. "No, I'm fine. I don't need any clothes."

"Which is good, since we're not here for you. I just thought you'd want to know."

"I already know my measurements."

"I don't believe you."

To prove his point, Emory spouted off his neck, arm, waist and pant leg measurements, and as he did, Peter compared them with Jeff's. "Except for the neck and chest, you two are practically twins."

Jeff continued questioning Peter while he grabbed shirts and pants from the racks. "Do you like where you live now?"

"Can't say that I do. I haven't found a place to really call home again. I don't know that anywhere here could ever feel like home."

"I'm kind of new to the city myself. Any idea where I could take someone for a nice romantic view of the city?"

Red-faced, Emory blurted out, "Don't you have enough clothes to try on?"

Following a slight jump at the outburst, Peter pointed behind them. "You can try them on over there."

His arms laden with clothes, Jeff headed toward the dressing room but stopped once he realized Emory wasn't following. "I'm going to need your opinion."

Emory frowned and followed him to one of the rooms but stood outside the curtain door. Jeff entered and looked back. "Come in with me."

"No. People might think... something's going on."

"Oh good god, just get in here." Jeff grabbed his arm and dragged him inside.

Emory whisked the curtain shut with such force, the other end jerked to the middle of the bar. He closed that end with a gentler tug before facing Jeff. "What the hell was that?"

"What?"

"It was embarrassing! Why were you hitting on him?"

Jeff hung the clothes on the wall hooks. "Is that what you think? I thought you were an investigator."

Emory paused a moment before sighing. "He's on your list. Why didn't you just tell me that from the beginning instead of lying?"

"I didn't lie. I am here to shop, in addition to questioning a suspect on *my* list."

"You could've told me before I made a spectacle."

"Sometimes I come across as flirty when I'm actually just trying to put the other person at ease. I didn't mean to make you jealous."

Emory bleated an unconvincing laugh. "I'm not jealous."

Jeff snickered. "Okay, but something is bothering you." He held up a powder-blue linen shirt with a Cuban collar and checked out the look in the mirror. "This won't work for me. It might work for you. You should try it on."

Emory brushed it aside. "I don't need new clothes."

"We're here. Just try it on." Jeff handed off the shirt to a begrudging Emory. "So what's wrong?"

Emory took a deep breath before whispering, "This crotchety old woman I questioned today… cursed me."

Jeff roared with laughter. "Oh my god, that's funny! Tell me everything."

Emory gave him the quick highlights, ending with, "She really rattled me."

"Seriously? Rattled by a few mean words from a little old lady?"

"I'm sorry, but I've never been cursed before. How am I supposed to feel?"

"You don't believe in curses, do you?"

Emory looked to the mirror and focused on the new shirt he was now trying on. "No."

Jeff gasped into a grin. "Oh wow, you do!"

"I don't know, and don't laugh at me." Emory pulled the shirt off and reached for another one. "I'm from the mountains. Spell-casters and curses are part of the lore I grew up with. My granny didn't believe in fairy tales, so at bedtime she'd tell me stories of Cherokee vengeance that always started with a curse and ended with a grisly death. It's no wonder I'm an insomniac. Her favorite one was about Hugo Hickory."

"Who?"

Emory sighed as he tried on a pair of beryl-blue pants with a window-pane pattern. "It's a long story. I'll tell you later."

"Whatever. Now that you're an adult, you should realize curses aren't real. There's no escaped lunatic with a hook hand looking to slice up kids who are making out in the woods. By the way, those pants look great on you."

"That hook hand story has nothing to do with a curse." He gave a few tugs to the bottom of the shirt. "I don't like how this bunches up at the waist." He pulled the shirt off and let the pants drop to his ankles. "Poo-poo it all you want, but there are real, documented curses. King Tut's tomb, the Crying Boy painting, Tecumseh, the Busby chair."

"Take some bus chair?"

"Tecumseh and the Busby chair. They're… Never mind." Now in his underwear, Emory tried on another pair of pants from Jeff.

"If this alleged curse bothers you so much, just get her to take it back." Jeff handed him another shirt. "This will be good with those pants."

"How do I make her take it back?"

"Go make nice with her, and give her what she wants."

"I can't give her back the land."

"No, but you could give her closure." Jeff pointed at the mirror. "I knew that combo would work for you."

"I look fat." Emory removed the shirt in a single pull.

"What are you talking about? You've got like a twenty-eight-inch waist."

"Which is why I don't want a fat shirt." Emory removed the last shirt from the hanger. "How do I give her closure?"

"From what you've told me of her, I'm betting she didn't know – or refused to believe – that the sheriff was actually going to come to kick her out, so she probably didn't have a chance to say goodbye to her home. Take her to say goodbye."

Shaking his head, Emory looked at himself in the mirror, his eyes dropping to his bandaged hand. "I don't want to see her again."

"Then live with the curse." Jeff snapped his fingers. "Ooh! I have an idea. You could go to that fortune teller down the street from the office. Maybe she could lift the curse for you."

Emory shot him a derisive look. "A fortune teller? Really?"

"You believe in curses but draw the line at fortune tellers?"

"Let's just drop it and get back to the case."

Jeff handed him a pair of black corduroy pants. "Try these on."

Emory removed the pants he had on but dismissed the new pair without trying them. "I don't like those. I've been thinking maybe Corey's death had nothing to do with his current work project. Unless you find out something provocative from Peter out there, I say tomorrow we should focus on his personal life."

"Works for me." Jeff swooshed open the dressing room curtain.

"I'm not dressed!" Emory shouted as he hurried to get his own clothes on.

Jeff slapped the side of his own butt cheek and clenched his hand. "I guess it's up to me to provoke Peter."

By the time they left the dressing room, Emory had four wardrobe changes in hand, while his partner had none.

Jeff reached Peter first. "We left the items we didn't like in the dressing room."

"I'll rerack them."

"Forget about that. Tell me, Peter, did having to move into a tiny motel room with your wife and four kids drive you to kill the man who took your home?"

Peter's lips seemed unable to find each other in order to form a single word, but that didn't stop a guttural "Huh?"

"I do understand. I've met your kids."

Peter grabbed Jeff's collar with both hands. "Who the hell are you?!"

CHAPTER 9

"MR. WEST!" THE attention of Peter West and the two PIs shot to the red-faced little man in a suit scuttling toward them. "What are you doing?"

Peter released Jeff's collar. "Mr. Hall, I—"

Wearing a nametag with a manager title emblazoned in red, Mr. Hall turned his attention to Jeff. "Sir, I'm very sorry for my employee's outburst."

Jeff responded with a laugh and a dismissive wave of his hand. "I'm the one who should apologize. I started it."

"I don't care who started it. That's not how we interact with our customers." Mr. Hall glared at Peter. "What are you even doing in men's wear, Mr. West?"

Jeff interjected, "No, you misunderstand. Peter and I are old buddies. From high school. That's how we always greet each other. It's an inside joke that would take much too long to explain."

The manager jabbed his small fists into his robust waist. "High school? How many years were you held back, Mr. West?"

In obvious desperation to save his job, Peter joined in the ruse. "Uh… I was his coach."

"I don't recall seeing that on your resume."

"I uh… only did it for one season. Part time. It uh… wasn't really worth mentioning."

The unclenching of the manager's body signaled he was going to give him the benefit of the doubt. "Well, enough time visiting. You have work to do."

Jeff nodded toward Emory and his armful of potential purchases. "He's helping implement a much needed wardrobe revision for my friend here."

Mr. Hall reiterated, "This isn't his department."

Jeff nodded to Emory. "Okay. I guess we'll just put all this back."

"Very well." The manager pointed to Peter. "Finish up with your friend, and then return to your own department." Mr. Hall toddled away but didn't stray from eyeshot of the trio.

Emory held up his laden arms. "I don't need new clothes."

"You have to buy them now. Do you want Peter to lose his job?"

Emory pursed his lips. "You planned this, didn't you?"

Jeff flashed a smile of success. "We're ready to check out."

"This way." Peter led them back to his register.

As Emory unloaded the clothes onto the counter, Jeff continued his verbal poking. "That's quite a temper you have there, Peter. Verging on murderous."

Peter glanced at his manager, who was still watching from sportswear, and he plastered a pleasant expression over his gritting teeth. "What in the hell are you talking about?"

"Corey Melton, the TVA manager who took your land. He's dead."

"Huh." Peter scanned and folded Emory's new clothes. "How'd he die?"

Emory frowned at him. "Mr. West, I have to say, you seem unfazed by the news."

"Sorry, but I didn't know the guy. Never met him. He was just a signature on a letter I received."

Jeff wiggled his hips. "I'm sure you're doing a little happy dance in your head."

A sneer cracked Peter's veneer. "I don't wish anyone ill. I wasn't happy about him and the TVA taking my house, but they paid me a fair price for it. And it's for a good cause." He announced the total cost of the purchases, and Emory inserted a card into the chip reader of the credit card machine.

Jeff flared his left eyebrow. "And you're not upset at being forced to live in a tiny motel room?"

"It's temporary. We're looking for a new place now."

Emory picked up the full shopping bag from the counter. "Just one more question. Can you tell us where you were between eight-thirty and nine this morning?"

Peter's eyes shifted between the PIs. "Here. I get in at eight-thirty."

"Thank you for your time, Mr. West." Emory glanced at his partner and nodded toward the exit. As they walked away, he asked, "What happened to putting people at ease so they want to talk to you?"

"I never said that. I said that I make people realize they want to tell me what they know. That doesn't rule out provocation."

Naked, Emory strode across his apartment, opened his laptop and dropped onto the comfort of his unyielding modern couch. As his fingers touched the keyboard, he heard the vibrations of the ringing phone atop his desk. "Damn."

He put the laptop aside and popped back up to answer it. "Hello?"

From the Smoky Mountain town of Barter Ridge, Sheriff and Lula Mae Rome huddled around the speakerphone in their kitchen. "Emory, this is your mom and dad." His mother always began phone conversations with Emory in a giddy tone – a tone that promised exciting news but only delivered on rare occasions.

"Hi Son," greeted the sheriff.

Their voices lifted the corners of Emory's mouth and peeled the day's tension from his back and shoulders. "Hi there. What are y'all up to?"

"Nothing much, sweetie."

"Son, how was your first day at your new job?"

Emory moved the phone from his ear. *Damn, Dad always shouts when he's on speakerphone.* "It was... okay."

"What's wrong?" his father asked.

"Nothing." Emory returned to the couch and his laptop. "I don't know exactly what I was expecting. I guess I just miss my old job." He typed in the search engine, looking for information on curses.

"Well, is there any way you could get your job back?" The giddiness dropped from Lula Mae's voice.

"No." Emory pressed the Enter button on his keyboard, and as soon as he did, an ad for Mourning Dove Investigations popped up on his screen. He groaned when he saw Cowboy Emory smiling at him. "Son of a..."

"What was that, Son?"

"Nothing, Dad."

Lula Mae pressed him on the subject of his former job. "Honey, you never did tell us exactly why they let you go."

"They just said I didn't fill out a report correctly."

The sheriff tsked at his answer. "It seems like such a small thing to get fired over."

As his back tightened, Emory sighed away from the phone. "Mom, Dad, I'm sorry to rush, but I have a lot of work to finish before bed."

"That's okay," said Lula Mae. "We just wanted to hear your voice."

"Take care, Son."

"We love you," Emory heard his mother say before he hung up

the phone. He closed the popup ad on his computer and cursed Jeff for the ridiculous campaign.

His web search brought up multiple listings for do-it-yourself charms and spells, as well as ads for palm readers and spiritual guides.

Emory glanced at the bandage on his hand and closed his laptop. "I'm being stupid."

The sheriff twitched his lips when he heard the dial tone. "Now that's worrisome."

"I know." Lula Mae placed a caressing hand on her husband's forearm. "We should help him."

"I don't think he needs our money."

"No. I mean you should offer him a job. He'd be a great deputy for you."

"Lula Mae, you know what his answer will be."

She removed her hand and jabbed her fingertip onto the tabletop. "No, I don't, and you don't either. He could just be waiting for you to ask."

"I'll ask, but I wouldn't count on Emory ever moving back here."

CHAPTER 10

EMORY DARTED FROM his apartment determined to get to work early. Even though he had a legitimate – and preapproved – reason for being late the day before, he wasn't about to give Jeff a reason to rib him further about his punctuality.

Hurrying down the sidewalk toward his car, Emory passed a parked SUV with tinted windows. His head whipped to the left when he heard the rustling of a wet wipe being pulled from a pop-up pack. On the other side of the car, a man in a tailored blue suit leaned over the hood, a wipe in his manicured hand, and reached for a splat of fresh bird poop on the windshield.

"I was just sitting in my car, minding my own business, when a mourning dove perched on my windshield wiper and laid waste on my windshield," the handsome man with slicked-back grey hair explained. "Do you think he was trying to impart a message to me?"

Since the man's eyes remained focused on the windshield, Emory wasn't certain he was even speaking to him. Just in case, he muttered, "I don't know."

"Mourning doves are the most hunted species in America." The man faced Emory and pointed at him with his wipe-clutching hand. "I can see you're skeptical, but I assure you it's a verifiable fact. Hunters kill more than 20 million of my avian attacker's friends every year. Maybe that's why their song is more of a dirge."

Emory stopped walking and stared at the man. *I know him.*

"Do you suppose that's how your new partners dreamt up that rather unusual identity for their establishment?" The man pulled a baggie from his pocket, stuck the soiled wipe inside and pocketed it. "They consider themselves prolific hunters?"

"I've actually never asked that question, Mr. Alexander."

The man grinned. "You know who I am."

"Anderson Alexander, the director of the TBI. Your picture hangs in the TBI office where I used to work."

Anderson used another wipe to clean his hands as he approached Emory. "Of course. I would've made an appointment to see you at your new office, but I prefer to chat away from any prying eyes."

Whose prying eyes? Am I being watched? "What about?"

Anderson shook hands with the former special agent. "I'll get right to the point. I'd like for you to come back to the TBI."

Emory wanted to laugh, but he held it back. "I didn't leave of my own accord, Mr. Alexander. Eve Bachman fired me."

"I was recently made aware of the circumstances surrounding your dismissal. I've verbally reprimanded Eve for her behavior. I've also done my homework on you. I've seen your test scores, and I've read your files. Mr. Buckwald might have been the senior partner, but his success rate jumped sixty-two percent during your tenure together. How would you like to lead your own division?"

"What?" Emory could no longer contain his grin. "Are you serious?"

Anderson waved a finger at him. "My offers are never textured with frivolity, Mr. Rome."

Emory nodded like a scolded child. "Sorry."

"Art Pulaski, the special agent in charge of our Memphis division has his heart set on retiring to San Diego in two years. He'll groom you to be his replacement. You would become the youngest special agent in charge in the bureau's history."

"I can't believe this. It's too good to…" Emory had a sudden realization. "You know about the lawsuit." Anderson revealed a silent poker face, but that was enough. "But how? My lawyer said he wasn't even filing the paperwork until the end of the week."

"I don't share Eve Bachman's beliefs, but if you pursue this lawsuit, I will have to publicly stand behind her and defend the official reason she gave for firing you as legitimate."

"Thus the *verbal* reprimand, so there's nothing on record. So all of this was just a bribe to shut me up."

"Mr. Rome, I didn't politic my way to the top. I earned my position, and I would never dole out a meritless promotion to anyone in my purview. I meant my every word. You're an impressive young man whose career took a slight detour. I'm here to set you back on the right path – the one you set for yourself when you joined the TBI." Anderson laughed. "In five years or so, you could be resting your nameplate on my desk."

Emory thought for a moment before answering. "I appreciate your coming to see me. I need to think about it."

"Understandable." Anderson opened the back door of his SUV and handed Emory a business card. "You don't have to tell me right now, but you do need to tell me soon."

Emory hadn't noticed it before, but now he could see the silhouette of a large man in the driver seat. As the SUV pulled away, he looked at his phone. *So much for getting to work on time.*

Despite the chill in the March morning air, Jeff jogged down the street wearing shorts that exposed his tremendous legs and a light sweatshirt that didn't hide the outline of his pecs bouncing as he ran. When he turned the corner, he could see the front of

Mourning Dove Investigations, but he missed the man sitting on the sidewalk and tripped over his legs. He regained his balance before he fell, and checked the condition of the homeless man he had kicked. "Sorry Phineas. You okay?"

With his back to the brick wall, Phineas brought his legs closer to his body and clutched his grimy trench coat tighter to his chest. As long as you didn't hit my guitar. I'm chill." He nodded to the instrument propped against the wall at his side.

"Do you want some coffee to warm you up?" Jeff's hands reached for his pockets before he realized he had on basketball shorts. "I don't have any money on me now. I'll bring some out to you."

"Thanks man."

Jeff continued jogging until he reached the front door to his office.

Emory's tiny desk wobbled under the weight of his forearms as he thought about his unexpected visitor. *Anderson Alexander is offering me everything I want. Can I trust him?* He snapped back into the moment when the front door to the office opened.

His sweaty partner entered and didn't miss a beat before berating him. "I know you had to be punctual when you worked at the TBI. Why are you finding it so difficult now?"

Emory put on his most innocent, wide-eyed expression. "Why are you assuming I wasn't on time?"

"No assumptions. I came down when the office opened, and Virginia was the only one here." Jeff glanced at Virginia's empty desk. "Where is she, by the way?"

"She went to check on Becky, and you're one to talk about being late. You were jogging instead of working."

"I was power jogging, ruminating on the case. I think you're right about adjusting course and looking into Corey's personal life.

We should start with that holistic center that was helping him get over his acrophobia."

"Before we do, I was thinking we might as well check out his other job too. Swing by the natural history museum."

"Where Corey sold his morbid art pieces?

Emory nodded. "I want to interview whoever was his contact."

"Wouldn't that be his wife?"

"Virginia said Becky's the ticket cashier at the museum. She didn't have anything to do with the displays."

"Fine." Jeff pointed to Emory's desk, to a personal item atop it. "Glad you're making yourself at home."

Emory glanced at the framed photo he'd placed on the desk moments earlier. "Just a picture of my mom."

Jeff removed his sweaty shirt and lopped it over his left shoulder, revealing his marbleized torso. Emory tried not to look, but his eyes wanted to take advantage of the opportunity to adore the most perfect body they had ever seen. They were mesmerized by the effect his respiring lungs had on his square pecs, made more brilliant by the soft office lights that glimmered through the tiny drops of sweat clinging to the hairs that adorned his chest.

As Jeff stepped closer to look at the framed picture, he must have noticed Emory's stare. Smiling, he picked up the frame, flexing muscles unnecessary for the task, as if he couldn't help it. "That's not Mrs. Rome. Oh, you mean your birth mom."

Singed along the sides, the photo featured a smiling woman in her early thirties with straight black hair draping past her shoulders. Her dark brown eyes rested on extra-high cheekbones, complementing beautiful sienna skin. "This can't be your birth mom. You're so pale."

Emory grabbed the photo from him. "I take after my father."

"Your mom was Native American?"

Placing the frame back on his desk, Emory scowled at him. "I'm surprised Virginia didn't tell you I'm half-Cherokee."

"She told me you said that, but everyone in Tennessee claims to be part Cherokee. But you're legit."

"My grandparents were part of the Eastern Band of Cherokee, a tribe in North Carolina just on the other side of the Smoky Mountains. They moved to Tennessee when my mom was a baby."

"How cool." Jeff cupped his right ankle in his hand and pulled the heel of his foot to the perfect curvature of his right butt cheek, stretching after his run. "So the picture was in your granny's house when it burned down?"

Emory nodded. "One of the few things I was able to salvage. No pictures of granny though."

Jeff switched to stretching his left leg. "Why don't you ever talk about your real dad? Did you not know him?"

With more forceful mental prodding, Emory's eyes obeyed him and looked to the laptop on his desk. "I've met him. Let's talk about this later."

"God, you put the private in private eye." Jeff stopped stretching and pressed his palms onto Emory's desk, flexing his triceps and pecs. "I'll agree only if we talk about this." He pointed to Emory and to himself.

"What do you mean?"

"Well, we had an incredible night together, we solved a triple-murder, you were fired from the TBI and now you're here. We haven't talked about *us* since that night."

Emory closed his laptop. "You're right. I have been thinking about it, and I honestly don't know what the answer is."

"I'm curious. What's the question?"

"How do we put that night behind us and have a professional relationship moving forward?"

"Huh." Jeff clenched his jaw and pushed himself away from the desk.

"What, is that not what you were thinking?"

"Almost, although I was thinking more, 'When are we going on another date?'"

Emory's eyes darted around the room, looking for anything besides the disappointment now displayed on Jeff's face. "That's not really the same thing at all."

Jeff leaned over and kissed Emory, cradling the back of his head in his hand.

Emory kissed him back, gliding his hand over Jeff's right arm to rest on his shoulder.

Once their lips parted, Jeff stepped away and headed toward the bookshelf to the right of Emory's desk. "You think again about which question you want answered." He pulled the only non-mystery book on the shelf – John Knowles' *A Separate Peace*. The bookshelf door to his office swung open. "Oh, I almost forgot! I promised Phineas some coffee money, and my wallet is upstairs."

"I'll take care of it."

"He's the homeless guy."

"I've met him."

As Jeff disappeared behind the bookshelf, Emory pulled a five-dollar bill from his wallet and stepped outside into the cold.

When Emory and Jeff walked through the glass double doors of the Knoxville Natural History Museum, they found a petite redhead seated behind the ticket counter.

Emory greeted her with a nod. "Good morning. We're looking for the curator."

"Claire? She's here somewhere."

Jeff half-smiled at her. "Uh, it's a big place."

"Well, she's here somewhere," the young woman repeated.

"Thanks for your help." Jeff headed for the hallway to the exhibits. "I guess we just wander around."

"Excuse me," the woman called. "Tickets are $10 for adults. Each."

Jeff whispered, "Let's just find a backdoor and break in."

"We're not breaking and entering." Emory returned to the table, pulled a twenty from his wallet and paid her.

The woman rang up the sale on the cash register and handed him two tickets. "Enjoy the museum."

"I need a receipt."

The woman sighed. "For real?"

"It's a business expense."

She ducked behind the counter and came back up with a new role of register tape. "I ran out." She opened the printer cover on the register. "This is going to take a minute."

"Emory, forget it. I'll verify your purchase." Jeff waved his arms forward. "Let's go."

During the next several minutes, the PIs searched for an employee among the museum's handful of early visitors until they reached an exhibit of regional fauna, including dozens of skeletal representations with pictures and details of each animal. Emory pointed to a tailless skeleton about the size of a full-grown husky on a marble stand with a picture of a baby black bear. "I'm guessing the skeletons in this room are Corey's work."

Jeff scanned the displays. "Do you think they all died of natural causes, or were they actually killed just for this?"

Emory shook his head. "I don't want to think about it."

"Let's go." Jeff led him to the next room, an area devoted to the ancient human inhabitants of Tennessee known as the Mound Builders. He hurried past the exhibit of pottery, arrowheads and a bisected model of a burial mound, stopping when he found a door marked *Staff only*.

Jeff turned the knob and pushed the door open a crack. He looked back at the frown on Emory's face and said, "It's just entering. No breaking."

Emory followed Jeff into the warehouse. Once the door shut again, the only sound he heard other than the gentle hum of the lighting high overhead came from an indiscernible conversation deep within the room. He almost rolled his eyes when Jeff held an unnecessary silencing finger to his lips before proceeding between two of several rows of ceiling-high shelves, stocked with boxes, artifacts and life-sized sculptures of prehistoric humans in animal skins. As they neared a clearing, Emory could see over Jeff's shoulder two people talking – a hulking clean-cut man in a brown leather jacket and a woman with a museum badge on the lapel of her skirt suit and brunette hair tamed within an inch of its life around her head.

"We should wait until tomorrow," the woman said. "It's too soon."

The man argued, "I need the money now."

"Be patient." She placed a caressing hand on his arm. "Monty, we're going to be okay."

"This whole thing should've never happened."

"You should go. I need to get on the floor."

Without warning, Jeff stepped out of the shadows and interrupted the conversation. "So what *whole thing* are we talking about here? Corey Melton's murder?"

The woman jumped when she heard Jeff's voice, but Monty lunged for the intruder while reaching inside his jacket for something. Within two bounds, he had Jeff pinned against the end cap with a forearm to the chest and a twelve-inch hunting knife about to prune his Adam's apple. He snarled within an inch from Jeff's face, "Give me a reason not to slit your throat!"

CHAPTER 11

"I'LL GIVE YOU one," said Emory as he pressed the barrel of his black M1911 pistol into the carotid artery of Jeff's attacker. "Back away now."

Monty's eyes darted between Jeff and Emory, but nothing else moved.

"Monty, put it down!" the woman ordered from behind him. "Please."

The large man backed away from Jeff but kept the knife in a menacing grip at his side. He blocked the woman from the PIs' view and asked, "What do you want?"

Jeff relaxed his shoulders. "Geez, guy. Overreact much?" He rubbed his neck, checked his palm for blood and heaved a relieved sigh when he saw none.

The woman stepped beside Monty. "I apologize. Monty's just very protective. Please, put that thing away."

Emory holstered his weapon. "I think we all got off on the wrong foot here. We're looking for Claire."

"I'm Claire. Now who are you?"

"I'm Emory Rome, and this is Jeff Woodard. We've been retained by Becky Melton to investigate the recent death of her husband."

"Retained?" asked Monty. "So you're not cops?"

"We're private investigators," answered Jeff.

"Then get out of here. We don't have to answer your questions."

"Monty, it's fine." Claire patted his shoulder. "Just go. I'll take care of this."

With a shake of his head and warning glares for the PIs, Monty exited the backdoor.

"Gentlemen, let's walk and talk." Claire slipped between Jeff and Emory, heading toward the door through which the PIs had come. "I'm curious. Why did Becky send you to speak to me?"

"She didn't send us," answered Emory. "We're just checking out every aspect of his life to get a better picture of who he was and try to decipher his death."

"Didn't he kill himself?"

Jeff held open the door that led to the museum. "Common misconception."

"Oh. Well, I'm not sure how much help I can offer. Corey provided some pieces for us. I can show you if you'd like."

Jeff waved off the offer. "We've seen them."

Emory asked, "Do you know anyone who had any ill feelings toward Corey Melton?"

"I'm sorry. Corey seemed like a nice enough man, but I honestly didn't know him that well. I barely know Becky, and I see her just about every day."

"So do you run this place?" asked Jeff.

"The director officially runs the museum. He usually leaves decisions concerning the displays to me."

Jeff cocked his head. "Usually?"

Claire stopped walking and crossed her arms. "Gentlemen, I think I've been very accommodating, considering you're not actually law enforcement. I do have a job to do, so if you can show yourself to the front door…" With that Claire left for another room.

As they started for the entrance, Jeff told his partner, "Must've hit a nerve."

"What were you thinking?" asked Emory.

"I've thought of a lot of things. Could you be more specific?"

"The way you just barged onto the scene when Claire and Monty were talking."

"I just thought I'd catch them off guard and maybe get the truth from them before they could concoct a lie."

Emory pushed open the front door. "You could've been killed."

"I knew you'd have my back."

Virginia exited the backdoor to Becky Melton's house and found her friend wearing a terrycloth robe and sitting on a small swing set with a slide. As she rocked a few inches forward and back, one hand held a cell phone to her ear, while the other clutched the hanging chain and a lit cigarette. Virginia sat in the swing next to her and waited for her to finish talking to the funeral home. Once her call ended, Becky buried the phone into the pocket of the robe and took a deep drag from the cigarette.

Virginia said, "I didn't know you smoked."

Becky exhaled a cone of smoke into the chilly air. "I haven't since college. I found an old pack in a cedar chest when I was looking for something for Corey to wear." She puffed again on the cigarette. "Did you meet my in-laws?"

"I wouldn't say *met*. Your mother-in-law let me in. Are you... okay?"

"I'm a twenty-five-year-old widow. I don't know what I'm doing. I've never arranged a funeral before."

"Do you need help with the arrangements... or money?"

Becky took a final puff before crushing the cigarette on the sole of her white slipper. "My parents' flight landed a few minutes ago, so they'll be here soon to help. Corey had a small life insurance policy through work, so that should cover the expenses."

Virginia placed a hand on her friend's. "Becky, why didn't you tell me about Corey?"

"What do you mean? I told you not more than an hour after I found out myself."

"I'm not talking about his death. I'm talking about what he did to you."

The widow squinted at her. "I'm not following."

"I saw the bruise on your shoulder." Becky reached for her left shoulder, which elicited a gasp from Virginia. "You have a bruise on that shoulder too? How long was this going on? You could've come to me."

"Virginia, you've made a big ole leap here. Corey never laid a hand on me like that. He was a gentle man."

"Then where'd you get the bruises?"

"I backed into a piece of equipment at the gym. You know how clumsy I am."

Virginia lowered her chin and looked at Becky through her upper lashes. "What machine?"

"I don't remember. What does it matter? I'm telling you, Corey was an exceedingly gentle man."

Becky pushed off the ground to give momentum to the swing before dragging her feet on the ground to end it. "This swing set was left here by the previous owners. I asked Corey several times to take it down, had it on his list of chores ever since we moved in two years ago, but he somehow never got around to it. I think he secretly hoped we'd have children someday and be glad it was here." A tear dripped down her cheek as she slipped out of the swing and plodded over to an object on the ground. "You might want to get up."

Virginia pulled herself out of the swing. "What are you doing?"

Becky picked up the sixteen-pound sledgehammer by its hickory handle, stumbling as she adjusted to the weight. Holding the head up to about her waist, she spun around in a complete circle before hammering one of the swing's support posts.

"Becky?"

The widow continued with her task until the post buckled, at which point, her knees did the same.

In an examination room of the Knox County's Regional Forensic Center, Cathy Shaw pushed a corpse-laden rack into the body refrigerator and closed the door. "I have time to get an early lunch now."

A technician entered pushing a gurney in front of him and pulling one behind him. "Cathy, I have a double homicide for you."

The petite medical examiner's shoulders drooped in her lab coat. "Are you serious?"

"Sorry." The technician gave her an odd grin before leaving her alone with the sheet-covered corpses.

"No lunch today." The nose on her vulpine face twitched as an unexpected aroma tickled her nostrils. "What is that smell?" She gave the nearer body a sniff through the sheet before moving to the other. "Smells like hamburger." She grabbed the top of the sheet and lowered it a quarter of the way down the body.

Before she could focus on the face, the corpse spoke. "Hi Cathy."

She screamed and backed into the other gurney. "Jeff?"

Jeff held up a bag. "We brought you lunch."

"We?" The corpse behind her ascended like a black-and-white movie vampire's rise from the grave. Cathy screamed again. "Emory?"

Emory pulled the sheet from his face. "Sorry Cathy. We didn't mean to scare you. We just wanted to make sure no one else was in the room first."

Jeff hopped off the gurney and handed her the bag. "His asshole ex-partner left Emory's picture with the front office staff and told them to keep him out. We bribed the tech to sneak us in."

Cathy hugged Emory. "I heard what happened. I'm so sorry."

"Don't feel too sorry for him." Jeff slapped his own chest. "Now he gets to work with me full-time.

"That's true, handsome. Thank you guys for lunch and for going through so much trouble to see me."

Emory straightened his suit. "To be honest, we had another reason for coming. Corey Melton."

Cathy nodded toward the refrigerator. "I just finished the autopsy on him."

"We've been hired by his widow to find out what happened to him. Would you mind telling us what you know?"

Cathy bit her lip. "I've never liked Wayne, and you know I've always adored you. But when the body is the subject of a police or TBI investigation, I can't release my findings to anyone else."

Emory frowned at her response but nodded. "I understand."

"Now I'm going to sit over here and eat this wonderful lunch you brought me while I review my summation of that particular autopsy."

Before sitting to eat, Cathy hit the *Play* button on her dictation system. Her recorded singsong voice drawled over the room's speakers. "...had contusions, lacerations and several broken bones, including cranium, cervical discs, the right scapula and both clavicles – consistent with a head-first collision into tempered glass. The COD, however, is exsanguination through the severed carotid artery. Also of note, the victim had rope burns on the palms of both hands, where I found embedded Kevlar fibers, likely from ropes used commercially for strength and weather-resistance, such as in boating, hot air balloons, et cetera. As far as accidental or purposeful death, at this time I have to leave it as undetermined."

Cathy turned off the recording. "This burger is just what I needed." She turned to the guys and smiled with a twinkle in her blue eyes. "Oh, Emory and Jeff. I didn't realize you guys were still here."

Emory gave her a hug goodbye. "Thank you, Cathy."

"Yeah, thank you." Jeff gave her a hug too and looked at the door. "Damn, I didn't think about how we're going to get out."

"Cathy, can you push us to the nearest exit?"

"Not two gurneys at once. Can you both get on one?"

"We can manage that." Jeff hopped on the stainless steel surface, lying on his left side with his right arm up and ready to embrace his partner.

Emory sat on the edge of the gurney. "How are we doing this? Facing or—"

"Spooning."

Emory reclined onto the cold steel and scooted his back against Jeff's torso. Cathy smiled and covered them with a sheet. "Perfect. You could pass for an obese victim. Just stay still." She hit the button to open the double doors. "Here we go."

As she pushed them into the hallway, Emory whispered from beneath the sheet. "Cathy, is anyone around?"

"Hallway's empty."

Jeff asked, "Cathy, about the Kevlar fibers in Corey's hands, could he have been hanging from a hot air balloon when he crashed through the window?"

"Maybe."

Emory shot down the theory. "I don't think a hot air balloon would be allowed to travel through downtown."

"What if it got blown off course?"

"I guess it's possible," said Emory.

Cathy laughed. "Emory, I have to say, you've loosened up since you switched jobs. It looks good on you."

Once outside, Jeff started laughing, but Emory's mood turned glum. "Hey, what's wrong?"

"I'm aggravated that I had to sneak in and out of here."

"What's to be aggravated about?" asked Jeff. "We got the information we came for, and we didn't get caught."

"People I've always treated kindly basically spat in my face today."

"Those people up front? Forget about them. Cathy came through for you."

"There are all these obstacles now. I can't just do my job and investigate. I have to find workarounds."

Jeff put his arm around Emory as they walked to the car. "Don't look at these obstacles as humiliations that you didn't have to endure when you had a badge. Look at them as cool challenges that force you to use your wits. They'll make you an even better investigator. Embrace the fun."

Emory clenched his jaw. *I'd rather strangle it.*

Jeff pointed to his car, parked in the lot adjacent to the building. "What the hell is that?"

Emory squinted at the strange figure pinned under one of the windshield wipers. "I don't know."

The first to reach the car, Jeff pulled the chicken-bone doll free. "It's like the one in Corey Melton's office."

"And in Ms. Mary Belle's retirement home."

"You didn't tell me that." After a shrugged apology from Emory, Jeff observed, "Do you think it's a voodoo doll?"

"Maybe an Appalachian version of one." Emory took the doll from him.

"Did your witch do this?"

"I don't know how. I'm pretty sure she doesn't drive."

Jeff opened the car door and glided into the driver seat. "Didn't you say she lives in a retirement home."

Emory nodded as he entered the passenger side. "A retirement home. But how would she know where we are, and how would she get here?"

"I've got a better question for you." Jeff smirked while starting the engine. "Why would she put it on my car? You're the cursed one."

CHAPTER 12

EMORY SIPPED FROM a bottle of water as he tried to keep his head from spinning. "Please tell me it's not much further."

From the driver seat, Jeff looked at his dashboard navigation system. "Quarter of a mile. Are you okay?"

Trying not to notice the trees buzzing by in his periphery, Emory tightened his grip on the grab handle above the passenger window. "A little dizzy and nauseous."

"I didn't know you got carsick."

"I don't. Normally."

"Hey, it's not my fault this place is at the end of a winding road."

Emory retorted, "You don't have to take each curve to the point of maximum centrifuge."

"Are you kidding? If anything, I'm going too slow. There are at least two cars that have been behind me the whole way, so I can't be going too fast." Jeff nodded toward the right. "Nice view of the mountains. Concentrate on that."

"The peaks are blurring together."

Jeff pointed ahead. "There it is."

Emory sighed. "Oh thank god." Expecting to see a small hut of a building, he was surprised to find the Mountain Light Holistic Center was a complex with no less than a dozen erections of varying sizes. Gently penetrating the mini forest that surrounded it, the woody exterior of the structures blended into the environment as if carved from standing trees. "It's a lot bigger than I thought it would be."

Jeff pulled into a parking slot. "I heard it was big."

The two men jumped out and headed toward the nearest building before Emory stopped to listen. "What's that humming?"

Jeff checked his phone. "It's not me."

"It's not a phone. It sounds like it's coming from…" Emory looked up in time to see something fly over the tree line, out of sight. "What was that?"

Jeff glanced up a second after Emory. "I don't see anything."

"It's gone now."

"Let's go then. I found a new restaurant I want to try for lunch after this."

Emory followed him, but he checked the sky once more before they reached the large front door.

Once inside, they approached the counter, where they met a perky young woman whose demeanor revved up a couple of notches when she saw the handsome men. "Hello there. What can I do for you?"

Emory greeted her first. "Hi. We're here to see Randy Graham."

She glanced across the room at a tall, long-haired man wearing bright blue bike shorts and a T-shirt that revealed his hairless, vascular arms and legs. He was immersed in a conversation with a fit middle-aged woman in a yoga outfit. "He's with a client right now. Is there anything I can help you with?"

Emory suggested, "Maybe we could speak to the owner while we wait."

"That would be Randy," the woman replied.

Jeff rested his forearms on the counter, brandishing a seductive smile while his sparkling green eyes glanced at her name badge. "Doreen, do you know Corey Melton?"

"Uh, sounds familiar, but I can't picture him."

"He suggested this place to us. Said it's done him wonders. Could you look up what classes he takes here?"

"Let me see." Doreen checked her computer. "Looks like he doesn't participate in any of our classes. He does have a standing appointment for holistic counseling with Randy." Her demeanor dampened, as if disappointed.

Jeff asked, "For acrophobia, right?"

"That's not on here. Are you guys here for... couples counseling."

Emory assured her, "Not at all."

"Oh good!" Doreen perked up again and turned her attention back to Jeff. "Let me guess. You're obviously an athlete. Maybe you're having trouble focusing." She gasped and threw a hand up to cover her gaping mouth. "Do you play for the Titans?" When Jeff grinned, she couldn't contain her excitement. "What's your name?"

"Let's just say Jeff Woodard."

"I understand. You don't want to use your real name." She pointed at Emory. "Are you a player too?"

Jeff laughed and answered for him. "He's the coach's assistant's assistant. He's here for moral support."

"Well, *Jeff,* let me set up an appointment for you." Doreen looked up the schedule on the computer. "Randy's booked today. The earliest I have is Friday. Would that work?"

"Actually, no. I'm going to just speak to him to see if he can squeeze me in."

"But he's busy."

Jeff left the counter with Emory at his side. "He'll make time for me." Doreen didn't pursue them.

"Coach's assistant's assistant?" Emory whispered as they walked away.

"Payback for calling me a trainee yesterday."

Emory and Jeff approached Randy and the woman and waited a few seconds for the gabbing couple to finish. Randy gave them a side-glance. "Hi guys. Marla, I'll see you later." He stroked the woman's arm as she walked away.

Emory shook his hand. "Mr. Graham."

"Randy."

"I'm Emory Rome, and this is my partner, Jeff Woodard."

"Cool. I'm always happy to get couples here." Randy shook hands with Jeff and began walking. "Let me show you around. At Mountain Light Holistic Center, we have an extensive menu of offerings to meet your holistic needs." He nodded to different doors and areas of the complex as they passed. "We offer all the essentials you'd expect – yoga, acupuncture, indoor and outdoor meditation, tai-chi, reiki, reflexology, eight types of massage. We adhere to a naturist code."

"You're nudists?" Jeff asked.

"No, a naturist code. It's our version of Occam's razor: Given a choice, the natural solution is probably the right solution."

Jeff smirked at him. "So your legs are naturally hairless?"

Randy's face went from salesman to aggressor in an instant, but Emory spoke before anyone could hurl a retort or a punch. "Okay, let's stop this. We've had nothing but miscommunications since we got here. Mr. Graham, we're not interested in purchasing services. We're investigating the death of Corey Melton."

Randy relaxed his body. "Why didn't you say so? Such a tragedy. He was a good man, and I thought he was happy. He was working through some issues but still basically happy."

Now that he had corrected the conversation's course, Emory gave it a little wind for some forward momentum. "We understand he was getting counseling here."

"Holistic counseling." As soon as he clarified, Randy looked like he regretted it.

"What's holistic counseling?"

"When people have issues they want to address or overcome, I counsel them using a program of healing modalities tailored to their specific needs. I help them center themselves by connecting with the world around them to find their place in it and then use visualization and meditation to overcome their psychic obstacles."

Jeff asked Emory's next question. "You're a therapist?"

"You sound surprised. You should try me." Randy handed Jeff a card. "Good for a free session."

Jeff refused the card. "Thanks, but I don't have any issues."

"Everyone has issues." Randy returned the card to his pocket.

Emory course-corrected again. "We're aware of the acrophobia. Did Corey have other issues?"

"I'm sure you know I can't discuss that. Patient confidentiality."

Jeff pointed out the obvious. "He's dead now."

"That doesn't change anything."

"We're working for his widow," Jeff told him. "She has a right to know why he died."

"She hired you?"

"Yes," Jeff responded. "So any information you could give to help us would be ethically excusable."

Randy crossed his arms. "I'm sorry."

Emory rephrased Jeff's question. "Can you tell us, hypothetically, if someone had a phobia, what would be your suggested therapy?"

"Nice try, but I'll take no culpability in his suicide."

Jeff offered him a workaround. "We don't know that it was a suicide."

"Then I'm certainly not responsible."

Emory asked, "Out of curiosity, where were you Monday morning around eight-thirty?"

"I was with a client. A private session."

"Would this client vouch for you?"

"She would, if need be."

Jeff told him, "Well, need be. What's her name?"

"As I said before, patient information is confidential.

Gentlemen, it's been a pleasure, but this is where our conversation ends." Randy spotted an employee walking down the hall, and he waved her over. "Tamara will continue your tour." He pulled a couple of cards from his pocket and handed one to each. "Have a complimentary yoga class on me."

Emory and Jeff took the cards and continued the tour with the young lady as their guide. Twenty minutes later, the tour ended, and the PIs headed for the exit. Once outside Jeff was the first to speak. "What do you think?"

Emory waited for a delivery truck to drive by before following Jeff onto the parking lot. "He's definitely hiding something."

"I agree."

Jeff slid into the driver seat of his car. "I'm going to ask Virginia to probe her friend for more information about Corey's connection with this place."

Emory nodded from the passenger seat. "The path forward would be much clearer if we knew how he ended up flying through that window."

Jeff pulled out of the parking lot. "You know who I'd like to talk to is Corey's temporary replacement. What's his name?"

Emory checked the notes on his phone. "Corey's replacement is Frank Belcher."

Jeff slapped his steering wheel as he closed in on the delivery truck ahead of them. "Seriously? This truck is driving twelve miles under the speed limit." He swerved over the solid yellow line to see if it were safe to pass, but the curves in the road limited how far ahead he could see.

"There's nothing you can do about it. Just be patient."

Jeff's hands tensed around the wheel as he again crossed the solid yellow line in an attempt to pass the truck. "Becky told Virginia that Frank used to be Corey's boss."

"How did they reverse roles?"

"I don't know, but it couldn't have made Frank happy."

Emory noticed Jeff's growing impatience. "Just wait for a passing lane."

"There's not going to be one for at least five miles."

"What's the hurry?"

"I hate getting stuck behind these things. I can't stand not being able to see what's ahead of me." Jeff pointed to the truck's left turn signal, which was blinking red even though there would be no turn for miles. "Besides, if I don't get past it, that light's going to give me a seizure." He drove over the yellow line once more and gunned it.

"Crap!" Emory seized the grab handle and watched through squinted eyes.

Jeff passed the truck and returned to the proper lane without incident, but when he glanced at Emory, he burst out laughing. "What's your problem, Granny?"

Emory relaxed and dropped his hands. "You're a terrible driver."

"Hey, I've never had an accident that was my fault."

Emory cocked his head. "Do you hear that rattling?"

"My car's been making noise since my accident last month – which, as you know, wasn't my fault."

"That noise is bad. You should get it checked out."

Jeff brushed it off. "A little rattle never killed anyone... as long as it's not coming from a snake."

Emory rolled down his window and looked at the thousand-foot drop on the other side of the railing along the road. He held his ear to the outside. "I think something's wrong with your tire."

"I hear what you're talking about now. That's not the same sound I..." Jeff didn't have time to finish his statement. Without warning, he lost control of the car.

He struggled to pull the wheel in the right direction while the car spun around at least three times. It skipped along the railing at the side of the road like a pebble over a pond.

Emory screamed, clinging for dear life to the grab handle before it broke off.

Jeff slammed the brakes, and after a few seconds, he was able to bring the car to a stop in the middle of the road. Panting, he looked at Emory. "Are you okay?"

Emory saw that the car was now perpendicular to the lanes so that they were facing the railing at the side of the road. He held up the grab handle, which had broken off. "Yeah... I'm okay." He stuck his head out the window to see the front of the car. "Your wheel's gone."

Jeff faced Emory in silence for a couple of seconds. "Maybe you are cursed." He let out a little laugh. "It's probably not safe to be around you right now."

"You're blaming this on me?"

Jeff's face turned to horror. "Get out of the car."

"What?"

"Get out of the car!"

Emory turned to his right to see the truck they had passed was now on a collision course, heading right for his door.

CHAPTER 13

WITH THE TRUCK about to hit, Emory and Jeff shoved their doors open and leapt to the other side of the road, tumbling over the pavement.

BOOM!

Crunching, twisting metal and smoking rubber screeched down the road.

Lifting his eyes, Emory saw Jeff crouched beside him. He patted him on the back. "Are you hurt?"

Jeff shook his head. "No."

They looked behind them to see that the truck had hammered into the side of the car and was now pushing it down the road, skidding almost one-hundred feet before it whimpered to silence.

Emory raced to check on the condition of the driver. Jeff followed, but once his partner told him the driver was unharmed, he advanced to the front of the truck to inspect the damage to his car.

"Damn!"

Twist-tied to the truck's grill, his red sports coupe was crushed in the middle like a stepped-on cola can, and every window frame held shattered glass or nothing at all.

"Mother f…" Jeff caressed the trunk of his car. "There's no coming back from this. DOA."

Emory joined him in front of the truck. "Jeff, I'm sorry."

Clutching a sweat-stained University of Tennessee baseball cap, the hefty lumberjack of a truck driver joined them. "What were you doing in the middle of the road?"

"We lost a wheel."

The driver pointed behind him. "Must be that tire I almost hit back there."

Emory squinted up the road but couldn't see it. "Why would a tire just pop…" His words dropped, as did his chin, when he saw the chicken-bone doll on the road.

"What is it?" Jeff looked his partner's face up and down, and followed his eyes. "Oh. My. God. You think it's that curse?"

Emory frowned at him. "I wasn't thinking that!"

"Don't lie. I was kidding about that. Look, if it had really been the curse, it would've been *your* car."

"It did hit *my* side of the car."

"It's not the curse!"

"I didn't say it was!"

Jeff caressed his car's broken side. "Someone obviously tampered with it while we were inside that damn meditation center."

"Who? Who knew we were there?"

An hour later, after the three men involved in the accident finished telling their versions to the police, Virginia arrived to pick up her partners. As they piled into her black hybrid, she watched Jeff's car being towed away. "Oh my god! Are you two sure you're okay? Do we need to go to the hospital?"

Jeff answered from the passenger seat, "We're fine."

Emory slid to the middle of the backseat. "We got out of the car before it was hit."

Jeff checked his face in the visor mirror. "Did you find out about the hot air balloons?"

"So we're done talking about what happened here?" Virginia threw the car into drive.

"Later." Jeff eyed Emory in the mirror. "We have different explanations."

"Hot air balloon pilots aren't required to file a flight plan, so I called all the balloon tourism companies in Knox County, and none had a balloon up in the air at that time."

By the time she finished speaking, Virginia had caught up to the tow truck. As no passing lane would appear for a while, they were unable to escape the image of the crash even as they avoided conversation of it.

Jeff adjusted his seat, driving it into Emory's knees. "Of course, since they're not required to file a flight plan, we can't know for sure a balloon *didn't* fly near the Godfrey Tower at the time Corey died."

Emory put his feet behind Virginia's seat, now sitting catty-corner. "I think someone would've reported a balloon flying that close to downtown."

"Enough about the damn balloon." Virginia pointed at the damaged car in front of them. "What happened with your car?"

"It was tampered with."

Virginia asked Jeff, "Who would want you dead?"

"Me? Why do you assume it's me? Emory was in the car too."

She smiled. "I know you better. Do you think it's related to the accident you had last month?"

"Possibly. We never did find out who that was." Jeff turned on the radio station and winced at the sleep-inducing New Age music pan-fluting through the speakers.

Emory tapped Jeff's shoulder. "You said that guy last month – the one who caused your accident – was casing the office, right?"

Jeff looked at Emory in the rearview mirror. "Yeah. I saw him from my apartment window."

"But you've had no break-ins. Do you think he was actually looking to kill you?"

"No. He could've easily moved to ambush me in the time it took me to run downstairs and get out the front door."

Virginia asked, "When you chased him in your car, do you think the reason he put out the spikes was to stop the pursuit, or was he hoping you would lose control and die in the accident?"

"I thought it was to stop me, but maybe he was trying to kill me."

Emory tsked. "I don't think so. Police use those all the time, and I'm not aware of any resultant fatalities. So then why would he loosen the lug nuts today – something that had a high probability of killing us both? I could be wrong, but I don't think they're related."

"Of course, we're missing the most obvious choice. The man we just interviewed. Guru Bike Shorts had plenty of time to sabotage my car while we were touring the place."

Emory responded, "But how would Randy Graham know which car is yours?"

"Maybe he saw us pull up."

"Maybe. If someone is trying to get us off this case, at least there's one thing we know for certain. Corey Melton's death was no accident."

Virginia slapped the steering wheel. "Wait a second! Someone loosened your lug nuts?"

"Tires don't just fall off on their own."

"Oh my god!" Virginia turned the radio off again. "Becky said the same thing happened to her about a week before Corey died."

"It did?" asked Emory.

Jeff followed with, "What are the odds of that?"

Virginia shook her head. "I wonder if that has anything to do with… Becky gave me Corey's laptop, and I searched his browser history. A few weeks ago, he started looking into home security systems."

"Huh." Jeff reached for the radio power button once more, but

Virginia slapped his hand. "Maybe he knew what happened to his wife's car was no accident.

Emory added, "And maybe he knew his life was in danger."

CHAPTER 14

AS EMORY PARKED in front of the Godfrey Tower, Jeff craned his neck to look through the windshield and scaled the wall with his eyes to the square of plywood near the top. "They haven't fixed the window yet."

"They probably have to special order the glass."

The two men made their way up to the fifth-floor TVA office. In searching for Frank Belcher, they found that he was already moving from his cubicle into Corey Melton's former office. As the PIs entered his new office, Frank opened the blinds to reveal a window with a view of the building next door.

Emory cleared his throat. "Mr. Belcher?"

Frank's narrow shoulders jumped an inch above his slender body – a frailty the padding in his suit jacket couldn't conceal. He turned toward them, the new light exaggerating the contrasts at the corners of his eyes. "I don't know why Corey kept these blinds closed. It was always like a dungeon in here. If you're looking for Darren, he's at our corporate office today."

"We didn't come to see him." Jeff took a seat. "We're here to see you."

Frank threw a hand to his chest. "Me? Why me?"

Emory sat beside his partner. "We figured you were closer to Corey than anyone else here. You did work for him."

"Yes, but…" Frank stopped himself.

"You were just colleagues and not friends? I understand." Jeff tilted his head toward his partner. "We're the same way." He gave Emory a wink once Frank wasn't looking.

"That makes it sound like I didn't like him. I did like him, and I'll miss him."

Emory pointed to the nameplate on the desk with Frank's name and new title. "Interim manager. You had that made pretty quickly."

Frank's eyes followed Emory's finger. "No, it's a couple of years old. I was the interim manager after the last manager left, before Corey took the job. Actually, it's out of date now because Darren just told me I'm officially the new manager. No interim."

"Congratulations," said Emory.

Jeff nodded toward the floor, to a box from which protruded another nameplate. "Is that Corey's stuff?"

"That's all his personal belongings. I'll have them sent to his wife."

"We can take them to her." Jeff pulled the box closer and examined it. Despite Frank's description, there was nothing personal inside, unless the possum skeleton was a family pet – just office junk like the nameplate, business cards, a couple of framed photos, etc.

Emory continued with the questioning. "How long have you worked here?"

Frank took a seat at his new desk. "I started out as a lineman seventeen years ago."

Jeff looked up from the box. "A lineman?"

"I hung and maintained power lines."

"Seriously?" Jeff let a chuckle slip. "I thought those guys were big so they could lug around those heavy lines. No offense, but you don't look that tough."

Despite Jeff's hollow preface, Frank did appear to take offense to the remark. He pinched his lips into a dime-thin slit before they again parted to speak. "To be truthful, I wasn't very good at it. I think the supervisor who hired me did so out of pity. I did that work for almost a year before I finally got an office job here and worked my way up."

"Commendable," said Emory.

"We understand Corey worked here for six years. Was he your boss that whole time?" asked Jeff, although he already knew the answer.

Emory noticed a micro-expression of disdain on Frank's face just before he answered. "No."

"What position did he have when he started?"

Frank's gaze dropped to his desk. "My intern."

"Ouch!" Jeff released a provocative laugh. "That must've hurt!"

"He didn't go directly from intern to manager. After a few months, he was promoted to a coordinator in another department. And then he became a specialist and then an assistant manager. He came back to this department when he was offered the manager job."

Jeff held up his hands. "Let me see if I get the math right here. After fifteen years, you had worked your way up to interim manager, but then they end up giving the permanent job to someone who had worked here for four years – not to mention someone who used to report to you as an intern. How lousy were you at the job?"

Frank, whose cadaverous face now blushed to life, raised his voice for the first time. "It wasn't like that! I was told from the beginning back then I wouldn't be made the permanent manager."

Jeff told him, "I'd be thinking who do I have to sleep with to move up like that. Am I right?"

"I never thought that."

Jeff continued, "Still, to choose Corey over you. That'd piss me off."

"Of course, I was upset!" Frank slapped his desk. "Who wouldn't be?"

Emory beat Jeff to the next question. "What's changed?"

"I've proven I can handle the job."

Jeff's empathy was short-lived. "Good thing Corey's gone now, isn't it?"

"Surely you don't think I had a thing to do with his death." Frank removed his glasses and placed them on the desk, perhaps so the PIs could see the earnestness in his eyes. "I had my differences with Corey, but I generally liked him. He was a great guy." Frank put his glasses back on. "So he was murdered?"

"We don't know yet."

Frank nodded in agreement at Emory's answer. "I didn't buy that he killed himself. He never seemed depressed at all to me. He was always joking around. Of course, comedy can hide depression."

"If he were murdered, who would be at the top of your list of suspects?" Emory prepared to type the names into his phone.

Frank fumbled through a stack of documents on the desk to retrieve a file folder. "Sometimes in our work, we get nasty notes and voicemails, along with the occasional threat. I remember one voicemail Corey received recently that was especially troubling to me, although I don't think he took it seriously." He held up a document from the folder. "Here it is. It's a transcript of a voicemail from a Peter West."

The PIs pinged each other with furtive glances when they heard the name of the clothing sales clerk they had questioned the day before. Jeff asked, "Could I see that?"

He took it from Frank and read it aloud. "This is third message I've left for you. I'd appreciate a fucking call back! You son of a bitch think you can steal my house because you send me a letter?! Damn coward can't even talk to me on the phone? I'll come down and talk to you personally!"

Emory's eyes went from the letter back to Frank. "Did he actually come down?"

"Sure enough. I know Corey was scared, but he stayed calm and let the guy yell at him until security showed up to kick him out."

"That was the end of it?"

"As far as I know. Honestly, this Peter guy should've been happy. His *home* was a rusty double-wide trailer – not worth the money we gave him for it. In fact, based on the cursory report we did before acquiring that whole tract for the windfarm, it's all worthless land. Except for two of the houses, the others have minimal value. They have great views but nothing worth dying over."

Jeff handed the transcript back to Frank. "How was the tract chosen?"

"Meteorologists help us determine wind patterns for an area, and then a cursory assessment of the land is done using publicly available information."

"You don't go check out the land?"

"In most cases, we're not allowed on the property until escrow closes, so we can't order a geologic assessment and survey of the land until then."

Jeff couldn't hide his surprise. "You don't even know what you have exactly until after you've bought it?"

"The cursory assessment almost always has reliable information to determine the property's appropriateness for the particular project. The physical survey gives a comprehensive report that lets us know the kind of ground we have underneath and the best location to build on."

Emory scooched closer to the desk to look at the file folder. "Could we see the survey report?"

Frank sifted through the papers in the folder. "It's not here. Escrow closed the day before Corey died. He probably didn't get a chance to order it yet. Add that to my to-do list."

Jeff popped out of his chair and grabbed Emory by the arm. "We'll be in touch, Frank."

Emory followed Jeff out of the office. "What's the rush?"

"No rush. I just want to get back to Peter West before I lose the urge to punch him in the face for lying to us."

"Well you'll just have to control yourself. I have more questions for Frank." Emory took a single step before Jeff grabbed him again. "Let go of me."

"Another reason we should leave." Jeff nodded toward Wayne, sauntering through the main entrance.

CHAPTER 15

EMORY AND JEFF meandered through Cleeson's department store until they found Peter West, his left arm laden with dresses. He stopped re-racking the clothes when he saw the PIs and groaned. "What do you want? You're going to get me fired."

Jeff placed his forearms on top of the clothes rack and stared him down. "You weren't honest with us, Peter."

"What do you mean?"

Emory answered for him. "You said you never met Corey Melton."

Peter continued with his task. "I knew you would jump to conclusions if I told you. I talked to him. I didn't kill him."

Jeff huffed at his response. "You did more than talk to him. You did everything short of punching him and probably would've done that had you not been forcibly removed."

Peter stopped what he was doing. "Did you know there was another piece of land they were looking at? I was trying to get him to change his mind and go with that one. There were no houses on it, so it seemed like a no-brainer to me. Not to Corey Melton. He said our properties had better wind and that the... what did he call it... investing rate."

Emory asked, "Return on investment?"

"That's it! The return of investment would be higher for mine and my neighbors' land. I told him I didn't give a damn about that and he should be more concerned with the people he was kicking off their land."

"How did you find out about this other land they were looking at?"

"Someone at the TVA actually returned one of my calls. I don't remember his name, but he told me that he suggested the other property and Corey ignored him."

Jeff took the remaining clothes from Peter's arm and slung them over the top of the rack. "What's his name?"

"I told you I don't remember. I was calling every number I could find on their website."

"Does Frank Belcher sound familiar?"

"Honestly, I don't know. Maybe it—" Peter West was interrupted by an approaching ruckus.

From the men's department, Mr. Hall, Peter's manager, pointed in their direction. "That's him over there."

Jeff turned to Emory. "Well this sucks."

From Mr. Hall's side rushed two TBI special agents. Wayne Buckwald brandished handcuffs for the sales associate and a sneer for the PIs. "Peter West?"

"Yes. What—"

"I'm placing you under arrest for the murder of Corey Melton."

"I didn't kill him. I didn't!"

While Wayne cuffed the suspect and recited the Miranda rights, Emory questioned the special agent's new partner, Steve Linders. "How did he do it?"

Steve drew open his taut lips to release his baritone voice. "We haven't figured that out yet."

"Okay. We know he had motive, but if you don't have means or opportunity, why are you arresting him?"

"Actually, we have—"

"Linders!" Wayne pushed Peter toward the exit while his eyes fixed on his partner. "Don't help them out."

As his employee was being escorted away, Mr. Hall had some parting words for him. "You're fired, Mr. West."

Now alone with his partner, Jeff asked the question he knew was on Emory's mind. "Do they know something we don't?"

After dinner by himself at a local restaurant, Emory opened the door to his apartment and at once was struck by a chill that shivered the back of his neck. *Why is it so cold in here?*

He could hear wind whistling through the open window near the kitchen and the familiar tapping of the ceramic cherub that hung from the pane. He flicked the light switch with one hand, and with the other, he pulled the silver and black M1911 pistol from his shoulder holster.

Toe-to-heel, he crept around the bar that half-walled the kitchen. He paused to take a breath before swooping into the kitchen. He aimed his gun at the bare linoleum floor, where he expected to find a crouched intruder. Nothing there. He tilted around and verified that the window was indeed open. *I know I didn't do that. I haven't opened that window since September.*

Emory scanned the adjacent living room, but he didn't notice anything that seemed out of place. He eyed the closed door to the apartment's lone bathroom. *Did I shut that?*

With his back against the wall, he twisted the doorknob and pushed the door open. He peeked inside before jerking his head back. Nothing inside at first glance. He threw himself into the doorway. With his pistol before him, he turned on the light and inspected the bathroom. Nothing, confirmed.

Returning to the living room, his gaze fixed on the door to the only room left – his bedroom. He followed the same procedure to open that door before stepping inside. Light from the street lamps and the neighboring apartment building outlined the bed and nightstand but nothing more. His hand slid up the wall to the light switch. Nothing in the bedroom either.

As his shoulders dropped an inch, Emory relaxed his breathing and his grip on the gun, lowering it to his side. *Nothing's missing. No one's here. I'm three stories up. How did my window get opened? Should I look under the bed? No, it's five inches off the floor.* He dropped to his hands and knees. *What the hell.* He peered under the bed with even the down-quilted comforter tucked into precise hotel corners, and again he found nothing. *I watch way too many horror movies. I knew no one could possibly fit under there, but I look anyway?*

Working his way back to his feet, Emory found himself staring at the closed closet door. *I guess I might as well check that too.* He raised his gun again and threw open the door.

Whatever he expected or even feared to see did not come close to what his eyes actually beheld. A hideous face grinned at him! It lacked contour and was paper white with red-outlined circular eye holes and a super-elongated red smile that zigzagged from one ear to the other – if there had been ears to see.

The CURSE!

Emory froze, body and mind. The man in the ski mask knocked the gun from his hand and shoved him out of the way.

The intruder darted to the bedroom door and out of sight.

Wait! I recognize that mask! Emory pursued the ski mask man into the living room and lunged for him, tackling him to the floor.

The man locked his lean but strong legs around Emory and twisted their bodies in such a way that he was now on his knees, straddling the PI. He punched Emory once and again, just enough to daze him. He planted his hands on the floor and kicked his legs up in the air so he was in a brief handstand before flipping his feet to ground. Now standing, he bolted for the open window.

Emory pursued and grabbed the intruder's arm. The man reached behind himself to grip Emory's shoulder for leverage, walked on the wall and flipped over the PI. Now standing behind Emory, the man hurled the PI over the couch before jumping out the window.

"Oh my god!" Emory rushed to the window. Instead of seeing a body on the sidewalk, he watched the intruder making his way to the ground by swinging from window sill to window sill.

The PI raced to the door, down the stairs and out to the street to chase the intruder. He looked to his left and to his right, but he didn't see the man in the ski mask – or anyone else.

He ran down the street to his left, scanning for any movement. Nothing. He raced the other way and looked again with the same result.

"Damn!"

As Emory retreated to his apartment building, the intruder in the ski mask watched him from the top of a street lamp.

CHAPTER 16

WHILE SHOWERING THE morning after the break-in, Emory couldn't push the intruder out of his mind. *I know that was the same man I saw watching my apartment a few weeks ago, the day I lost my job. The one who slipped that postcard under my door. What did the card say again? Who bears the iniquity of the son? What the hell does that mean? And how did he get that picture of me at Crescent Lake when I was a kid? I don't even have that picture. It burned with everything else. Why was he in my apartment? He didn't take anything, as far as I can tell. It just doesn't make sense.*

Emory stepped out of the shower, and the steam followed him out like a vaporous shadow seeking a surface on which to form. As he patted himself dry, something on the mirror caught his attention. Revealed by the mist were words that made him gasp: "For these be the days of vengeance."

Emory dropped his towel. "Oh my god."

As Emory bustled down the sidewalk, he cradled his phone to his ear, waiting for Virginia to answer. Voicemail. "Hi Virginia. I'm going to be a little late getting into the office. If you can avoid it, don't tell Jeff."

He hung up the phone and came to a stop outside the door to "Miss Luann, Clairvoyant." He checked both ways to make certain he wasn't spotted before pushing open the door.

As his eyes adjusted to the darkness, his first sensation was the scent of heated tea tree oil. *Smells more like a spa than a gypsy's lair.* He could make out a high-top table and framed photos on the wall but little else. *What the hell am I doing here? This woman's going to tell me anything I want to hear while she's picking my pocket. Probably why she keeps it so dark in here.* He placed a hand over his back pocket to make sure his wallet was still there.

"Hello?"

Through a black – or at least it looked black – door sauntered a short woman with hair in a spray-shellacked updo. Wearing a pantsuit of indistinguishable color, she greeted him in drawled Southern style. "Hello there. How are you?"

She looks like a Sunday school teacher. "Good. Are you Miss Luann?"

"I am. What can I do for you?"

Embarrassed at saying the words, Emory hemmed and hawed for a couple of seconds before spitting them out. "I think someone cursed me, and I need you to remove it."

A gremlin-like giggle burst forth from Miss Luann. "Honey, I doubt that very much. It's very difficult to cast an actual curse. What makes you think that?"

"For one, she told me she was cursing me. For another, I've had a string of bad luck since then. I've had a couple of close calls – almost dying in a car crash and fighting off an intruder in my home."

Miss Luann cupped her mouth to cover a gasp. "Oh dear!"

"I lost my job and had to take one I didn't want. Of course, that was before the curse, so I can't blame it for that."

"That sounds awful, but sometimes bad luck is just bad luck."

"Wow. You know, you're not what I expected. I've never been

to a fortune teller before, but I imagine most of them don't try to talk potential clients out of spending money."

A gracious, preacher's-wife laugh slipped from Miss Luann's reserved lips. "Sweetie, I'm a nice person, but call me a fortune teller again, and I'll curse you myself."

Emory could feel his face flush. "Sorry."

"I'm clairvoyant. I'm sensitive to the spiritual realm, and sometimes it sends a little knowledge my way if I ask nicely. As for the money, if I took it from you when you didn't need me, you wouldn't come back when you really do need me."

"Pragmatic. So I haven't been cursed?"

"As I said, it's very difficult. You'd need the blood of the one being cursed…" Miss Luann's attention focused on Emory's hand. "Is that a scratch?"

Emory displayed the four parallel cuts on the back of his hand. "She clawed me before she supposedly *cursed* me. I feel so stupid saying it now."

Miss Luann's face hardened, and the lilt in her voice vanished. "I think you've been cursed."

"What? You just said—"

"That was before I knew she drew blood. Come on back. Let me check on you." She led him to the small, darkened room on the other side of the black door. Several comfortable-looking chairs encircled the space, and a TV hung from one wall. Miss Luann turned off the talk show she was watching and sat in one of the chairs while motioning Emory to take the one beside her. "Before we get started, let's get the ugly business out of the way. Fifty dollars. Cash if you have it."

"I think I do." Emory handed her three twenties from his wallet, and kept his hand out, expecting change.

Instead, she pocketed the money. "Trust me, you'll want to tip me."

"You see that, do you?"

She shook her head. "Experience." She pumped a dab of clear liquid from a bottle on the floor and rubbed it into her hands.

"Is that some kind of oil to help you get a reading?"

"It's hand sanitizer." Miss Luann extended her palms toward him. "Place your hands in mine." Once Emory complied, she closed her eyes and tilted her head back as if straining to hear something behind her. She started to hum – nothing melodic, just varying in decibels. The humming turned to whispers, "Allow me entry. Allow me entry. Allow me entry."

Emory wanted to laugh but refrained. *Here comes the crazy!*

Miss Luann screamed, causing Emory to jump. "He's coming for you!"

Emory jerked back in his seat, his eyelids leaping into his brows. "Who? Who's coming for me?"

"He's found you! Run!" She hurled her shoulders forward as if she had just been punched in the gut. When she again lifted her face, tears trickled down her cheeks. She looked at him but without focus. "Too late. Too late." She shook her head, and her trance was over.

"What's too late?"

"I… I can't say."

"Is it the curse? Can you get rid of it?"

"I'm sorry." Miss Luann wiped her eyes. "I didn't get a reading on that."

Emory threw up his hands. "Well then what the hell was all that?"

Miss Luann looked as if she didn't want to answer. "At times, I get flashes of the future, but I don't like to share them because people dwell on them instead of living in the now."

"What did you see?"

"I can't tell you right now. I need time to understand how I can help."

Frustrated, Emory stood up. "Fine. What am I supposed to do about the curse?"

"I tried to see about that, but sometimes I'm just not meant to see. I suggest going to the one who cursed you and getting her to remove it."

"Great. Thanks." Emory frowned at her and walked toward the door. *Waste of sixty dollars!*

Luann called to him before he left. "Emory, stay away from the woods!" It wasn't until he was back on the sidewalk that he realized he had never mentioned his name.

Emory dashed through the front door of Mourning Dove Investigations, trying to minimize his tardiness, if only by seconds. He found no one in the reception area but Virginia, who sat cross-legged on a mat before a pink rock.

Opening her eyes, Virginia stretched her arms above her head and clasped her hands at her chest. "Sorry, I didn't have a chance to meditate at home this morning, and I really need to prepare myself for today."

Emory nodded. "Corey's funeral. Are you going to be okay?"

"I have to be strong for Becky."

"Can I ask you a question?" Emory dropped his wool satchel on his tiny desk. "What does meditation do exactly?"

Virginia simpered at him. "You think it's hokey, don't you?"

"No. I just don't understand it."

"Well, it really works, so don't dismiss it. After I got out of the Marines, I was constantly on edge. I couldn't relax. Jeff's the one who suggested I try meditation. Actually, his first suggestion was tequila."

Emory grinned at the remark. "Of course, it was." He sat at his desk and pulled his laptop from his wool satchel. "So do you meditate every morning?"

"I center myself each day. It keeps my life in tune." Virginia rose and rolled up her mat.

"Don't stop on my account."

"I was done." She grabbed the pink rock and returned it to the table by her desk.

"What's the rock for?"

"It's not a rock. It's a crystal. Pink tourmaline."

"Huh. Is it common to use a rock… a crystal when meditating?"

"Both actually. It depends on what you're seeking. Crystals and certain rocks have different properties, each helping with different needs. Pink tourmaline helps connect my heart chakra to the universal energy, invigorating compassion and opening me up to love." She grinned. "I'm totally ready to meet someone."

Emory thought back to something that happened earlier in the week, and his eyes widened. "What would someone use to get over a phobia?"

"I'm not sure. Let's find out." She sat at her desk and searched on the computer. "Looks like the best is rutilated quartz."

"Quartz. Is it translucent?"

"Yes, in some of these pictures I'm seeing. In others, it's almost clear like glass, except it has strands of brown filaments in it."

Emory came over to see the images. "That's it! I need to go."

"What is it?" The intercom on Virginia's phone buzzed. "Hang on." She hit the speaker button. "What is it, Jeff?"

"Was that Emory at the front door?"

"I'm here."

"Good afternoon, Mr. Rome. So nice of you to mosey on in to work. Could I see you in my office?"

Emory displayed his displeasure at Jeff's tone with an exaggerated frown. "I'll be right in." When he entered Jeff's office, he found his partner looking in a wall-mounted mirror, fussing over his tie. "Wow, I've never seen you in a suit before."

Jeff untied the knot and started over. "For the funeral. By the way, I'm thinking of changing our hours of operation to open the office an hour later. Maybe that way you could get here on time."

"I was fifteen minutes late."

"So why were you late this time?"

"I'd rather not say."

Jeff finished tying the knot, but the pointed hem was about two inches above his belt. "My dad only taught me one knot, the double Windsor. Is there a single Windsor so I can get my tie longer?"

"There's a half Windsor."

Jeff jerked the knot loose and removed the tie. "So it jumps up from a half Windsor to a double Windsor? That doesn't make any sense. If it's a double half, it's a single."

"It's one of life's great mysteries. Right up there with flammable and inflammable meaning the same thing. Give it to me. I can tie a half Windsor." Emory took the tie from Jeff and knotted it around his own neck. "While you guys are at the funeral, I'm going to check something out."

"You're coming with us. The deceased is our case, the widow is our client and the killer – if there is one – could be in attendance. We all have to go."

"I'm not dressed for a funeral."

"You are always dressed for a funeral." Jeff pointed with his right hand at Emory's charcoal grey suit. "Look at you. Why aren't you wearing any of the new clothes we bought the other day?"

"You mean the clothes you forced me to buy." Emory handed Jeff the tie with a clean half Windsor knot in place. "They're at the dry cleaners. Look, I'm tired. I didn't get much sleep last night."

"Is your insomnia back?" Jeff pushed his head through the loop in the tie.

"It's not that. I had an intruder in my apartment."

"An intruder?!" Tightening the knot around his neck, Jeff's hand jerked the tie down too fast when he heard the word, eliciting a gagging cough. "What?" He curled two fingers between the tie and his neck, and gave it a slight pull. "Way to bury the lead! What happened?"

Emory sat on the edge of Jeff's desk as he recounted the events of the previous night to his spellbound partner.

"Did he take anything?"

"Not that I've noticed."

"You must've came home before he had a chance."

"Maybe. The worst part about it, when I saw him in that creepy ski mask, the first thought to come to my head was, 'The curse!' I froze for a second, and that allowed him to get the upper hand on me."

"Ski mask? What did it look like?"

"It was white with red stitching."

Jeff squiggled a line over his mouth with his finger. "Jagged smile, circle eyes?"

"You've seen him too?"

"Oh my god!" Jeff jabbed his finger into Emory's chest. "He's the one who caused my car accident last month."

"You never told me that guy wore a mask!"

"I didn't?"

"No." Emory looked away as he remembered his encounter with the ski mask man from before – an event he had yet to share with Jeff. *The same guy slips the postcard under my door, cases this building, causes Jeff's accident and breaks into my place without taking anything. What the hell does he want?*

"What, have you seen him before?"

Emory snapped out of his own thoughts. "On the street outside my apartment the night you came over to ask me to join the agency."

"You didn't tell me that."

"I didn't think it was important." *No need to tell him about the postcard.*

Jeff began to pace. "Who is this guy? And what does he want?"

"If he's been stalking us these past few weeks, it isn't connected to our current case."

"It's personal. But personal for who? Me or you? He's gone after both of us."

"I don't know." Emory thought about the postcard and knew he himself was the target.

CHAPTER 17

THICK, GRAY CLOUDS veiled the midmorning sun, offering a dearth of daylight to those below – fitting for a day of mourning. Emory checked the sky as he held open the door to the funeral home for his partners. "It's going to rain."

Jeff didn't even glance up. "No, it isn't. Those clouds will make it to the mountains before dropping their load."

"Guys, who cares?" Virginia gave them both a look of warning. "Be reverent." Once inside, they were directed to the room where Corey Melton's funeral would be held and found most in attendance had not yet taken a seat. "I don't see Becky. I'm going to look for her."

When she left, Jeff scanned the room. "Remember, if he was murdered, his killer could very well be here. Look for any clues in their actions and demeanor."

Emory's gaze locked on a familiar figure. "There's Frank Belcher."

Jeff's eyes followed Emory's but were drawn to the person next to Frank. "Damn, who is that mammoth woman next to him?"

"I bet it's his wife."

"She's like a foot taller than him. Maybe Lady Macbeth killed Corey so her husband could be promoted. Oh look, there's our buddy, Randy Graham."

"Is he actually wearing a tank top under his sport jacket?" Emory asked with a scowl.

Jeff snickered. "Maybe he thinks no one will realize with his jacket buttoned."

Emory noticed a conspicuous absence. "You know who I don't see is Corey's boss, Darren Gleeson."

"You're right. Mr. Warm-and-Fuzzy is probably pissed his staff took off work to attend the funeral."

Emory's phone dinged, and he saw it was a text from his lawyer. *The paperwork for your lawsuit is completed. Are you ready for me to file it?*

"What is it?"

Emory pocketed the phone. "Nothing important."

Virginia left the bathroom after checking the stalls for Becky, and she bumped into a mutual acquaintance heading in. "Hey, do you know if Becky is here yet?"

Wearing a black sari with silver trim, the young brunette pulled a paper towel to dry her hands. "She's here, but I haven't seen her in a while."

"Thanks." Virginia kept looking around until she came to a closed door. On the other side was an empty viewing room – at least she thought it was empty at first glance. There in the corner, she found her friend embracing a man she had never met but recognized from her online research. It was the TVA's director of generation resources, Darren Gleeson.

When Jeff and Emory left the funeral home to continue their investigation, Virginia opted to stay with her friend as the mourners proceeded to the cemetery. Even as Corey Melton's body was being lowered into the ground, her mind was replaying his widow's embrace with his former boss. *I should've told the guys. No, then they would've thought that Becky had something to do with it. I need to find out myself.*

Following the burial, several family members and close friends retreated to Becky Melton's tiny house, bringing food and comfort. After most mourners left, Virginia broke away from a living-room conversation with Becky's mom to find her friend alone in the kitchen. "Becky, I can take care of the clean-up."

"That's okay. It gives me something to do." The widow unspooled a copious sheet of aluminum foil to cover a tuna casserole. "I don't know why I'm saving this. I can't handle cooked tuna even when my stomach isn't twisted in knots. Do you want to take it home?"

Virginia waved a hand in front of her face. "I'm with you on that. The smell alone makes me nauseous. I could give it to Jeff, if you don't mind."

"Take it." Becky moved on to the plate of deviled eggs and grabbed the plastic wrap.

Virginia placed the casserole next to her purse on the kitchen table. "Becky, I need to ask you something."

Becky ran her fingers around the edge of the plate to seal the plastic. "What is it?"

"Before I ask you this, please know that I don't for one second believe you had anything to do with Corey's death, but Darren might have. That's why I need you to be honest with me."

Becky squinted her eyes almost to closing. "Darren? What do you mean you don't believe I killed my husband? Why would you say that?"

"Because it's true, and I felt I should preface my question with that."

"What the hell could the question be?"

Becky's sudden anger prompted Virginia to lower her voice to a whisper. "Are you having an affair?"

The de-escalation trick didn't help, as Becky's tone grew more confrontational. "Why the hell would you ask me something like that?"

"I saw you two together at the funeral home."

"And?"

"You were alone in a room together."

Becky stamped over to the purse on the kitchen table, pulled out a sealed envelope and threw it on the counter. "Corey's colleagues at work started a collection for me, and he was giving me the money. He didn't want to embarrass me by handing it to me in front of everyone. I was overwhelmed, and he was trying to comfort me. As far as the kiss goes…"

Virginia perked up at the word. *Kiss?! What kiss? I didn't see that. Oh my god!*

"Haven't you ever just kissed someone and not have it mean anything?"

"Honestly, no."

"Well I have, and that's exactly what happened. I was vulnerable, and he was there. For god's sake, it's not like he took me right there in the funeral home with my husband's body in the next room! It was just a kiss."

"I believe you. But I noticed that you still haven't answered my question about the affair."

"I'm not having an affair with Darren!"

The way she said the last two words bothered Virginia. *Why didn't she end the statement at affair?* "Your response seems purposely specific."

Tears stormed from Becky's furious eyes, down her reddened cheeks. "I just buried my husband. If you can't offer your support to me now of all times, maybe I misjudged our friendship."

"Becky, I—"

"Please, just leave."

Virginia grabbed her belongings and scurried away.

CHAPTER 18

WHEN EMORY TWISTED the doorknob, the wind slammed the door open and rain pelted his face. "Not going to rain, huh?"

Jeff followed him onto the rooftop of the Godfrey Tower. "I'm not a weatherman. Why would you listen to me about that? I'm still not sure what we're doing back up here. If there was a clue here, your ex-partner must've found it, and that's why he arrested Peter West."

"I wouldn't bet on that. Wayne medaled in jumping to conclusions. I saw something the last time we were here and didn't think anything of it..." Emory stopped in his tracks and pointed. "Oh my god!"

"Did you find something?" Jeff looked to where his partner pointed, and a grin stretched across his face.

"Are you kidding me?!" screeched Emory. "The bus stop wasn't bad enough?"

The object of his consternation was the huge rooftop billboard. Gone was the hair product ad, and in its place was now one for Mourning Dove Investigations. It was similar to the bus stop ad he had seen days ago, but in this one, his face was gigantic.

A beaming Jeff proclaimed, "It looks amazing!"

"It looks ridiculous!" Emory threw up his hands and forced his eyes to look away. "Forget it. We have a rock to find." He headed toward the flagpole near the edge of the roof, to where he had tripped before.

"A rock? Is that why you brought me up here?"

Emory searched the rooftop. "Remember what Randy Graham was telling us about his holistic counseling? He uses meditation and visualization to help them overcome their obstacles. What do you want to bet he had Corey meditating up here to overcome his fear? Virginia got me thinking about it when I saw her meditating with a crystal. Here it is!" Emory found the rock in a puddle of fresh rainwater and held it up.

Jeff shrugged his broad shoulders. "It's a rock."

"It's rutilated quartz. See the brown filaments in it. It's used in holistic circles to overcome phobias."

"Okay, if that was Corey's, you really think he could make it this close to the edge?"

Emory's attention was drawn to an incessant clanging. The weeping wind was blowing the short rope dangling from the flag-pole's pulley, causing the snap hook near top to bang against the aluminum pole. "The halyard."

"Halyard?"

"The rope. He could've used it as a crutch, a security blanket."

Jeff stretched to grab the end of the rope as it swayed in the wind. "You saw him. He was a short guy. He wouldn't have been able to reach this. It's not even long enough to hoist a flag up. That's why the pole's empty." He felt the tip. "This rope's been cut."

Emory extended his arm. "Hold my hand."

Jeff smirked. "You want to fool around up here?"

"I need you to steady me." Emory poked his head over the edge to look at the wood-covered window below. Once he erected himself again, he faced Jeff with a wild look in his eyes. "I know what happened!"

"Well? Spill!"

"First, let's search every possible hiding spot up here."

"What are we looking for?"

Emory pointed at the flagpole. "The rest of that rope."

The two PIs split up to search the roof, and within three minutes, Emory heard a pronouncement from the other side of a ventilation system. "I found something!" He met Jeff to find he had removed one of the panels from the side of the system. He grabbed something from inside it. "It's a gym bag."

"Open it up."

Jeff pulled from it some blue fabric. "It's a blanket."

Emory thought back to Virginia's meditation mat. "Maybe Corey sat on it to meditate."

Jeff removed a long length of rope from the bag. "The rope!"

Emory grabbed the rope and returned to the flagpole, followed by Jeff. He held the end dangling from the pole. "It matches! Not only that, but notice how it doesn't stretch. It's Kevlar."

Jeff slapped the right side of his butt and clenched his fist. "Hot damn! Like the fibers Cathy found in Corey's hand!"

"This proves it was murder. Here's my theory. Randy Graham was helping Corey overcome his acrophobia by having him come to the rooftop of the building, where he meditated during his breaks, or judging from the time of his death, before he started work each day. He probably began near the door the first time, gradually working his way closer to the edge each time he meditated. He eventually made it to the edge, but he would hold onto the flagpole rope as a security blanket. The day of his murder, someone followed him up here, likely waiting for him to be in full meditation before approaching him. Here, sit down like you're meditating."

Jeff reached out a hand. "Give me your jacket."

"Why?" Emory started unbuttoning his black field jacket.

"The ground's wet. I need something to sit on."

Emory took a step back. "You're not going to sit on my jacket!"

Jeff waved a hand over the rooftop. "The water's not going to hurt it. If it does, we'll stop by the thrift store and get you another one."

"Use your own jacket."

Jeff patted the breast of his pea coat. "This doesn't touch the ground."

"Then just pretend you're sitting!"

"Fine!" Jeff crouched, facing the edge. Emory continued, playing the part of the murderer. "So the killer came up from behind Corey Melton, grabbed the back of his collar and his belt and then flung him over the edge before he had time to react."

Playing Corey, Jeff stood and pretended to be hurled toward the edge. "The killer would have to know that Corey came up here, and he'd have to be strong enough to throw him."

Emory nodded. "Like you said, Corey was a small man."

"That doesn't explain how he crashed through the window. He would've still fallen straight down."

"Not if he held onto the rope and was hurled out far enough. He would've shot away from the building, and once the rope was taut, he would've come flying back toward the building, giving him enough speed to crash through the window."

Jeff picked up the story, "Once he did, the killer drew the rope back, cut it off and hid any evidence of Corey being on the roof. That explains the rope burns on his palms."

"Except he didn't pay any attention to the rock, just like we didn't the first time up here." Emory saw Jeff grinning at him. "What?"

"We did it! We know how he died."

"Now it's just a matter of figuring out who."

Jeff reached again for the rope dangling from the pole. "The killer has to be at least six-foot tall to reach where the rope was cut."

"And strong enough to hurl Corey at least ten feet from the building. That narrows our list of suspects. Peter West definitely fits that description, and the TBI must have something on him to have arrested him."

"True, but I wouldn't close the case based on your ex-partner's assumptions. Randy Graham is about six-one, he's strong enough and he could've known Corey was coming up here."

"Again, we're lacking motive. There's also Corey's boss, Darren Gleeson, although he has no apparent motive either."

"Don't forget Lady Macbeth, and she does have a motive – so Frank could move ahead at work. Is that it for our suspect list?"

"Your friend from the museum could've done it, but he has no known motive."

Jeff grabbed his own neck at the mention of the man who held a knife to his throat. "He definitely has a hair trigger on that anger of his."

"Plus, I still have a couple of people to check off my list of ejected land owners because they weren't home the other day."

"I have one of those too. We should get to those after we leave here, so we can hopefully have a complete suspect pool to focus on."

"Agreed."

Jeff advanced toward his partner and stole a kiss. Emory didn't fight it, but he did end it. "See, this is exactly the type of thing we shouldn't be doing now that we're working together."

"Why n—" Jeff didn't have time to finish his question as Emory's lips returned to his to deliver a longer, more passionate kiss.

Emory backed away and shook his head. "I don't know. You always do this. You confuse me."

"I've never had more clarity." Jeff wrapped his arms around Emory's waist. "How about we put that blanket to use?"

"Here?"

"Why not? It's the tallest building. No one will see us."

"It's raining."

"Which makes it sexier."

"It's freezing rain." Emory broke from him. "And we can't have sex on evidence. Crap, I need to call Wayne."

"Way to ruin the moment. Why would you mention his name now, and why on Earth would you call him?"

123

"We have to turn the evidence over to the TBI."

"What? Why?"

"Keeping it would be tampering with evidence."

"Haven't we already done that?"

"We have an obligation to let the proper authorities know. I'm calling." Emory pulled out his phone and called. "Voicemail."

"He's probably screening."

Emory left a message and returned his attention to Jeff. "If I don't hear from him in fifteen minutes, I'll call the police and let them take care of it." Before putting away his phone, he looked again at the text from his lawyer and thought, *I don't know what to do. Do I trust Anderson Alexander, or was the offer just to get me to drop the lawsuit? If I take him up on it, would he find another way to get rid of me? What about Jeff? What would this do to him? To us?*

"Hello!" Jeff waved his hand in front of Emory's face. "Are you zoning out on me?"

"Sorry. Just thinking. Hey, would you want to come over to my place for dinner tonight?"

Jeff brandished an incredulous look. "Man, you're giving me mixed signals here."

"Sorry, but I can explain it tonight."

"Explain what..." Jeff's words drifted off when he saw two men come through the door to the roof – Wayne Buckwald and Steve Linders.

Emory turned to see what had captured Jeff's attention. "Wow, that was fast."

Steve must have overheard him. "Wayne just got your voicemail. We were downstairs to talk to Darren Gleeson, but the office is closed."

Emory greeted him with a handshake. "Today's Corey's funeral."

Steve nodded. "That explains it."

"Stop telling them stuff!" Wayne moved between his partner and the PIs. "Where's this evidence you found?"

Emory and Jeff showed them the items and where they found

them, as well as how the rope matched the rope on the flagpole. Emory shared their theory of how Corey was killed.

Steve congratulated Emory with a literal pat on the back. "Thank you for your help. We knew Peter did it and why, but we didn't know exactly how."

"What makes you certain Peter did it?" asked Jeff.

Wayne got in his partner's face. "Stop telling them things!" He thrust his arm in the air with his index finger inches from Emory's face. "This asshole was drummed out of the bureau for good reason! He's a lying son-of-a-bitch."

Jeff shoved his body in front of Emory. Looking down into Wayne's beady eyes, he snarled, "If you don't want to see firsthand the scenic route Corey took to the twenty-ninth floor, I suggest you holster that stubby little finger!"

Trying to look unfazed, Wayne couldn't hide the sudden nervousness in his glare. "Are you threatening an officer of the law?"

Emory scooched in between them. "No, he's not. Jeff, take a breather."

Jeff walked away as his phone started to ring. "Hello?"

Emory turned his attention back to his former partner. "Wayne, we were never friends, but I was a good partner. What did I ever do to you?"

"You weren't a partner! You were a glory hog. Well, you're not getting any of it this time. I'm warning you. Stay away from my investigation!"

"I never threw myself into the limelight."

"Well you made damn sure I didn't get any of it!" Wayne pointed to the billboard. "And you're really going to say that while your twenty-foot face is staring down at us?!"

"Emory!" Grinning, Jeff hurried back to them. "I have some great news."

Emory looked over his shoulder at the embarrassing billboard. "I had nothing to do with that."

Jeff grabbed Emory's arm and led him away. "Forget about him. I have a surprise for you."

"What is it?"

"I got us booked on *New Dawn, Knoxville!* Tomorrow morning."

"What?"

"They're devoted a segment to Mourning Dove."

Emory was surprised but didn't share Jeff's excitement. "No way. I can't do it."

"Don't start panicking. Virginia and I will be right there with you. Just take a pill before you go on, and you'll be fine."

Emory frowned. *That reminds me, I need to get a refill.*

Naked, Emory emerged from the bathroom, his lean, muscular body still steaming from the shower. He saw a blinking light emitting from the phone on his desk and checked it to see a text from Jeff that read, "Might be late. You must be rubbing off on me."

Emory smiled. "Jerk." He read the text from his lawyer again and debated how he would answer. *Why am I hesitating? I know what I want. It's all I ever wanted. I could be back at the TBI doing what I was meant to do. Besides, if Jeff and I weren't working together, there'd be no more conflict. He could see it as a good thing.* He shook his head and sighed. "Who am I kidding?"

A knock on the door interrupted his thoughts. "Crap!" He peered through the peephole. "Jeff, hang on!" He ran to the bedroom, threw on a pair of boxers and returned to greet his guest.

Jeff took one look and quipped, "I thought we were going to eat first."

"I thought you were going to be late."

Stepping inside, Jeff produced a bouquet of blue roses. "I didn't know how long it would take to get you these."

"Oh wow. I've never seen blue roses. They're beautiful." Emory held the flowers to his nose and inhaled. "Subtle scent."

Jeff grinned. "Like their bearer."

Laughing, Emory took the bouquet to the kitchen. "Beautiful, yes, but I wouldn't say you have a subtle scent. I don't think I have a vase."

"What, do I stink?" Jeff sniffed his underarms.

Emory found a lemonade pitcher in a cabinet. "This will work. No, you don't stink. The opposite actually." He half-filled the pitcher with water.

Jeff cocked his head. "I'll take that. Is it too sappy, bringing you flowers?"

"Not at all." Emory couldn't help but grin as he placed the pitcher with roses on his kitchen counter. "I think it's a wonderful surprise. As a matter of fact, I've got a surprise for you too."

"For me? What is it?"

"Later. Would you like a drink?"

"Sure. V—"

"Vodka cranberry. I remember."

While Emory mixed the drink and a gin and tonic for himself, Jeff picked up Emory's anxiety medication from the counter and shook the empty bottle. "How long have you been on this stuff?"

Emory lied. "A couple of years."

"You've been seeing a psychiatrist for two years?"

Emory served Jeff's drink with a garnish of annoyance. "Thereabouts."

"Because of whatever happened to you as a kid?" Jeff waited a few seconds for response. "Why won't you tell me what happened to you?"

"I will. One day. Maybe I'll even let you read my journal. Moving on." Emory clinked his glass against Jeff's. "Cheers."

"Cheers." Jeff sipped from his drink "You keep a diary?"

Emory sighed at the persistence of the subject. "I kept a

journal. My first psychiatrist made me keep one to write down everything that had happened. To help me get through it." Emory noticed Jeff's eyes darting about the place. "Don't bother looking for it. It's at my parents' house."

"I wasn't looking for it."

"Uh-huh. Changing subjects. Are you ready for your surprise?"

"Should I sit down for it?"

"Sure, but I mean, it's not anything big."

Jeff plopped onto the couch and waved off his concern. "I was born with no preconceived notions."

Emory gulped his drink. "I'll be right back." He disappeared into his bedroom, leaving Jeff to his vodka-fueled imagination. Four minutes later, Emory reemerged wearing the cowboy hat and outfit from the picture used in the ad campaign.

Jeff's jaw dropped, and he rose to his feet. "Oh. My. God. I thought you didn't have this anymore."

"I lied."

"Can I ask you a favor?"

Emory stepped closer to him. "What is it?"

"Can we postpone dinner for a few hours?"

As Emory led him into the bedroom, he didn't notice the blinking red light hovering outside his window.

CHAPTER 19

"WHERE IS HE?" Jeff glanced again at the wall clock in the green room for *New Dawn, Knoxville*.

"He'll be here. He's not going to let you down." Virginia gave her makeup a final check in the mirror. "Oh, I forgot to tell you, I did a background check on Randy Graham. He misled you guys about the type of therapist he is. He's not licensed in psychology or counseling or anything else outside of driving. He never even graduated from college."

Jeff stopped pacing and faced Virginia's reflection. "That shaved-legged liar. Trying to pass himself off as a therapist."

"He is a therapist. A certified reiki therapist."

"What on Earth is reiki?"

"It's like an aura massage – no touching."

"Seriously? That's like sex without an orgasm. What's the point? I can't believe you can actually get certified in massaging people without laying a hand on them. Sounds like a racket."

Virginia again faced Jeff. "I might've oversimplified."

"I assume then that reiki therapists aren't covered by patient confidentiality."

"Not even a little."

Jeff gave the clock another glance and pulled out his phone. "I'm going to call him."

"Are you sure he knew what time to be here?"

"I told him this morning before I left." As soon as he said the words, Jeff turned away to hide his face, hoping she didn't pick up on it.

She did. "Before you left? Did you two spend the night together?"

"Can I claim partner confidentiality and not answer that?"

"Not even a little. Spill."

"Not now, and please don't mention it to Emory. You know how private he thinks he is."

Virginia held up her right hand. "I promise. Why didn't you two just come here together?"

"I had to go home to get ready. I wasn't expecting to spend the night, so I didn't bring a change of clothes with me, and I wasn't about to wear anything from Emory's closet on TV."

"Ooh, I don't blame you."

Virginia and Jeff both cracked up laughing just before Emory rushed into the green room, offering a preemptive apology. "I'm sorry I'm late."

Jeff looked at the clock on the wall. "We're getting used to it."

Emory's eyes fixed on Jeff. "I need to talk to you."

Virginia looked at the clock again. "We have three minutes before we go on."

Jeff pointed to Emory. "Remember, no mention of being fired. You left the TBI because you knew you could help even more people in the private sector."

Emory blurted out, "I don't know if I can go through with this."

Jeff walked behind him to massage his shoulders. "You're just nervous. Did you take one of your pills?"

A redheaded college-age girl entered carrying three clip-on microphones. "Time to get y'all miked up."

As the production assistant clipped the microphone on Virginia, Emory stammered for words. "I... I am nervous, but that's not it. Uh... It's difficult to say."

"If it's that heavy, why don't you just wait until after the show?"

"I thought about that, but I don't want to go on TV and be disingenuous about the future."

"The future? The future is we're going to get all the exposure we can out of this pro bono case so we can start getting clients that count – the kind with money. What future are you talking about?"

"I don't know what to do about the lawsuit."

Jeff unbuttoned his shirt so the PA could clip the microphone to his collar and hide the wire underneath. "We already discussed this. You're dropping it. It would be bad for business."

"That's not why I'm debating it. If I don't go through with the lawsuit, I'll have another decision to make."

"What do you mean?"

Emory shifted his weight from side to side with each heavy breath. "Anderson Alexander came to see me the other day."

"How do I know that name?"

"He's the head of the TBI."

"He came to see you? To talk you out of the lawsuit?"

The PA made her way to Emory to mike him. "That, and to offer me another job with the TBI."

As Virginia gasped, Jeff could feel the color draining from his face. He felt as if he'd been punched in the gut and were incapable of exhaling enough breath to form words. At long last, he uttered, "How did you respond?"

"I told him I needed to think about it."

"Really?" Red rose from Jeff's neck like a thermometer touching a light bulb. "What's there to think about? They fired you! Threw you out! And I…" He waved his hand toward Virginia. "We gave you a lifeline. Opened up our business to you."

"I was there. I know what happened. That's why it's a difficult decision." Emory sighed. "Look, this could be a good thing for the agency. If I do take the job, I'd have access again to—"

"Don't try to spin this as something you're considering for the good of the business! Your reasons are completely selfish!"

The PA shushed them. "Please! You're going to have to keep it down." She pointed toward the open door. "We're live."

Virginia wedged herself in between the two men. "Guys, can you just put this issue aside for a few minutes? We're about to be on TV."

Jeff told her, "I don't care about the show."

Emory scoffed. "Publicity is the one thing you do care about."

The PA clapped her hands to get their attention. "It's time, people. Follow me."

Jeff glared at him. "Oh, is that it? The one thing? What does any of it matter now? You're done with us."

Emory tried a conciliatory tone. "You know, I never said I was taking the job."

"Don't play semantics with me. We both know you're taking it."

"There's a lot to consider."

"I'm sorry." Jeff embellished his tone with sarcastic empathy. "I didn't realize how difficult this is for you. Let me make it easier. Take the damn job! We don't want you."

"There's no reason—"

"Here's a reason for you." Jeff followed Virginia to the door. "We got along just fine without you, and we'll do much better without your annoying stick-up-your-ass pomposity!"

"Fine! I'll finish this case, and then I'll walk my pompous ass back to where I belong." Emory stormed past them but turned around long enough to say, "I'm taking the rest of the day off."

CHAPTER 20

WHILE THE FIGHT with Jeff looped in his head, Emory roamed the halls of Willow Springs Retirement Home, searching for room 165. When he spotted the number on the wall next to an open door, he saw Mary Belle Hinter inside. Seated in front of a window, the Crick Witch stared at the lone, leafless tree on the small patch of land visible past the walls that obstructed most of her view. "Ms. Mary Belle."

The old woman broke her stare and coughed out a raspy laugh. "Sweet sassafras, I told m' nephew, I knowed you'd be back."

"Why did you think I'd be back?"

"You wantin' me to take the curse from ya. I tell ya how – for a price."

"Let me guess. You want me to take you to your property."

The old woman nodded.

"Already taken care of. If you're up for it, we're going to drive up there right now."

A spark of hope glimmered in Mary Belle's cautious eyes. "Don't play wi' me."

"I told the woman at the front desk I needed your help for a murder case I'm working on, and she said you could go for the day."

"That squirrelly gal?"

"That's the one." *Of course, she'd prefer I take you away from here permanently*. "Mind you, it's just for the day. I have to bring you back before supper." He lied about the deadline, knowing the facility would probably be happier if she never returned.

The old woman slumped back in her chair. "What the damn point then?"

"I was thinking it would give you an opportunity to say goodbye to your land. The way it is now. Before they start building on it." When she didn't respond, Emory added, "Do you really want the last time you saw your property to be your last memory of it? Why not go say goodbye to it properly?"

"That better 'n nothin' I s'pose." Mary Belle started to push herself from the chair, and Emory offered a helping hand. "Git that away from me! I ain't he'pless!" Once up, she grabbed her oversized purse and filled it with items from her chest of drawers.

Emory noticed the untouched food tray. "We can wait for you to finish your breakfast."

"I ain't hungry. Let's git."

He held the door open for her. "Should I lock it?"

"Don't matter. Ain't nothin' mine no more."

In a white room inside the Knox County Jailhouse, Jeff sat at a table with a suited man, who whispered, "I shouldn't be here."

His mind far away, Jeff snapped back into the moment. "Relax. You're a real lawyer."

The young man wiped his forehead with his sleeve. "You don't know that."

"Look," Jeff said to his former college roommate. "You're annoyingly smart. There's no way you didn't pass the bar exam."

"Well I won't know for sure until I get the results, which is why I shouldn't be doing this."

"Just act lawyerly."

The door to the tiny room opened, and a police officer entered with a handcuffed Peter West. When the prisoner saw the PI, he took a step back like he wanted to return to jail. "You! What are you doing here?"

Jeff pointed to his friend. "I brought a lawyer, Booby Hobbs."

"I go by Robert now," the lawyer told Jeff.

"I have a lawyer," growled Peter.

"A public defender. I know. Your wife thought you might like a real lawyer, like Booby here."

Booby spoke through gritted teeth. "My girlfriend hates that nickname, and it's not professional."

Peter nodded to the officer, who then left the room. "So you got me a lawyer?"

"Not really." Booby turned his attention to the email on his phone.

Jeff said, "I just needed him to get in to see you."

Peter took a seat at the table across from them. "Why?"

"Corey Melton died around eight-forty-five. You were at work at eight-thirty. Why is the TBI convinced you killed him?"

Peter shrugged and admitted, "I lied to you. The truth is I don't start work until nine-thirty. I'm just used to saying I punch in at eight-thirty because that's what I tell my wife."

"Why?"

"So I can get some time to myself. Man, you've seen our living conditions. Without that lie, I'd never get any peace."

"So what do you do during that hour?"

"Different things. Drive around. Hang out at a coffee shop."

"What were you doing when Corey was killed?"

"I parked at work and just walked around for a while."

Jeff slapped the table. "That's it then. There are cameras outside the store where you work. There should be video of you parking."

Peter shook his head. "Employees have to park in the north

corner lot. There are no cameras out there, and I don't think the ones on the building look out that far."

"Okay, where did you walk to? Did you buy anything?"

"No. I just walked through that little park. I sat on a bench for a few minutes. That's about it."

Jeff twitched one corner of his lips. "I assume no one saw you."

"There were a few people walking by but no one I know."

"Wow." Jeff sat back in his chair. "As far as alibis go, yours really sucks."

Peter locked in on Jeff's eyes as if to transmit his sincerity. "I didn't kill that man. I swear it! You've got to help me. Please."

"You know, I pride myself on my well-oiled bullshit-o-meter. I believe you. Unfortunately, it looks like the only way I'll be able to prove your innocence is by finding the real killer."

On the drive to Brume Wood, Emory could sense Ms. Mary Belle's growing excitement. In between anxious glances at indicators that her former home would soon be in sight, she enlivened the drive with folksy, if disjointed, vignettes of her youth. "Me and m' sister—"

"Luke's grandmother?"

"Jus' got the one." The Crick Witch raised her hands from her dirt-brown cloak, as if signaling the answer were obvious. "Anyways, we use ta hide come dusk 'cause we wouldn't wanna go inside. We'd stay ina woods all night if we got our way – dancin' with lightnin' bugs 'n' fallin' 'sleep by the crick. My daddy'd come huntin' for us. I 'member one night, he thought he heard us ina bushes, only 'tweren't us. It was a polecat!" Ms. Mary Belle laughed herself into a coughing fit. "Polecat chased 'im upa tree and still got 'im! Mama wouldn't let 'im step foot ina house fer two days on accoun' ofa stink."

Emory laughed too – at her delight more than the story. "Seems like you've always stuck close to home. Have you ever gone out of state?"

"Ain't nothin' out there I needa see. My daddy taught me howta live offa land 'n' take care a m'self. My mama, she was a spellcaster 'n' potioner. It's how she made money, he'ping out the town folk. She passed it ona me."

Emory turned up the windshield defroster to pacify the fogging clash between the higher elevation's chill and the heat emanating from inside the car. "What about Luke's grandmother?"

Ms. Mary Belle snorted. "My sister ain't ne'er had no gif', 'cept for leavin' us. Once we growed up, I wassa only one ta stick around. That's why daddy gimme it all." She sighed and stared out the side window. "M' paren's was good people. They both of 'em died in that house."

"What happened?"

Ms. Mary Belle gave him a what-do-you-think-happened look. "They was old. They didn't die toget'er. M' dad stuck 'round couple years past. But they both took they last breath on that prop'ty, an' I will too."

Emory took his eyes off the road long enough to read her face, trying to gauge the seriousness of her words. "Ms. Mary Belle, I hope you're not thinking of doing anything foolish while we're there. I'll turn around right now."

"Sweet sassafras! I ain't ne'er felt inclined for that. Well, one time maybe. When I wassa young'un, sixteen, se'enteen – don't 'member no more – I met me someone who... I was ina woods gatherin' pine cones for Christmas, to where it wasn't our prop'ty no more, anna heard somethin' ona wind. When I came upon what it was, I seen a hand reachin' out from this deep holler ina ground. The hand was grabbin' ona rope tied 'round a tree, an' then it pulled up the most beautiful sight any eyes e'er did see standin' afore me. Tall. Thick brown hair. Hauntin' green eyes."

Emory smiled. *Sounds like Jeff.*

"I thought it wassa specter until it spoke – an angel's voice couldn't a been more upliftin' to hear. Said it was 'xplorin' the ground holler on its new prop'ty."

"What's a ground holler?"

"You know." She brought up her arms and touched together her fingertips as if she were holding an invisible, oversized pillow. "A big ol' hole ina ground. 'Tweren't wide big but deep big."

"Like a well?"

"No, like a holler. Come a find out, we had new neighbors, an' Specter was their young'un an' was my age. From then on, we was always toge'er. Ev'ry minute we wasn't was plain agony ta me." Ms. Mary Belle tsked and shook her head. "I fell in love good an' heavy. I'd had done anythin' Specter wanted. We promised we'd never leave each other. I made a charm for m' Specter so no harm would e'er come. I wasn't as good at it as I am now 'cause it didn't work. One day her daddy caught us havin' relations in the woods."

Emory whipped his head around to face her profile. *Her?! Her love was a woman? I had no idea!*

"He grabbed Specter by the hair and dragged her away. I tried to fight 'im, but he hit me good an' hard. M' mama found me ina woods an' bringed me home. When I woke up the next day, I runned to her place an' banged ona door. Her daddy answered, brown bottle in his han' an' beer in his sweat. He tol' me he sent m' Specter off ta live with fam'ly in West Virginia. I knowed he's lying, so I broke past 'im an' run all through the house. I found her mama cryin' on m' Specter's bed but no Specter. He really done it, I thought. He sent her away from me. Next thing I knowed, I heard breakin' glass. Took me a second to know he broke the bottle on m' head. He picked me up an' threw me out the front door. He told me if I e'er stepped foot on his prop'ty again, he'd shoot me. M' folks had words with him, an' then they told me the same thing – stay off his prop'ty. Broke m' heart, but I ne'er did go there again, an' I ne'er did see her again. Later I went walkin' ina woods, to where we last was, an' then I heard her. She was moanin', like she was 'fore her daddy found us. When I heard it, I didn't know what he'd done with her, but I knowed she wasn't in no West Virginia." Ms. Mary Belle wiped tears from her. "I knowed she was dead. M' Specter she was for sure then, an' she was chained to the woods, to our woods – the last place she was happy. She cain't leave 'em, an' now she's there all alone."

Emory didn't know what to say, so he said what everyone did in that situation. "I'm sorry." He wasn't sure he should ask, but he had to know, "What happened to her father?"

"He got his. I cursed 'im – a curse seeded with hate for 'im and love for her. He died ina bar fight not long after."

Ms. Mary Belle pointed to a tiny café coming up on the right. Emblazoned with a dim neon sign touting, *Log Cabin Diner*, the steel-and-glass establishment offered no indication for the reason behind its name. "Stop here!"

Emory nodded toward the windshield. "We're almost at your place, and I thought you weren't hungry."

"I need me some good tea. All they got at that ol' home is skeeter piss – ain't got no taste."

Emory pulled into the parking lot, and a moment later they were seated at the counter. Ms. Mary Belle placed her order before the approaching waitress was within a reasonable range. "Sassafras tea."

Once she stood before them, the waitress wrote down the order. "And for you, handsome?"

"I'm good. Thank you."

"That's it then?" Emory nodded at the waitress' question. "To go?"

"Yes please." He turned to the old woman seated on the bar-stool at his side. "You like sassafras tea?"

"My fav'rite tea! No taste like it ina world. They don't make

139

it right here. Use some damn fake stuff 'stead of the root. But it'll do 'til I get to the prop'ty an' dig up m' own. Got lots of sassafras trees."

"Ms. Mary Belle?" A middle-aged woman dining at one of the tables came up to them. "I'd heard you moved."

"Louise." Ms. Mary Belle offered a grin that looked like the side of an old covered bridge with missing planks. "How you an' Ben?"

"Well, truthfully, Ben's not doing so well. His rheumatism is back. He can barely move his knee."

Ms. Mary Belle searched her crocheted purse and pulled out a small mason jar containing a brown jelly-like substance. "Gom some of this on it twice a day. He feel better after 'while."

"Thank you!" Excited, Louise took the jar to her table and came back with her purse. "How much do I owe you?"

Ms. Mary Belle didn't hesitate to extend her gnarled hand. "Twenty." Louise paid her and returned to her table.

Emory nodded the side of his head toward Louise's table. "So what was in the jar?"

"Healin' potion. Don't ask 'bout the fixin's 'cause it's a secret recipe m' mama taught me."

"Do you make good money selling your potions and spells?"

"Pert' near e'eryone in town come to me. From 'round the county an' outside too."

"You must know a lot of people."

"Ain't you got no friends?"

"Sure, I do." Emory took a few seconds for some quiet introspection. "Honestly no. I don't really have any close friends anymore. I've spent my time focusing on my career. I could control that, or I thought I had control over it. Things have gotten confusing lately. I used to know exactly where my life was headed. I had it all mapped out. Now, I'm not even sure what I want to do with my life." Emory stopped talking when he realized he was spilling out his heart to the woman who had cursed him.

"You need prop'ty."

Emory laughed. "I'm not ready to buy a place—"

"Not prop'ty like m' prop'ty. You need somethin' to love an' that loves you back." Ms. Mary Belle placed a calloused hand on his forearm. "Why you livin'?"

"What do you mean?"

"What you livin' for? Why you here on Earth? Know that, an' then you know what to do."

Louise returned to the counter. "Ms. Mary Belle, I'm sorry to bother you again."

"Ain't no bother. Need he'p with somethin' else?"

"Not me. I texted Bernadette Jenkins to let her know you were here. She had been wanting to get ahold of you for a while now. She's been having some awful trouble sleeping since her husband died in prison last month. I think she feels guilty for not going to see him, in spite of what he did. She says he's been coming to her at night, stealing her dreams. She was hoping you could help."

"Ain't got nothin' for spookin' on me, but I pick somethin' up from home an' drop it off."

"That would be great! Thank you so much." Louise returned to her seat.

"Speaking of spooking, can we talk about the curse you placed on me?"

Ms. Mary Belle laughed. "Been workin', ain't it?"

"Well, I'm not dead, obviously, but I've had a string of bad luck, if that's what you mean. I've had a home invasion, I was in car wreck, I lost a job I didn't want... much and I think I lost something else."

"That's how 'tworks. Plays with you. Takes away e'erythin' you care 'bout."

"Well, good job then. Now how about removing it?"

"I cain't."

"Why not? You said you could."

The Crick Witch shook her head. "Said I'd tell you how."

"So how?"

"A curse ain't a piece a tape you can take off when you want. It part of you now. Only way to git rid of it is to die."

CHAPTER 21

AFTER DROPPING OFF Booby, Jeff drove his rental car to the Mountain Light Holistic Center. Once he walked through the front doors, he saw at the counter a different woman from his previous visit. He was about to ask her for the location to Randy Graham's office when he saw the man himself heading for the front door. Jeff intercepted him. "I need to have a word with you, *Doctor*."

Randy nodded toward the door. "I'm heading off to an appointment in town."

"This will just take a moment."

"I really don't have time."

Jeff stepped in his way. "Have you been questioned by the TBI about Corey Melton's death?"

"Why would I be?"

"I wonder how you would explain to them the fact that you pass yourself off as a counselor with only a certificate for holistic voodoo you can get from a six-hour online course."

Randy crossed his arms in a faux show of confidence. "I've never claimed to be a licensed therapist. I've done nothing illegal."

"You're misleading people into thinking you're qualified to offer counseling."

"I give advice."

"I wonder if the authorities will buy your fuzzy semantics

when I tell them you were counseling, or *giving advice* to, someone who committed suicide."

"The police said Corey was murdered."

"That's just one of their theories. You hid behind patient confidentiality to avoid talking to us earlier, but that little certificate of yours doesn't grant you any measure of patient confidentiality protection. You're going to answer my questions, or I swear I'll publicize your credentials, get the authorities involved and do everything I can to shut you down."

Randy took a moment to weigh his options. "What do you want to know?"

"What was your therapy for Corey?"

"With fears, you want to address the root cause of the fear, but with a lot of phobias, a root cause is elusive or impossible to find. In those cases I help people focus on mastering that irrationality so they can face those obstacles from a place of peace instead of a place of fear."

"So you did direct him to go to the rooftop of the building where he works?"

"The only way to overcome fear is to face it, so part of the therapy is to meditate in a location of discomfort and to continue doing so for days, weeks or months – until you can walk up to that edge as calmly as you could walk down the street."

"How long had Corey been going to the roof?"

"He started about six weeks ago."

"Besides you, who knew that he was going up there?"

"No one that I know of. His wife, maybe. He joked a lot, but he was a very private person. It's not the sort of thing he would've talked about."

"Okay. Now about that alibi of yours."

"I'm still not going to tell you her name. I think we're done here." Randy walked out the front door and held it open, but the PI was stuck in place. "Aren't you leaving?"

Jeff pulled a card from his pocket. "I've been a little tense, so I thought I'd redeem this yoga coupon you gave me."

Randy sneered at him. "Enjoy."

"Oh, by the way, I'll make sure to check my tires and engine before I pull out of your parking lot this time."

"What's that supposed to mean?"

"Just an FYI." Jeff let the front door close and watched Randy walk to his car. He returned the card to his pocket and approached the woman at the counter. "Could you tell me where Randy's office is?"

The woman pointed to the front door. "You just saw him leave."

"Yes, but I forgot to give him my card."

"You can give it to me, and I'll make sure he gets it."

Damn! Jeff gave her one of his business cards, which she placed under the counter. "Aren't you going to take it to his office?"

"I'm working here. I can give it to him when he gets back. Is there anything else?"

Jeff slapped the yoga card onto the counter. "Where's the yoga class?"

She pointed to the hallway at the left. "In the Yoga Center. Go out the door at the end of this hallway, and follow the walkway to the next building."

"Thanks." Jeff followed her direction to the outdoor walkway, where he stopped an approaching employee. "Excuse me. I have a meeting with a Randy Graham. Could you tell me where his office is?"

The young man pointed to a one-story structure encircled by trees. "That's his office."

"The whole building?"

"Yes sir."

Jeff frowned at him. "Don't call me sir. I'm like three years older than you." He waited for the younger man to leave before heading to Randy's. He tried the door. Locked. He pulled from his pocket a home-fashioned L-shaped strip of copper and a custom-made pick with a tulipwood handle and aluminum blade. With little effort, he turned the tumbler and opened the door.

The office itself was unremarkable – a large desk in the center of tacky-art-covered walls. "Randy Graham has sippy cup taste on a crystal glass budget." Behind the desk was another door. He tried the doorknob, but it wouldn't turn. "Locked too. A bit of overkill." He picked the lock and flicked the light switch on the other side. "Oh my god!"

Filtered light exposed a room much more interesting than Randy's office. Jeff stepped inside and toured the sandalwood-scented space to take in all the tantric elements within its leather-quilted walls – erotic Indian artwork of copulating deities, a massage table with stirrups, a shower/steam room, a meditation circle with a trove of feathers and shelves holding a variety of oils, straps, Ben Wa balls and other sexual enhancements.

"Hello, Mr. Grey." Jeff turned off the light and locked the door again, returning to Randy Graham's main office.

He noticed a large monitor on the wall. The screen was black, but he could hear it running. *Sleep mode.* He tapped the keyboard on the table below it. A split screen of twelve different video feeds appeared, each showing high-definition views of various areas at the complex – including the parking lot. He watched cars coming in and out of the lot for a few seconds before commenting, "He could've seen us arriving and known which car was mine. He had plenty of time to screw with my tire. Of course, he didn't know us then so he would've never even noticed us."

Virginia prepared herself for her first encounter with Becky since she accused her bereaved friend of having an affair. *I'll just apologize.*

I know her parents and in-laws were leaving this morning, so she'll be all alone. No distractions. We can talk it out.

Virginia parked on the street and walked up the driveway to Becky's house and across the walkway to the front door. As she did, movement between the living room curtains caught her attention. She glanced at first before peering with urgent interest. *What?!*

Virginia couldn't believe her eyes. In the middle of the living room, Becky was seated in a chair from the dining room table, but not by choice. Standing before her, back to the window, was a man in a black ski mask. Becky was tied to the chair – a ball gag in her mouth and a knife held to the side of her neck.

CHAPTER 22

VIRGINIA SCURRIED TO the back of Becky's house, peeking in each window along the way for a better look at the intruder's movements. She opened the screen door and squeezed the knob to the back door. Unlocked! She nudged it open, hoping it wouldn't squeak. It didn't.

As she tiptoed into the kitchen, she could hear the intruder's voice but not discern his words. She scanned the room for a weapon and unsheathed the chef's knife from the knife block. Staring at her reflection in the blade, she wondered what the hell she was doing. She replaced the knife and looked for something less bloodying.

Arms shaking and brandishing a copper skillet, Virginia emerged from the kitchen. The intruder was now standing behind the chair, the crotch of his black jeans rubbing the back of Becky's head while he kept the knife near her throat. As Virginia crept toward him, she could make out what he was saying.

"Now I'm going to remove the ball from your mouth and give you something else to gag on." He walked around the chair to stand in front of Becky. "You're not going to scream. You're going to be a good girl… Holy shit!" Seeing Virginia upon him with the skillet held high, the intruder dropped the knife and jumped back.

Virginia took a warning swing with the skillet. "Stay back, or I swear I'll knock your head down so far, you can gag on it yourself!"

Becky looked up at her and tried to speak, but her words were muffled by the ball in her mouth.

Wearing a black thermal shirt that hugged his lean musculature, the tall man took another step back. "Look—"

"Just stay back!" Virginia kept the skillet high in her right hand and used the left to pull the gag from her friend's mouth.

"Virginia."

"Don't worry. I'm going to get you out of here." Instead of gratefulness, Virginia saw anger in her friend's eyes.

"What are you doing here?!"

The intruder took off his mask. "Tell her."

"Tell me what?"

Becky nodded toward the man. "This is Randy Graham. He's not an attacker. He's a friend."

Virginia knew immediately what she meant. *She is having an affair!*

Randy picked up the knife and ran it across his palm. "It's a fake knife. We were roleplaying."

At the sound of approaching sirens, Virginia gasped. "The police."

"You called the police?!" Becky started struggling in her chair. "Someone untie me!"

Randy rushed to loosen the ropes that kept Becky's hands behind the chair.

Virginia headed for the front door. "I'll talk to them, explain it was a mistake." She exited in time to see two patrol cars screech to a halt in front of the house. When the officers bolted forth, she put up her hands to calm the situation. "Hi. I'm the one who called."

An officer threw his body between her and the house. "Miss, get behind the car! He could have a gun!"

"No, he doesn't. I made a mistake. He's not an intruder."

The officer looked back at her as if trying to gauge her veracity and if she were under duress. "Stay back. I'll check it out." He entered the house, gun drawn, followed by three other officers. A moment later all four returned to the front yard, guns holstered, and walked past Virginia without saying a word.

Virginia went back inside the house to see Randy with his arm around her friend. "I'm so sorry, Becky. I didn't know."

"I've never been so embarrassed in all my life!"

"I really did think you were in danger."

Randy squeezed Becky. "It's okay. It was just a misunderstanding."

Becky broke from him. "That doesn't make it any better."

"I already said I'm sorry." Virginia hardened her tone. "Look, I asked point-blank if you were having an affair, and you lied to me."

"I said I wasn't having an affair with Darren."

"Exactly! I knew you were being purposely specific." Virginia sighed. "Becky, why? Corey loved you. I thought you loved him."

"I did love him. Don't ever question that. It's like I told you. He was a gentle man."

Virginia turned her attention to Randy. "You gave her those bruises."

Randy shrugged. "We got a little carried away."

The front door slammed open, and Jeff bounded into the room, his blue-barreled PD10 drawn and ready to fire. "Is everyone okay?! What's going on?"

Becky huffed. "You called your partner too?"

Jeff pointed to Randy. "What are you doing here?"

"I'll fill you in." Virginia grabbed Jeff's arm and led him out to the front yard, explaining what had happened.

"It makes sense. Randy's office looked like a padded cell for a sex-addict. So he was counseling Corey at the same time he was screwing his wife. I wonder if he told him to go to the rooftop just so he could kill him."

"Maybe. I don't know him."

"Do you think they plotted together to get Corey out of the way?"

"No. I mean, I would've never believed Becky cheated before all of this."

"Why don't you head back to the office. I want to talk to Christian and Anastasia in there and get the truth out of them."

"I'll help you question them."

"That's my job."

Virginia crossed her arms. "You know, I get a little sick of always being the one stuck in the office."

His face reflecting genuine surprise, Jeff asked, "Really? Where is this coming from?"

"I've been feeling it for a while now. You get to go do everything while I stay behind."

"That's what you wanted."

"Not anymore. When we made that arrangement, I had just left the service, and I was looking for peace. Well, I've found it, and it's boring."

"But without you there, who's going to watch the office?"

Virginia rolled her eyes. "Who's watching it now?"

"Exactly! We could be missing our next client because you're not there."

"Then why aren't you there? Why does it have to be me? I swear, I just opened up to you, and all you're focused on is having a body to greet clients."

"Because that's what we agreed to."

"Well, I don't agree to it anymore!"

Jeff grabbed her shoulders. "I'm sorry. I didn't know you felt that way. We can talk about you doing more field work. Of course, that means we'd have to hire a secretary to be there full time."

"See!" Virginia broke from him and jabbed a finger into his chest. "I knew that's what you thought of me, that I'm just a secretary."

"I don't! Bad choice of words. Look, can we talk about this later? I need to interview them before they decide to leave."

"*We* need to interview them."

Jeff blocked her as she headed for the front. "No. I'm serious. You're too close to this. I need to do it alone."

Virginia hesitated before relenting. "Okay. But I'm taking the next lead we get."

"Okay."

She walked back to her car but had one parting word. "Alone."

Jeff rapped on the front door to the Melton house. Becky opened it just enough to poke her face through and say, "I don't want to talk about it."

"That's okay. I'll just use my imagination to fill in the blanks when I tell the TBI how you and your boyfriend conspired to kill your husband."

"What?!" he heard Randy shout from behind the door. "I didn't kill anybody!"

Becky sighed and opened the door to let Jeff enter. Randy came to Becky's side as if they were dinner hosts greeting guests. "I know this looks bad."

Jeff entered the living room and inspected the chair where Becky had been held captive. "What it looks like is a motive for murder."

Becky waved back and forth between Randy and herself. "This is not a motive for murder! I loved my husband."

Jeff eyed her paramour. "I can see that."

Randy picked his props off the floor. "We're just having fun. But even if we were serious, we wouldn't have had the oppor..." Mid-sentence, his words collided into a stern look from Becky.

Jeff grabbed the fake knife and pointed it at Randy. "Wait

a second. Are you telling me she was your Monday, eight-thirty session?" When Randy didn't answer, Jeff pointed the knife at Becky. "You were having sex with him while your husband was being thrown off a building?"

Becky lowered her head. "Yes."

Jeff thought about it for a second. "I'm not sure I believe you."

Becky looked up at him with more anger than shame. "Why on Earth would I lie about that?"

Randy spoke up for her. "She's telling the truth."

"If you two are each other's alibi, then as far as I'm concerned, neither of you has an alibi. Well, Becky does just because she couldn't have physically thrown him with the necessary force." He pointed to Randy. "You, on the other hand, are still on the hook."

"I didn't kill Corey." Randy held up his right hand. "I swear it. I honestly liked the guy."

"Not enough to keep your hands off his wife." Jeff waited for a response, but it never came. "While we're on the subject of motives and alibis, let's talk to you about the accident I had after leaving your place the other day."

"What accident?"

"While at your holistic center, someone loosened the lug nuts on one of my tires. The tire came off and almost killed me and my partner."

"And you think I had something to do with it? That's ridiculous."

"Is it?" Jeff handed him the knife. "Maybe you're right. I have to say, your center is very impressive."

"Thanks. I put a lot of work into building a comprehensive facility with everything you could possibly want."

"Here's a question that's been bugging me. How did you afford it?"

"I worked for it."

Jeff laughed to get a rise out of him. "Get serious. How much money could you possibly make as a trainer/pseudo-therapist?"

Becky spoke up for him. "Just tell him the truth, Randy."

"I am. I work hard."

Becky rolled her eyes. "His parents gave him the money. They're rich. Tobacco money."

"They gave me the money to start, but that's it! You think I liked taking it? That my whole upbringing was financed by the death and misery of others? I've devoted my life to health, to making sure other people are healthy. That investment was a way for my family to make amends. That's how I justify it. I haven't taken a dime from them since, and I won't."

Jeff tightened his lips to think for a moment. "You know, *that* I believe." He turned his attention to Becky. "One more thing. I understand Corey had been looking into security systems before he died."

Becky pointed to the panel near the front door. "We bought one. It was installed last week. I never remember to turn it on."

"What prompted that decision?"

"I honestly don't know. He just brought it up one night over dinner. He said something about break-ins in the neighborhood, but I hadn't heard anything about them."

"I can answer that." Randy hesitated before elaborating. "Corey had become paranoid."

"How do you mean?" Although Jeff asked the question, Becky looked like she was curious to hear the answer.

"He was convinced he was being watched."

"Watched? Like someone was following him?"

"Not exactly." Randy chuckled at what he was about to say. "He thought drones were following him."

Becky joined Jeff in asking the next question. "Drones?"

"Yeah, he said he saw one hovering overhead once when he was driving to work."

"That doesn't mean it was watching him."

"That's what I told him, but he obviously didn't like that

answer, so he embellished the story. He said he also heard one outside at home – here – and when he looked out his bedroom window, the drone was right there watching him."

Becky aimed her palms at the floor. "Here?! Why didn't you tell me?"

"Because I didn't believe him. Why would anyone want to watch Corey?"

"You still should've told me."

"What he told me was confidential, just like I didn't tell him what we do."

Jeff rolled his eyes. "This is why he should've been seeing a real, licensed therapist." His phone chimed, and he checked it to see a picture had been texted to him. "Oh my god."

Becky clutched her chest. "Now what?"

CHAPTER 23

WHEN EMORY TURNED onto the gravel road leading to Mary Belle Hinter's former property, he caught another glance of her right hand, which had been vise-gripped on the door handle for the past five miles. With her free hand, she pointed. "M' driveway's up ona right."

Emory looked where she directed and noticed an obstruction. "There's a chain across it. I'll just pull off the side of the road up here." He drove past her driveway before parking.

As soon as the car stopped, Ms. Mary Belle shoved the door open and fled like a teenage shoplifter. Emory grinned and stepped out of the car. The chilly mountain air gave visible form to his breath before the cutting wind dispersed it into nothingness. Although past noon, the ground on both sides of the road still glistened white from the morning's frozen dew. Ms. Mary Belle's property had no fence around it so the boundaries were unapparent. Not that it mattered. Everything in the immediate area now belonged to the TVA.

In her haste, the Crick Witch hadn't bothered to walk back to the dirt driveway. Instead, she raced over the frozen wild grass toward a weather-battered cabin – or shack, however you looked at it.

Opting to forego the brush in favor of a clearer path, Emory headed back to the driveway. Once at the chain, he saw a sign posted in the center. "Notice of auction. Property and contents." The sign gave a date of the coming Saturday.

Emory snapped a picture of the sign with his phone and texted it to Jeff with the message, "???"

When he caught up with his companion, he found her banging a rock against a padlock that had been placed on the front door. "Ms. Mary Belle! Ms. Mary Belle, we can't do that." As she raised the rock again, he snatched it from her hand.

"Someone locked m' house!"

"I'm sorry, but we can't go in there. I brought you here to say goodbye to your property, but we can't break into the house."

She jabbed a gnarled finger toward the door. "It's *my* house!"

"Not anymore." The words started her crying, and Emory fell into backtrack mode. "I'm sorry."

"Kicked me outta m' own home. Woke me up an' dragged me out. M' 'longings in there."

"I thought your nephew got your belongings out."

"He didn't know what's 'mportant. I got 'mportant stuff here."

Emory frowned and let his eyes creep to the lock. "Maybe there's an open window."

"I cain't climb through no window."

"You're right." Emory glanced at the door and the rock in his hand. He hurled one mighty blow, and the lock clanked to the grey-wood porch. He opened the door for her. "After you."

The house's interior was better kept than the exterior, but the homemade furnishings were less than aesthetic to the eyes. The place looked as if Ms. Mary Belle had just returned from a walk in the woods, although many of the cabinets and drawers were open, some half-emptied. Emory figured Luke must've just packed what he could in the amount of time the sheriff gave him and that he was smart to leave the furniture. He rubbed his hand along the rough, slatted surface of the kitchen table and was rewarded with a splinter to the index finger. His hand snapped up at the prick.

As he dislodged the wooden shrapnel from his finger, Ms. Mary Belle grabbed a tattered carpet bag from the hall closet. She pulled jars, bottles, rocks and objects Emory couldn't discern from various cabinets and buried them in the bag.

"M' nephew left all m' potions an' charms. Cain't make no livin' w'out m' wares."

Emory picked up an errant rock on the kitchen counter. "Charms? You mentioned you gave your Specter a charm to keep her from harm. Would one of those work for me to reverse the curse?"

The witch snatched the rock from his hand. "To'd you, you have ta die."

"Not much for loopholes, are you?" Emory opened a cabinet and found a chicken-bone doll in the back corner. He pulled it out and asked, "What is this for?"

"It's a blessin' tal'sman." Ms. Mary Belle took it from him.

"It's for luck?" Emory glanced inside her bedroom to see a multi-colored, crocheted quilt on the dimpled bed. "Do you need any help?"

She grunted at him and continued her work. After a few moments, she closed all the cabinets. "I'm outta tea. Gotta go dig me some more. Where's m' 'andbasket?"

Dig tea? Emory pointed to a spool table in the corner. "Is that the handbasket you want?"

The witch grunted and picked up a basket woven from thistle branches from the table. She reached behind the front door for a cane made of copper. "Let's git."

Emory grabbed her carpet bag and followed her outside. Shutting the door behind him, he tried to return the broken padlock to the latch, but each of his three attempts ended with it jangling back onto the porch. "Forget it."

He looked toward his car but didn't see his elderly companion. "Where'd she go?" He spotted her heading toward the woods at the side of the house. "Ms. Mary Belle!" He ran to stop her before reaching the edge of the tree line. "What are you doing?"

The witch twisted her head back while pointing forward. "I need to attend to m' trees."

As sweat grated through the pores on his forehead, the private investigator scanned the woods from side to side, trying to judge how expansive they might be. "How far are they?"

"Just yonder." She pointed and continued walking.

Damn. I hate the woods. Emory reached for a pill bottle in his pocket before he realized it wasn't there. *I forgot to get a refill.* He shook his head and forged ahead, following the old woman.

Wind whistled through the holes in the hollow cane clutched in the Crick Witch's gnarled right hand, laying down an eerie score to their sylvan trek. They trudged over the frozen mud and occasional icy puddles between the trees. After a few non-verbal moments, they came upon a creek, frozen on top and running from a boulder with an unusual shape.

Ms. Mary Belle pointed to the creek. "M' trees are b'hind Crow Rock."

Emory snapped his fingers when she said the name. *That's what it looks like.* The boulder was indeed shaped like a hunched-over crow with greenish water flowing from its beak, as if it were regurgitating food for an imagined chick.

He followed her around the creek to a grove of leafless sassafras trees in an area of land pockmarked with numerous shallow holes. "Was this all your property?"

She nodded toward a clearing several hundred feet away. "T'where the woods end." The old woman dropped her thorny basket and steadied herself with the copper cane, waving aside Emory's helping hand, as she dropped to her knees near the trunk of one of the trees. She ran her free hand down the tree trunk, along a large root that reached across the ground two feet before disappearing into the dirt. She gripped her cane with both hands and rammed it into the root.

What the hell is she doing?

She struck the root and the ground beside it again and again. Clink! The cane hit something hard, which she pulled from the dirt and tossed over her shoulder.

Emory picked up the lustrous blue and white rock that landed at his feet. *Pretty. I wonder if this could be used for meditation. Maybe it's good for healing or luck or fortune. Where do they come up with which rock is good for what purpose anyway? Maybe I should take up meditation.* Emory dropped the rock and turned his focus back to the crazed digger before him.

Ms. Mary Belle drove the cane into the ground again and again, several times throwing aside other bothersome rocks. When at last she dropped the cane, she placed the pieces of the root she had chipped off into her basket.

Now that the cane lay silent, another sound came to Emory's ear. It was faint at first, but it grew with the wind. He tilted his head to get a bead on the source. "Ms. Mary Belle, do you hear that?"

The old woman stood, clutching her full basket, and her face cracked into a grin. "That's m' Specter."

The faint moaning quivered the air, wheedling goosebumps from Emory's skin. His mind screamed as he realized she wasn't imagining it. The spirit of her deceased love haunted the woods!

Emory watched Ms. Mary Belle close her eyes and embrace herself in proxy for her lost love. He found himself mesmerized by the witch as she swayed to the moaning of her Specter as if it were melodic. The wind gathered strength, blowing through her long grey hair and raising the hem of her brown ankle-length skirt. Her swaying morphed into slow rotations, and she raised her arms over her head before extending them at her sides.

The cell phone ringing in his pocket slapped Emory's attention away. He glanced at the caller ID and walked away from Ms. Mary Belle before answering. "Jeff, did you see the picture I sent you?"

Still at Becky's house, within earshot of both her and Randy, Jeff answered Emory over the phone. "Why would the TVA be auctioning off property after going through all that trouble to acquire it?"

"I have no idea, but we need to find out."

Jeff waved to Becky and headed toward the front door. "I'm on my way to talk to Frank Belcher now. By the way, what are you doing out there?"

"I brought Mary Belle Hinter here so she could get some closure."

Jeff slipped into the driver seat of his rental. "I'm glad to see you took my advice. Is she going to lift your so-called *curse?*"

"Don't poke at me."

"I wasn't."

"I heard that tone."

Jeff smiled at himself in the rearview mirror. "That was concern. Not ridicule."

"Whatever. Apparently, the curse is set in stone."

"She can't break her own curse? What kind of witch is she?"

Emory glanced at the witch, who was now singing to the wind. "A very odd one."

Jeff barged into Frank Belcher's office without knocking or waiting for an invitation. "So the TVA is into flipping properties now?"

Hunched over his desk reading a document, the startled man gasped at the sound of Jeff's voice. "What?"

"You just kicked all those people off their land for the expressed purpose of building a windfarm, and now you're selling it?"

Frank removed his glasses and placed them on his desk. "Going after that tract was a decision made by my predecessor – one I never agreed with."

"That's great. Why not just sell the land back to the previous owners?"

"Unfortunately, I can't reverse the purchase of those properties. They're owned by the TVA now, and the only way we can unload property is through public auction. On the bright side, the previous owners can probably get the land back at auction for less than we paid them for it. I'm calling all of them today to let them know about the auction."

"I suppose that's good for them." Jeff took a seat and relaxed his tone. "So you're prepared to take a loss?"

"The added energy produced at the new tract will more than make up for any loss."

"How did you choose the new tract so quickly?" Jeff felt his phone vibrate in his pocket.

Frank gurgled out what Jeff thought was a laugh, if not a well-executed one. "We always had two tracts we were considering."

"That's right. I remember Peter West saying something about that." Jeff saw that Virginia was calling him, but he let it go to voicemail. "Was that common knowledge?"

"It was publicly shared knowledge. In the paper. On our website."

"So why did you disagree with Corey's choice?"

Frank sat back in his chair and interlocked his fingers over his sunken waist. "Corey had a tendency to make decisions with his gut instead of basing them solely on the facts at hand. A meteorological report comparing the two tracts clearly shows higher average wind speeds at the tract I chose."

"Could I see that report?"

Frank tilted back toward the desk. "It's publicly available information." He shuffled through papers on his desk and handed Jeff the document.

Jeff glanced at the annual wind speeds for both tracts. "The difference is just 0.01?"

"Trust me, it's significant."

"I make it a rule never to trust someone who begins a sentence with those two words."

Frank cleared his throat. "Ultimately, Corey said he chose the other tract because it's flatter, and so he thought it would be cheaper to build on."

"Is that not the case?"

"Yes, but we'll make up the difference with the extra wind."

"When we last spoke, you mentioned a report you get from a physical inspection of the land after you've purchased it. Could I see that report on the original tract?"

"It's the survey report, and I actually haven't received it yet. The contractor was supposed to give it to me yesterday. It's a moot point now anyway."

"Who's the contractor?"

"We use a company called Rutherford Geophysical Survey Company. Why?"

Jeff rose from his seat. "Just curious. Thank you for your time." He stopped shy of the door and turned. "By the way, did people in the office here know about Corey's rooftop meditations?"

"He didn't announce it, but I don't think it was a secret. He had been coming in half an hour before the official start of the workday, opening his office and then disappearing with a gym bag for twenty minutes or so before returning to the office. There's no gym in this building, so I asked him once where he went and he told me."

"You must get here really early."

"First to arrive and last to leave. I take my job seriously."

"Thanks again for your time." Jeff exited the office and pulled out his phone to call Virginia back when he saw that she had left him a voicemail.

"Jeff, this is Virginia. I think we should add Becky to the list of suspects. After that incident at her house, I guess you could say I took off my blinders. I did some digging, and it turns out the more I find out about her life, the less I know her. She told me that Corey had a small life insurance policy, and I figured it was just enough to pay the funeral expenses with maybe a little left over. Jeff, it's for $750,000."

CHAPTER 24

VIRGINIA PARKED ON the street in front of Becky's house and started up the walkway.

The front door opened ahead of her, and Randy Graham exited the house, wearing a sleeveless, quilted vest. "Hello again."

Virginia grumbled at him before a black object fell from his vest pocket. "You dropped something."

Randy one-eightied and picked it up. He grinned at her, holding up the ski mask he had worn during the role-play fiasco as if it were an enticement.

Virginia rolled her eyes and continued to the front door.

Becky answered in a bathrobe. "Virginia. Why are you back here? I was just about to take a shower."

"I won't keep you long. I need to talk to you."

Becky stepped back to let her in, but Virginia gave her head a gentle shake and stood in place. "Are you here to apologize?"

"No. Why didn't you tell me about Corey's life insurance policy?"

"I did."

"Yes, but you didn't tell me how much it was."

"Only because I didn't know at the time. I was shocked when the insurance company told me."

Virginia shrugged. "Well now that his death is officially

a murder and not a suicide, there's nothing to keep you from cashing in."

"I'm telling the truth! Look, before Corey started contracting with the museum, we were barely making ends meet. I knew he had some life insurance through the TVA, but he never told me how much. I guess he wanted it to be a surprise."

"How much more work did he have to do for the museum?"

"The contract was for a year, but the director was really happy with his work, so there's no reason he wouldn't have renewed it after that."

"How many more pieces did he have to provide?"

"There was no limit. The museum replaces them regularly and sells them off to other museums. The curator, that stuck-up bitch Claire Beckett, always says, 'Stagnant exhibits lead to dropping attendance.' I bet she couldn't wait to give Corey's contract to her husband."

"Her husband does those animal skeleton things too?"

Becky nodded. "He used to supply them before Corey got the contract."

"I don't like to ask this, but how much was he making from the museum?"

Becky shrugged and answered, "He was averaging about $3,000 a month."

"Wow! I would've never guessed that much."

"It's funny what people will pay for."

"Okay, thanks. I'll let you get to your shower." Blank-faced Virginia turned away.

Becky grabbed her arm and widened her eyes. "Hey, don't leave like this. You're my friend. I'm sorry if I haven't been the best to you since this whole mess began."

Her friend's description of recent events brought the expression raging back to her face. "This whole mess?" Virginia locked eyes with the widow. "Becky, your husband was murdered while you were sleeping with another man, and you've continued carrying on as if nothing happened. You betrayed him in life and in death."

Becky crossed her arms, and once her mouth closed, she spit out, "My marriage is none of your concern!"

"You're right. And neither is your friendship. Goodbye Becky."

Virginia wandered around the natural history museum until she saw a woman setting up a display with what looked like a coyote skeleton. She glanced at the woman's badge and stopped to speak to her. "A new piece?"

While adjusting it on the stand, Claire answered, "Yes, it just came in."

"Your husband's work?"

Claire Beckett stopped working and faced Virginia. "Who are you?"

"Virginia Kennon. I'm a PI investigating Corey Melton's murder. You met my associates."

"Yes, but I don't understand why y'all keep coming around here. No one here had anything to do with it. Unless it was Becky."

"Why would you say that?"

Claire shrugged. "Isn't it always the spouse?"

Monty Beckett entered the room carrying a skeleton Virginia couldn't identify. She nodded toward the approaching man and asked, "Speaking of which, is that yours?"

Claire pointed Monty to an empty display stand. "Just put it there." She turned back to Virginia. "Did Becky tell you how they stole the contract from Monty?"

"How did they steal it?"

Now empty-handed, Monty joined his wife. "Honey, everything okay?"

Claire didn't answer him. "She found out how much Monty was making and had her husband put in a lowball offer. My director will take any opportunity to cut costs."

Monty asked, "Who are you?"

Claire answered, "Another PI."

"Okay." Monty stepped in front of Virginia, glaring down into her brown eyes and pointed a finger an inch from her nose. "You need to go."

Virginia didn't budge. "You need to get that finger out of my face."

Monty jabbed his finger into Virginia's forehead. "Now."

Claire touched his arm. "Monty, stop."

"Do that to me one more time," Virginia dared.

Monty accepted the challenge and pushed her forehead again. Quick as a snap, she grabbed his finger and rammed it into her knee.

Monty yelped and jerked his hand back. "You bitch! You broke my finger!"

While Claire tended to her husband, Virginia told him, "It's just dislocated. Now, I'll go."

Exiting the museum, Virginia heard her phone ring. "Hi Jeff."

Jeff clicked on his turn signal as he talked on the phone over the car's Bluetooth. "Hi. I need a favor. Can you track down a report on the windfarm land? The Rutherford Geophysical Survey Company was supposed to do a complete physical survey of the land, but Frank Belcher said he hasn't received anything from them."

As she walked to her car, Virginia put the call on speakerphone and typed the name of the company on her mobile browser. "Do you think he's lying?"

"Possibly." After making a turn, Jeff pulled down the car visor to shield his eyes from the sun. "Either way, our best bet for getting our hands on that report is through the surveyors."

"Okay. I'll take care of it in the morning."

"Why not now?"

"It's late. I wasn't planning on going back to the office."

"Are you outside?"

Virginia took the phone off speaker. "I just questioned Claire Beckett."

"The museum lady? What about?"

"Apparently, Corey took the gig from her husband Monty, and neither of them is happy about it."

"Monty? That name sounds… That big guy's her husband?"

"Yes."

"She left out that little tidbit when we saw them. Wait a second, you questioned him? Virginia, that guy held a knife to my throat! You shouldn't have gone there by yourself."

Virginia hopped into her car. "I can handle myself, *partner*."

"Understood. Anyway, I'm calling it a day too." Jeff exhaled a heavy sigh, sending fluttering distortions to the other end of the line. "Hey, do you want to meet me at Bakwudz tonight? I need to drink, and I need to drink hard."

"Like ten o'clock?"

"Sure. I might get there a little early," Jeff said as he pulled into the driveway for the Bakwudz Bar.

Virginia hung up and looked at her mobile browser, where she had typed in the name of the survey company. "It's two blocks from here. Might as well take care of it now."

In Barter Ridge, Lula Mae Rome arrived at her house just as the sun was touching Crown-of-Thorns Mountain – named for the ring of twisted dead trees that encircled its barren peak. She placed her park ranger hat on the kitchen table and called for her dog. "Sophie!" She walked to the living room but didn't see the French bulldog. "Sophie?" She continued into the hallway and found the dog sitting in front of a closed door. "There you are. Why didn't you come?" Sophie looked up before returning her attention to the door. "Emory's not home. Why're you staring at his room?" Lula Mae saw light shining beneath the door. "Is he home?"

She turned the knob and opened the door. "Emory?"

Lula Mae shivered at the chilled wind blowing through the open window. She hurried to close it but slowed before reaching it. "Did someone break in?" She took a pensive step toward it. "Where's the screen?" She poked her head outside and saw the screen below, leaning against the exterior wall. She drew her head back in, shut the window and locked it.

Now shivering from fear, she turned around and scanned the room again for anything unusual. All she saw was Sophie now staring at the closed closet door. *Is someone in there?*

Rushing to the chest of drawers, Lula Mae opened the small box on top, where Emory always put his loose change, and she found a good fifteen dollars in coins. She grabbed one of his old socks from a drawer and poured the change inside. Clutching the mouth of the sock, she cocked her arm, preparing to swing the makeshift weapon.

Lula Mae crept to the closet door, shooing the stubborn dog away with her foot and gripping the door knob.

Sophie barked, sparked by Lula Mae's heightened stress and strange behavior.

Lula Mae took a deep breath, swung the door open and jumped back with her sock-wielding arm raised. Her eyes darted about, but from the top of the closet to the bottom, she saw nothing more than a cedar chest on the high shelf, Emory's old clothes hanging on the pole and several pairs of shoes aligned on the floor.

"Lula Mae?" Sheriff Rome called from behind.

She screamed and shot around to face her husband. "Nick!"

Sheriff Rome stood in the bedroom doorway. "Is something wrong?"

"I thought someone broke in."

"And you were going to attack them with a sock?"

"It's filled with change. It's supposed to hurt."

"Good lord, Lula Mae, you gotta stop watching those prison shows. What makes you think someone broke in?"

She pointed as she placed the sock on the nightstand. "The window was open, and the screen is on the ground."

"It was? Maybe Emory came back for a visit."

"Well, that's what I thought, but he's not here."

He looked around the room. "Nothing else is out of place or missing."

Lula Mae picked up Sophie and cradled her. "I know I didn't open that window, and I certainly wouldn't have left it open."

The sheriff drew his pistol, prompting a gasp from his wife. "Stay here."

Sheriff Rome left his wife alone with their dog in Emory's old bedroom to search the rest of the house for signs of intrusion. Following a cursory inspection, he returned to her and announced, "All clear."

Lula Mae bowed to let Sophie jump from her arms. "Thank goodness. Who do you think it was?"

Seeing the tension still in her brow, the sheriff lied to alleviate her concern. "You know, I might've done it. I came home for lunch, and it was a little stuffy in here. I think I did open it, and I guess I just forgot to close it."

Lula Mae's shoulders dropped. "Nick, how could you? Sophie could've gotten out."

"I'm sorry." Sheriff Rome caressed her shoulders. "How about we don't cook tonight? Change out of your uniform, and I'll take you to the Creekhouse to eat."

"But it's the middle of the week."

"It doesn't have to be a weekend for me show off my beautiful wife in town."

A luster of delight beamed across Lula Mae's face. "Give me five minutes."

When his wife left for their bedroom, the sheriff hurried outside through the kitchen door and scurried around the house to Emory's bedroom window. The snow coverage was minimal now, but even in the dusky light he spotted discernible shoeprints – tracks too big for him to have made. He pulled the flashlight off his belt and inspected the window. At the top of the bottom pane, just below the lock, he could see scrapes along the wood where the paint had been chipped away. There was no doubt about it. Someone had inserted a slender object between the two panes to jimmy open the lock. *Maybe a knife. But why?*

CHAPTER 25

AS THE SUN descended from view, a relieved Emory pulled his car up to Willow Springs. Earlier he had to pry Ms. Mary Belle from her former land, using gentle words at first and then pleading, bargaining and even admonishing – everything shy of physical force to get her back in his car. She only acquiesced once he asked her if she would rather be driven back by him or the sheriff. Apart from a stop to drop off an anti spooking charm for Bernadette Jenkins, she had remained silent the entire return trip.

Emory stepped out of the car and opened the door for her, but she didn't budge. "Ms. Mary Belle, we're here."

She clenched her eyes closed. "Gi' me a minute."

He notice her clutching her abdomen. "Are you okay?"

"Toucha the blue devils. Musta upset m' stomach."

Emory offered her a hand. "Do you need some help?" To his surprise, she accepted. He pulled her from the car, but before she straightened up, she heaved and threw up all over his pants. "Oh my god!" Seeing her legs buckle, he grabbed both her arms near the shoulder. "Are you okay?"

She coughed and heaved again. Ms. Mary Belle regained control but not her strength. "I need he'p."

"Okay, let's get you inside." Emory tried to help her walk in, but her feet weren't moving. "Ms. Mary Belle, I need to pick you up. Are you okay with that?" When she didn't answer, he took that as consent.

Emory picked up the ailing Crick Witch, who was lighter than he anticipated, and carried her inside. Lucy, the screaming woman from his first visit, stood behind the counter and clutched her chest when he opened the front door. "What happened?"

Emory explained as he sat Ms. Mary Belle in a chair. Lucy called for help, and within thirty seconds, two men arrived rolling a gurney between them. They loaded her onto it and wheeled her down the hallway.

"Where are they taking her? Shouldn't she go to a hospital?"

"We have a doctor onsite. Excuse me, but I have to make a phone call."

As Lucy dialed the phone on the counter, Emory looked at his soiled pants and whispered, "Bathroom?" She pointed to the door behind him. Over the next several minutes, the PI went through about twenty sheets of cheap brown paper towels that fell apart with three or four scrubs against his thighs. When he exited the bathroom, the calico-haired woman was still talking on the phone, so he took the opportunity to gather Ms. Mary Belle's belongings from his car. He returned just as Lucy hung up. "I don't understand. She was fine."

Lucy hurried toward the hallway on the right. "Well, that's how it happens."

"What do you mean?"

"I'm sorry, but I'm needed."

Now alone, Emory looked down at the thorny basket and carpet bag in his hands. He thought about placing them on the counter but feared they might not make their way back to their owner.

After a little meandering, he found his way back to Ms. Mary Belle's room. Placing the basket and bag on the tidy twin bed, his eyes took a brief jaunt around the space before his feet followed. The characterless room was quite different from Ms. Mary Belle's house – standard furniture, manufactured linens, painted walls. The dresser top, however, presented a few telltale signs of its occupant – jars of who-knows-what, rocks, sticks and yarn. He also saw a tiny frame with a black-and-white photo of two teenage girls standing in front of an old car. "I wonder if that's Ms. Mary Belle and the friend she lost. Her Specter. Maybe it's her sister." He returned the photo to its place and picked up one of the rocks beside it.

"What are you doing?" a voice asked from behind.

Startled, Emory turned to find Luke Hinter standing in the doorway. "Luke. Your aunt—"

"I know. They called me. She's in the infirmary now." The surfer in a suit stepped inside. "Why are you going through her stuff?"

"No, it's not like that." Emory nodded toward the bag and basket on the bed. "I brought in her things."

"I don't understand. Why did you have them?"

Luke was now close enough for Emory to see flecks of brown in his otherwise blue eyes. "I took her out to her to see her old house."

Luke sighed and crossed his arms. "Ah, dude, why'd you do that? She's never going to get over that place if she's able to visit it."

Emory held up the rock. "About that, I have some potentially good news. There was an auction sign on the property. It looks the TVA has changed plans, so now you can get it back for your aunt."

"Man, that's awesome! What a relief!" Luke nodded his head back toward the doorway. "This place keeps calling me to complain about her. I'm afraid they're going to kick her out, and I can't have her live with me."

"I know your aunt will be happy if she can return to her prop'ty... Uh, property."

In one fluid motion, Luke jumped onto the bed with his butt on the pillow, back against the wall and size-thirteen wingtips crossed at the end of his long legs. "But we better not get ahead of ourselves. There's no guarantee we'll have enough money to actually buy it back."

Emory's eyebrows arched upward. "Don't you still have your aunt's money – the money the TVA paid for her property?"

"Well yeah, but someone could bid more than what we have."

Emory's brows found their way home. "Of course, you're right."

"I could put in some of my own money, but I can't go much higher than what was paid." Luke interlocked his veiny fingers over his belt buckle. "No matter what, we shouldn't say anything to Aunt Mary Belle. She's frail enough as it is. Telling her she might get her property back and then snatching it away again could kill her."

"Speaking of her health, do you know what's wrong with her?"

"She has liver cancer."

Emory gasped at the news. "Is it treatable?"

"She won't have it. She doesn't believe the doctor. Thinks she's just homesick." Luke pointed at the thorny basket beside his feet. "The doctor thinks it's from all the sassafras tea she's had over her life."

"Really?" Emory looked at the chunks of sassafras root piled inside the basket.

"Yeah, there's some carcinogen in it. Uh, what's the name? Safrole. I think that's it."

"I should probably take this away then." Emory grabbed the basket. "How long does she have?"

"The doctor thinks maybe six months."

"I'm sorry."

Luke popped off the bed, not bothering to flatten the covers. "Me too. She kind of grows on you, you know?"

Emory chuckled. "I actually do. Well, I better get out of here. Oh." He handed the rock to Luke. "She might miss this."

"She definitely would." Luke held it up for inspection before returning it to the top of the dresser. "I don't understand her fascination with gravel."

Emory left Luke alone and found his way to the exit. As he

glanced up at the rising moon, he heard a ping and checked his phone. It was a text from Jeff – a picture of him in a bar, smiling and holding a green drink in the center of a group of smiling people. "See i don'tneeed u." That was followed by another, pictureless text, "lets doa shot to the end of our partnershhhp. celebraate. im at bakwudz."

He obviously turned off auto-correct. Emory closed his eyes and rested his forehead on the steering wheel. *This is all my fault.* He looked at his soiled, stinking pants and then texted back, "I'll be there in an hour. Don't drink anymore without me."

Emory pushed open the heavy alder door to Bakwudz Bar and stepped into an homage to the heritage of Southern mountain living. Above tables made from reclaimed barn wood hung photos of significant outposts in local postbellum history – damming rivers for power and flood control under the New Deal, bootlegging and the rise of auto racing, and Depression-era shots of impoverished families. A fake moonshine still emitted intermittent jets of smoke toward the ceiling, from which dropped several chandeliers of vintage lanterns.

Emory unbuttoned his black field jacket but kept it on, not expecting to stay long. As he searched for Jeff in the near-capacity crowd, he found himself mouthing the lyrics to the Roseanne Cash song he heard playing overhead – only it wasn't Roseanne Cash singing. It was a man's voice, and it sounded live. Moving closer to the stage, he saw a sign promoting karaoke night, and onstage at the microphone stood Jeff, singing "Seven Year Ache."

Oh my god. He stopped to watch and listen. *It's beautiful.*

More eyes turned to the stage, and noisy patrons fell into scattered whispers. The audience appeared enraptured by Jeff as he poured his heart into the song, imbuing his voice with the dejection of the lyrics. For Emory, the haunting croon was like a satin rope to his chest, tugging him closer. As soon as the last vocal note ended, Jeff dropped his forlorn expression and flashed his incredible smile – like an actor hearing, "That's a wrap!" from the director. The audience delivered a vigorous applause, intensifying the shaky hand of the man who grabbed the mic afterwards.

Emory wormed his way through the crowd to get to Jeff, who headed toward the bar. "Jeff."

"Emory!" Jeff grinned and threw an arm around his neck.

"I can't believe what a great singer you are. Is there anything you can't do?"

"I sing better drunk. Do a shot with me." With his arm still hooked on his neck, Jeff led Emory to the bar.

"Don't you think you've had enough?"

"Interesting question. To put it in economic terms, maybe I've reached my point of satiety, but my goal is the saturation point, and I'm not dripping vodka yet." Jeff squeezed between two bar huggers and raised his hand to attract the bartender.

"You don't need more vodka."

"You're right." Jeff slapped the bar and held up two fingers. "Two tequilas." He turned back to Emory. "So what are you doing here?"

"You texted me."

"I did?" He squinted his eyes, searching for the memory. "Oh yeah. Sorry, Virginia stood me up, and I... You were next on the list." The bartender filled two shot glasses with tequila, and Jeff handed one to Emory.

Emory raised the glass. "Cheers."

"Wait!" Jeff blocked Emory's forearm with his free hand. "That's not how partners shoot."

"What do you mean?"

"You do me, and I do you." Jeff rested his free arm on Emory's shoulders and held his shot glass up to his partner's lips. "Now you do the same."

The sweet, oaky smell of Añejo tequila tickled Emory's nostrils, but he was more concerned with two pairs of eyes burning through the crowd at them. One belonged to a mid-twenties man with perfect hair, wearing a polo shirt with the sleeves cut off, while the other belonged to his denim-jacketed pal. "People are looking."

"Don't be so paranoid. No one cares. Now give me my damn shot."

"Fine." Emory threw his arm around Jeff's shoulders and popped his shot glass up to his partner's mouth.

Jeff jerked his head back. "Careful! Don't chip my teeth. My smile's half my charm." He touched his lower lip to the rim of the glass. "Cheers!"

After downing the tequila, Jeff exhaled and pounded his chest, while Emory winced at the burning trail the liquor cut down his esophagus. "Good, isn't it?"

Emory clanked the shot glass back onto the bar. "Aren't we supposed to chase with a lime and salt?"

"We don't do that. Just savor the flavor."

"Consider it savored. Listen, I'm sorry about this morning. I should've waited until later to tell you. How did the show go?"

Jeff laughed. "I was actually charmless, if you can believe that. My responses were terse and dull. Thankfully, Virginia picked up my slack, so the interview wasn't a total loss. I just hope there really is no such thing as bad publicity."

"I guess we'll find out."

Jeff looked down his nose at Emory. "Well, *we* won't. You're off to greener pastures. Why are you even here?"

"Remember, you texted me."

"But why did you come?"

Emory told him, "I don't want you to hate me."

"I don't hate you." Jeff placed an arm around his shoulders. "I need you to drive me home. You're in no condition to be alone."

Emory laughed. "Thank you for looking out for me. Where's your coat?"

"In my car." He broke from Emory and led him to the door.

Once outside, Emory shoved his coat lapels together while he scanned the parking lot. "Where's—"

Jeff bookended Emory's face with his hands, stepping on his toes as he tractor-beamed his partner's eyes with a bright green glare. "Are you one hundred percent certain that you want to return to that job? I was there after you got fired. I know how hurt you were. I'd hate to see you go through that again."

"Sixty-five percent."

Jeff dropped his hands and smiled. "Then thirty-five percent of you wants to stay. I can work with that."

Emory held a hand out to his shivering partner. "Where's your rental? I'll get your coat."

"I'm perfectly capable of getting my own coat." Jeff pulled the key fob from his pocket. "Just wait here."

Emory watched as Jeff staggered to the left and clicked the fob to disarm a compact to his right. His partner changed directions, waving back at Emory, and that's the last thing he saw before stars filled his eyes. Emory's legs buckled, but the wall behind him kept him from falling. *What's going on?*

Dazed, he spotted Jeff running toward him. "Are you okay?"

Emory wasn't sure. "What happened?"

Holding his partner's shoulders, Jeff nodded to his right. "That guy just walked by and clocked you with his elbow."

Emory hadn't noticed but sometime after they exited the club, the two guys who had been glaring at them as they shot tequila had followed. The taller one now wore a green jacket over his sleeveless polo, lighting a cigarette and laughing with his friend in the denim jacket.

Incredulous, Emory asked, "You hit me?"

180

The polo guy took a drag of his cigarette before responding. "You people don't belong here."

"You son of a..." Jeff lurched toward Emory's attacker.

Emory grabbed his arm. "You're too drunk. Stay here."

The polo guy laughed. "That's right. You don't want any of this."

The denim jacket guy chimed in, "Maybe he does."

Emory growled, "This is my fight."

The polo guy dropped his cigarette and readied his fists, while his friend seemed to sidestep the impending conflict. As soon as Emory stepped within range, the guy shot a fist toward his face.

Emory deflected it and torpedoed him with a torso jab and a left hook, dropping the polo guy to his ass.

The denim jacket guy came from the sidelines to shove Emory into the wall. He followed it with a barrage of erratic punches, most of which were deflected or inflicted minimal damage.

Before the polo guy could double-team Emory, Jeff rushed to his aid. The polo guy readied a fist for Emory but delivered it to Jeff instead. Perhaps numbed from his blood alcohol content, Jeff didn't flinch when the knuckles connected with his jawline. Jeff responded in kind.

Again the polo guy ended up on the ground, soon followed by his friend.

As the PIs waited for the instigators to rise again, blue lights began strobing the scene. Emory turned to face the approaching police cruiser and noticed that a small crowd of onlookers had formed from the bar patrons. A few moments later, Emory and Jeff were being questioned by a policeman, while a second officer questioned the other two men.

The clean-shaven, red-headed policeman asked Emory, "So he just hit you out of the blue? No reason?"

"Honestly, I didn't even see it. My eyes were on the parking lot. Next thing I know, I'm seeing stars."

Jeff said, "I saw it all. He walked up from behind Emory and elbowed his face once he got beside him. That's when I came to help."

"Had you exchanged words with them?" the officer asked.

"No. Not until after he hit me."

"And then we kicked their asses!" Jeff yelled in the direction of the other guys.

"Sir, how much have you had to drink?"

Emory answered for him, "I came here to drive him home."

"If you had no previous contact, why did he hit you?"

Jeff responded, "Why do you think? He didn't like seeing us together."

The officer eyed them both before uttering, "Oh." He turned his attention to his approaching partner.

The dark-haired, mustached officer glared at Emory. "The young man said he was defending himself."

"What?!" the PIs responded in unison.

"He said you grabbed his ass."

"I did not!" Emory insisted. "I never touched him until he hit me, and I certainly never touched him anywhere below the belt."

"Well, it's your word against his. If we take him to jail, we're going to have to take you too. Do you want to go to jail?"

"That's bullshit!" yelled Jeff.

The mustached officer took a step back and placed a hand on his gun. "Lower your tone, or we'll take you too."

Seeing Jeff's mouth open, Emory shook his head in a warning not to say another word.

The officer dropped his hand before facing Emory again. "Do you want to go to jail?"

Emory grimaced at him. "No."

"Okay. We'll consider this matter dropped."

Once the officers walked away, Jeff asked, "Why did you do that? You're innocent!"

"Which we might be able to prove later but not before spending a night in jail." Emory saw the mustached officer shaking hands with his grinning attacker. "Let's just go."

A young man in a beanie approached the PIs and told Emory, "Dude, you need to know something. That guy you were fighting said that you two are gay, and then that cop with the mustache told him to say that you grabbed his ass."

"He did?" asked Emory.

"Yeah man. You should file a complaint or something." The man in the beanie held up his phone. "I took a picture of him if you want it, and I don't mind being a witness."

"Absolutely," said Jeff. "Thank you."

Emory shook his head. "I appreciate it, but I just want to forget it."

"Forget it?!" Jeff grabbed one of Emory's shoulders. "Are you crazy?"

"Drop it!" With that, Emory walked away.

Virginia woke up shivering. As she crawled her way out of a dream state, she wondered why the right side of her face was numb and why she had such a headache. She rubbed her forehead, trying to massage the pain away, but all she got was a wet hand.

"What is that?" she uttered in a raspy voice.

She pushed herself out of bed, but it wasn't her bed. In fact, it wasn't a bed at all.

Her hands were in an inch of snow, and she was sitting on the ground. She looked around for a light but saw only darkness. She peered toward the sky for starlight, but all she saw was a circular patch of stars above her head. "Oh my god. I'm in a hole!"

With hands stretched before her, she walked to the nearest side and felt it for a way to climb out. Every surface was too smooth to grip. "Damn!"

She heard something. Something faint. Now it was gone. She heard it again – only this time it was louder and longer, like moaning.

She tripped and fell on top of something – something that crackled under her weight. Her eyes adjusted until she realized she was now face to face with a skeleton.

Virginia screamed.

CHAPTER 26

WITH A FEW exceptions during a recent bout of insomnia the previous month, Emory Rome always woke up before his alarm went off – sometimes by mere minutes and other times by an hour or more. Regardless, he set the alarm every night – either because he didn't trust himself or he didn't trust what had always been would continue to be.

As soon as he awoke, he walked into his living room to turn on music from the Bluetooth speaker synced to his phone. From there, he proceeded to the bathroom for a shower. As the water pelted his body, he noticed intermittent anomalies with the sound. "What's wrong with the music? Is it echoing?" The longer it went, the more it bothered him – not enough to step out of the shower but enough to rush through it.

Still dripping and with a towel cinched around his perfect waist, Emory stepped into the center of the living room. *Sounds like I'm in a stadium.* He snapped his fingers to see if he could determine the location of whatever was picking up the sound and sending it back to the speaker. He snapped again and again as he walked around the room until he found the origin of the reverberation. It was a painting of two silhouettes walking down a puddled, lamp-lit street inside a carved wooden frame. Emory pulled the painting from the wall and examined it. He noticed one of the street lamps was out. He drew his eyes closer and realized that something black and circular was stuck over the light. He tugged at it and peeled off an electronic device about half an inch in diameter and a quarter-inch thick. He clasped the device within his fist and mouthed the words, "A bug!"

His mind flashed to the ski-masked intruder. *That's why he was here!*

Emory ran into the kitchen and put a glass under the tap. As it filled with water, he squinted at the bug to discern any identifiers that would indicate who had planted it. He saw some markers, but they weren't clear. Turning off the water, he held the bug at the rim of the glass and contemplated dropping it inside. *If I do this, they'll know I found it. I should wait until I find out who's behind it.*

Startled by a knock on the door, he lost his grip on the bug, and it sunk to the bottom of the glass. *So much for that. Who could that be? Maybe they realized I found the bug!*

From the shoulder holster hanging over the corner of his desk's hutch, he pulled out his gun and crept toward the door. He looked through the peephole and lowered his weapon to answer the door. "Mom. Dad. What are you two doing here?"

"Emory!" Lula Mae was about to hug him when she saw the gun in his hand.

Sheriff Rome eyed the weapon and scolded Emory with his eyes. "You always armed when you answer the door?"

"Sorry." Emory didn't have a convenient place to put it, so he holstered it at his waist inside the hem of the towel.

While his wife hugged Emory, Sheriff Rome explained the reason for their visit. "I had to come up on business to file some papers with the state, and Lula Mae called in sick so she could join me."

As his mother broke away, Emory saw that her blouse was damp from his wet torso. "I'm sorry, Mom."

"Lord, don't worry about it. It'll dry."

"Perhaps we best shake." The sheriff extended his hand. "We thought maybe we could take you to breakfast, but it took us longer than expected to get here."

"Breakfast sounds great." Emory returned his gun to its holster.

Emory heard his mother ask, "Don't you have to get to work?" as he retreated to the kitchen to fish the bug from the glass of water.

"Don't worry about it." With the bug concealed in his hand, Emory reemerged from the kitchen. "I have time for breakfast. I'll just give the office a call and let them know I'll be late."

The sheriff shook his head. "Son, we don't want you to be late."

Emory picked up his cell phone from his desk. "It's fine. It'll keep up my streak." He dialed the number, and as it rang, he found his magnifying glass in the top drawer. He was about to speak on the phone when he realized Virginia wasn't talking on the other end. "It's going right to voicemail. Virginia, this is Emory. My parents drove up from Barter Ridge, and I'm going to take them to breakfast before I come in. I won't be too late." He hung up the phone. "Y'all just make yourself comfortable, and I'll get dressed."

Once inside his bedroom, Emory gave the bug a closer inspection with the magnifying glass. *Oh my god.* He found the telltale sign. Along the edge of the bug was an etching of three intertwined triangles. *Aesir. This is the TBI!*

With gentle steps, Jeff descended the spiral staircase from his apartment to his office. Although showered and dressed, he moved like a sloth and squinted his eyes as if he had just fallen out of bed. *Wake up!* He slapped himself a couple of times and carved out a smile before entering the reception area, but his cheeks dropped when he found the room empty. "Where the hell are they?"

Jeff checked the clock to verify his two partners were indeed late. He saw a silhouette in the sunlight transuding through the heavy cotton curtains covering the window by the door. "Who is that?" He unlocked the door and opened it to see an old woman standing there. "Could I help you?"

From the pocket of her mud-colored cloak with tattered hems, Mary Belle Hinter presented the business card Emory had given her. "I wanna see Em'ry Rome." She entered the office, pinging the floor with her copper cane as she walked. "I didn't think you was e'er gonna open. Don't git people who don't greet the morning's blessing."

Jeff retorted, "It's just after nine."

"Sun rises for a reason." She walked around the place as if she were looking for something. As she did, she snarled at the décor, grazed the furnishings with her crackled fingers and sniffed the books. "This here writhen shop gits me swimmy-headed, but it smells good."

"Okay, I have no idea what you just said. Who are you?"

"Mary Belle Hinter."

How do I know that name? That's it! She's one of the displaced property owners. The witch. "Why are you here?"

"Guessin' your ears ain't up yet." She raised her voice to repeat, "I'm waitin' for Em'ry Rome!"

Jeff covered his ears. "Not so loud. Look, I know you're here for Emory. I'm his partner. Since Emory isn't here yet, is there something I can help you with?"

Ms. Mary Belle gave the place another quick glance. "You seen m' 'andbasket?"

"You didn't have a handbasket with you?"

"I knowed that! I ain't a fool!"

Jeff covered his ears again. "Seriously, inside voices. What's so important about this handbasket? Is it your ride to Hell?"

"Em'ry took it. I wan' it back."

"Well, you're going to have to talk to him about that because I haven't seen it. And before you ask, I don't know when he'll be in or even if he'll be in."

"I ain't got time ta wait more. Home folks come lookin' fer me. You need ta he'p me with m' one other problem."

Jeff smirked at her. "You just have one other?"

"Paper said they auctionin' m' land. I gotta git it back. I'm worried someone's gonna snatch it from me. I need to git there and spell it so no one'll want it."

Jeff touched his chest. "And you want me to take you?" Ms. Mary Belle nodded. "You have a nephew that's caring for you, right?" He didn't wait for the answer. "Can't he take you?"

"He ain't answerin' his phone. Left messages."

"Can't you just spell the property from here?"

"Better if I'm there."

"But if you're as a powerful a witch as I've heard, couldn't you just maybe hold something that came from there?"

The old woman thought for a moment before speaking. "I do got m' charms."

Jeff crossed his arms. "I haven't seen them."

"They in m' purse." She creaked onto a chair and pulled a bluish rock from her crocheted purse.

"What's that?"

"Glowstone. It has magic prop'ties. Channels it." Clasping the rock in her contorted fingers, Ms. Mary Belle closed her eyes and chanted.

Jeff pointed his palms to the floor. "I didn't actually mean *here* here. Wouldn't you be more comfortable outside?"

"Shh! Spirits cain't hear o'er your yammerin' on and on."

"Can you let them know they don't have an appointment?"

"Hush!"

Resigned, Jeff took a seat at Emory's desk and waited for the stubborn woman to finish her vain act of repulsion. His eyes wandered from her to the framed picture of Emory's birth mother.

Emory has your cheeks. Your eyes. Same shape, same determination, same suppressed fear – like an escaped captive. What happened to you? To you both?

When he again glanced at Ms. Mary Belle, she was still entranced. *How long is this going to last? I don't have time for this.* He pushed away from the desk and opened the bookshelf door to his office. Taking a seat and scooting up to the desk, he turned on his computer and searched the shared case file for a phone number. The cell number listed for Luke Hinter went right to voicemail, so he called the work number.

"Neyland and McKay," the woman on the other end of the line answered.

"Neyland and McKay? What kind of company is this?"

"We're a commodities brokerage. Can I help you?"

"Yes, I'm calling for Luke Hinter."

"Please hold. I'll connect you."

The phone rang three times before connecting to voicemail. "You've reached Luke Hinter. I'm out of the office on vacation until the fifteenth. Please leave a message, and I'll call you as soon as I'm back. If you need immediate assistance—" Jeff hung up before the message ended.

Still looking at his phone, Jeff opened his photo album and flipped to the picture that Emory's mother had sent him. The image of the cowboy hat and beautiful face beneath it ticked up the corners of his mouth. Jeff's modest mirth was momentary, as he felt a presence staring at him. "Whoa! What are you doing? Are you finished?"

Now standing beside him, Miss Mary Belle peered into Jeff's face. "I know that look." She retrieved another bluish rock from her purse, but this one was attached to a thin leather strap. "Here. Wear this 'round your neck. It gives the hurt a place ta go so it leaves you 'lone."

Her words sparked a subdued but genuine smile from Jeff, who took the amulet. "Thank you."

The old woman cranked open her palm. "Ten dollars."

"Ten... I thought it was a gift."

"Why would I gift you? I ain't sweet on you. Magic costs."

"Whatever." Jeff shook his head and paid her. "Are you done?"

She nodded. "Ready for you ta take me back."

"Me? How'd you get here?"

"Took the damn bus."

Jeff sighed. "Let's go."

CHAPTER 27

EMORY HAD NO sooner exited the backseat of his father's pickup, when he heard a delighted squeal from his mother. Lula Mae pointed to a Mourning Dove Investigations ad plastered on the side of a bus stopped at a traffic light. "Look! It's Emory! Quick, Nick, take a picture!" She grabbed a blushing Emory's upper arm with both hands. "Were you surprised?"

Emory feigned delight. "I definitely was."

"I just fell in love with the idea when Jeff called me." By the time Sheriff Rome pulled the phone from his pocket, the bus started moving. "Hurry, Nick! You're gonna miss it!"

The sheriff trotted along the sidewalk with his phone in front of his face. When he walked back to them a moment later, he was scrolling through the few pictures he'd captured. "I think they're all blurry, Lula Mae."

Her shoulders dropped at the news. "Oh no. I hope we see another one."

Emory led them to a diner with a pseudo-shanty exterior and the name *Dolly's* painted on a sign. He held open the front door for his parents. "After you."

Once inside the restaurant, his mother's demeanor recovered. "Emory, what a nice place." Her eyes roved around the Dolly memorabilia adorning every wall. To upbeat country music, a handful of waitresses shimmied among at least two dozen tables and booths, dressed as different versions of Dolly Parton – from her television days in the 1960s and 70s to her movie characters of the 1980s. Costumed as Porter Wagoner, the host greeted the trio of newcomers and led them to a table for four.

"Jeff introduced me to it."

"He's such a nice man. I really like him."

"I do too, Mom."

After they were seated and had ordered, Lula Mae wasted no time in steering the conversation. "Emory, we have a confession to make. The reason we're here is to talk to you. Well, for Nick to talk to you."

"About what?"

Sheriff Rome took a sip of his coffee and winced as he clinked the cup back onto the saucer. "Son, we were a little worried after our last phone call. You don't seem to be happy with your new job, so we were thinking you might consider working for me."

"You want me to be a deputy in Barter Ridge?"

Lula Mae answered for him. "You could live at home as long as you want."

The sheriff ripped open a packet of sugar and dumped it into his coffee. "We could definitely use someone with your expertise. You already know we couldn't have caught that murderer last month without you."

Emory glanced at Lula Mae's hopeful face before turning to his father. "I appreciate it, Dad, but I'm happy here. In Knoxville."

Lula Mae sank into her seat. "Emory this is about your birth father, isn't it?"

"No."

"That hateful man is gone now." She grew more passionate as she spoke, ending at the point of trembling. "I'm sorry to be blunt, but he's dead. You two saw him die. Everything that happened, it's over. There's nothing keeping you from coming home." She waited a few seconds for a response. "Unless you just don't want to be around us."

"Oh my god, that's not it at all." Emory hesitated before giving a reason. "I just don't need another job offer."

His father removed the coffee cup from his lips, forgoing a sip for a question. "Another one?"

"I didn't want to say anything because I'm still debating it, but Anderson Alexander came to see me."

Sheriff Rome perked up at the name. "Hey, I've met him. He's the head of the TBI."

"He offered to override my former boss' decision and reinstate me."

Lula Mae's elation returned. "Emory, that's wonderful!"

"Congratulations Son!"

"Thanks, but I don't know if I want to go back."

The sheriff added another packet of sugar to the coffee. "But isn't that what you've always wanted?"

"It is. I've always had a straightforward plan. I knew exactly how my career was going to go. Now I do feel... adrift. I took the PI job because it was offered to me on a silver platter, but I don't like the disrespect that comes with it. Karmic retribution I suppose. I can say that it hasn't been boring, and it's kind of freeing to be my own boss and not have to deal with the politics of the reporting structure. I do like being around Jeff." *Do I tell them I'm gay and have feelings for Jeff?* "I mean we argue all the time. Constantly, but..." *I can't.* "Still, it would be nice to be back on a course where I know the destination." Emory shook his head. "Being fired just left such a bad taste in my mouth."

A surprising expression of anger leapt out of the shadows to slap the sympathy from Lula Mae's face. "Honey, get some Scope and rinse it out. You belong in the TBI. Isn't it better than what you're doing now? Jeff is very nice, but you've always had higher ambitions."

"There's something else." Emory pulled the listening device from his pocket and placed it on the table. "I found it in my apartment this morning."

Lula Mae reached out to touch it but then recoiled as if it intended to bite her. "What is it?"

The sheriff took it from Emory. "It's a bug."

Lula Mae covered her mouth to ask, "Can they hear us now?"

"It's not a lip-reading machine, Lula Mae."

"And I've disabled it."

The sheriff retrieved his reading glasses from his shirt pocket and gave the device a closer look. "Who put this in your apartment?"

"I encountered an intruder earlier in the week—"

His wide-eyed mother talked over him. "An intruder? In your apartment?"

Emory nodded. "My first thought was that I had interrupted a burglar, but now I think he might've been working with the TBI. There's an Aesir logo on the side of the bug. It's the company that supplies the TBI with surveillance equipment."

Lula Mae gasped. "Why would they have you under surveillance?"

"I was about to sue them for wrongful termination."

Sheriff Rome handed the bug back to Emory. "So you think they're trying to find something to discredit you? That's not a legal reason to bug you."

"What if they came up with another reason? Eve Bachman, my old boss, has had this chip on her shoulder where I'm concerned. I wouldn't put it past her to fabricate an internal corruption investigation as a reason to surveil me."

"What if you're wrong? Surely the TBI isn't that Aesir company's only customer." The sheriff tested his coffee again and then sipped away.

"It's possible, but I don't know why anyone else would break into my apartment to plant a bug. I never really have guests, and my conversations with myself just aren't that interesting." Emory briefly flashed on his sexual encounter with Jeff, and his face reddened. *They must've heard all of that!*

Lula Mae shifted in her seat and pinched her face into a fretful expression. "Burglars, surveillance. That settles it. You need to come home and work with your father."

"Mom, I'm not running."

"Fine. Where's the ladies' room?"

Emory pointed it out. "Over there."

"I'll be right back."

As his mother walked away, Emory told his father, "Actually, I could use your professional help with something."

"Hang on. I need to tell you something before Lula Mae gets back. Someone broke into the house yesterday while we were at work."

"Oh my god!"

"I didn't know why until now. I think I need to check our house for bugs."

Emory frowned at him. "I can't believe the TBI would tap your place too."

"Maybe they're covering all their bases to find something on you."

"Maybe."

"So what did you need my help with?"

Emory handed him two plastic baggies – one containing a blank, used envelope and the other a photograph of Emory as a teenager at the former Crescent Lake. "This picture was slipped under my apartment door in that envelope about a month ago. By the same person who broke in the other night – at least he was wearing a similar mask."

"I've never seen this picture before."

"That's because it was taken before I met you, and it burned in my granny's house – along with all my other pictures. Or that's what I thought."

"How did this picture survive, and who had it?"

"The only other person at her house then, besides me and her, was my father."

"So he took it."

"That's what I figure, and then the TBI must've confiscated it along with everything else after he died. Read the back."

The other side of the picture was black with silver writing that read, "Who bears the iniquity of the son?"

The sheriff trained his eyes on Emory. "What does it mean?"

"I'm not sure, but it looks like someone is using my past to get to me today. Can you look into it for me? You have access to fingerprint records, and I think you can be more objective about it."

"Of course." The sheriff pocketed the baggies just as his wife returned to the table.

Lula Mae slid into the booth. "Did I miss anything?"

The sheriff put an arm around her. "I was just telling Emory he should take the direct approach. Go talk to Anderson Alexander. Make him lay all his cards on the table, and ask about the surveillance."

"I agree." Lula Mae tapped the table with her index finger. "Honesty's best. Get all this behind you, and get back to work."

"You're both right. I'll get this straightened out."

When Jeff returned to Mourning Dove Investigations after driving Ms. Mary Belle home, he was surprised to find the office still empty. "It's 10 o'clock. Where the hell are they?"

He continued on to his office, removing his grey pea coat as he walked. While hanging it on his coatrack, his face jerked upwards. "What was that noise?"

He heard Bobbie's muffled growling through the ceiling and scuffling. Jeff opened the bookcase door to the secret space behind the wall and pounded up the spiral staircase to his apartment. He shoved open the door and spotted someone in his living room. The ski mask with circle eyes and jagged red smile flashed his mind to the night of his car accident a month earlier. *It's him!*

The intruder tried to slip out the window, but the bobcat clung to his calf with her front paws and sharp teeth.

Jeff lunged for the man, grabbed the waist of his black pants and hurled him to the apartment floor. He jumped onto the intruder, straddling his torso, and punched him twice before reaching for the ski mask. "Who the hell are you?!"

The man uttered nothing but grabbed Jeff's wrists before he could pull off the mask. He bucked the PI up and slid from underneath him in one fluid motion. The man dropped his weight onto his palms and twirled his body to deliver a kick to Jeff's jaw, flooring him.

Bobbie, who had been waiting to pounce again, did just that. She leapt onto his left shoulder, but the intruder spun his body around, flinging her before she could dig in her claws.

Shaking the stars out of his head, Jeff took advantage of the distraction his bobcat provided and kicked the man's knee pits. The intruder's legs buckled, and he fell to prayer position.

Jeff scurried behind him and locked him into a sleeper hold. The masked man seized Jeff's right hand and bent it at the wrist, forcing it back enough for him to escape the hold. He dropped again to his hands and donkey-kicked the now-standing PI back onto the bar that separated the kitchen from the living room, knocking the wind out of him.

The man yanked the electric cord from the lamp by the couch. As the lamp crashed to the floor, he vaulted over Jeff's head with legs in near-perfect splits, wrapping the cord around the PI's neck as he did. Now on the opposite side of the bar, the man clutched the ends of the cord and forced the back of Jeff's head to the top of the bar so that his feet almost couldn't touch the floor.

Jeff grasped at the cord, trying to free himself before he could be strangled to death, but the man's grip and leverage were too much to overcome.

Perhaps sensing a call for help, Bobbie jumped onto the bar and attacked the man's arms. The intruder yelped and released his grip on the cord.

Coughing, Jeff threw the cord to the floor and turned to his attacker.

The man had backed away from Bobbie and was searching the kitchen drawers. A second later, he brandished a chef's knife and lunged toward the bobcat.

Jeff dove onto the bar to push Bobbie away. The blade missed her but sliced through his right cuff, grazing his wrist. "Son of a bitch!"

The man withdrew the knife, and Jeff hurried off the bar. The intruder whisked the knife in an arc before him, aiming for Jeff's chest, but the PI jerked back just in time to avoid it.

The man leapt over the bar, stamping his feet into Jeff's ribs. Although he stumbled back, Jeff didn't fall. The masked intruder tried to cut him again and again. Whisk! Whisk! Whisk! With each effort, Jeff dodged or deflected the blade with whatever was handy – couch cushion, coffee table book, picture frames. After a close swing, Jeff grabbed his wrist and jammed it into his knee.

As the knife clinked to the floor, the masked man shot toward the window. Before Jeff could catch him, he was gone. By the time he poked his head out the window, the man was already darting down the alley.

Jeff dashed down the stairs and out of the office to street. He started running to get around the building to the alley, but when he turned the corner, he tripped over something that sent him flying to pavement.

"Dude, are you okay?" a voice from behind him asked.

Jeff grunted as he pushed himself up. He turned around to see Phineas sitting there with his legs stretched before him and his guitar leaned on the wall at his side. "I'm fine. Did I hurt you?"

The homeless young man chuckled. "Man, I'm feeling no pain right now."

"Phineas, did you see someone running by here?"

"You mean besides you?"

"Yes!" Jeff clenched his impatient fists. "Wearing a white a ski mask."

"What? A ski mask?" Phineas exhaled to check the air. "You can't even see your breath."

Jeff exhaled, but in exasperation. "He wasn't worried about the temperature." He ran down to the alley and looked both ways before returning to Phineas. "He's gone." He took ten dollars from his pocket and handed it to the homeless musician. "For lunch."

"Thanks dude." He reached for his guitar. "You want me to play you a song?"

"That's fine." Jeff waved and headed back to the office.

Once he was alone, Phineas smirked and reached two fingers inside his guitar. From beneath the strings, he pulled out a white ski mask with a jagged red smile.

CHAPTER 28

"QUIT FLINCHING!" FLUSTERED, Emory again waited for Jeff to extend his arm.

Seated at his desk, Jeff opened his scrunched eyes. "Can't you use some antibiotic ointment? I hate alcohol."

Emory smirked at the comment. "It didn't look that way last night."

"Very funny. It's going to sting like a mother."

"Look, this is the only disinfectant in the first aid kit. Now hold still so we can get this over with."

Jeff squeezed his eyes shut and gritted his teeth as he held out his arm again. He grunted when Emory touched the alcohol pad to the shallow knife wound on his wrist. "Do I need stitches? I feel like I need stitches."

"It's not that deep. Are you sure he meant to hurt you?"

Jeff held his wrist up to Emory's face. "You tell me!"

Emory clenched the left corner of his lips. "It's just that I was thinking he might be working with the TBI."

Jeff laughed. "This guy seriously tried to kill me. He's not law enforcement."

"I don't get it then. Who is he? He's now broken into our apartments, and he's bugged mine."

"Caused my accident last month."

"In all fairness – playing devil's advocate – you were pursuing him, and he was just trying to get away, so even that could be explained away."

"Tell that to the four tires I had to replace, thanks to his homemade spike strip. Did you say *bug*?"

As he bandaged Jeff's arm, Emory filled him in on the listening device and almost everything he had discussed with his dad. He debated telling him about the picture that had been slipped under his door because he knew that would lead to more questions about his past – a place he was not prepared to revisit just yet.

Once he was done, Jeff reiterated, "Whoever he is, he's not in law enforcement."

"Then who is he?"

Jeff rolled his sleeve down and nodded toward the adjacent wall. "Go over to that painting."

"Why?"

"Just do it." As Emory complied, Jeff inspected the gash in his cuff. "This shirt is ruined now."

Emory stared at the painting and remembered that he had meant to ask Jeff about it before now. Within the frame a hooded woman held a lantern before her as she navigated a seaside clifftop under the watchful gaze of a raven perched on the ruins of a church. "Why this painting?"

"Not that one." Jeff pointed to another painting. "On the other side of the bookshelf."

Emory looked at the correct painting but stayed put until he got an explanation. "To get from my office to yours, you chose *A Separate Peace* because it's your favorite book. To get to your apartment upstairs, you pull on *The Secret in the Attic*, which is obvious. What's the significance of this painting to get out of your office?"

Jeff shrugged off the question. "I just like it." He walked past Emory to the painting to which he had pointed. "Come to this one. It's a forgery. The real one is hanging in the Yale Center for British Art."

Emory inspected the painting, which he had never had the opportunity to notice before. It was of a nude woman sleeping in a bed, on the side of which sat a clothed man with clasped hands and a look of contemplation or regret. "It's haunting."

"Beautiful," Jeff said at the same time. "What do you see?"

"A man had sex with a woman and waited for her to fall asleep before getting dressed. He obviously regrets what he's done, so the woman isn't his wife. Perhaps she's a prostitute."

"Very good! The first name of this painting was *What Shall We Do about the Rent?*"

"The first name?"

"This was painted by Walter Sikert. Do you recognize the name?"

Emory thought for a second before shaking his head. "No."

"You really don't read any crime novels, do you? Walter Sikert changed the name of this painting to *The Camden Town Murder* in reference to a real-life crime in which a man had sex with a prostitute, slit her throat ear-to-ear while she slept and then left in the morning. The murderer was never caught."

"Was Walter Sikert a suspect?"

"Not in this one, but the fact that he was so obsessed with murder and prostitutes and the fact that he lived in London in the late 1800s have led some to speculate that he might've been the real—"

"Jack the Ripper?"

"See, you just might have some talent for this PI business. Too bad you're abandoning it. Anyway…" He pulled on the frame, which was mounted to wall – or rather to a hinged panel that separated from the rest of the wall and lowered to reveal a hidden crime board. "Didn't know I had this, did you?"

Emory just shook his head as he checked out the details of the images tacked to the white board with magnets and the descriptors written on it. A picture of a white ski mask had been colored with a red marker to look more like the one the intruder had worn. The heading of each column named sightings of the man with the dates of each – outside the office (which led to the pursuit that damaged Jeff's car), outside Emory's apartment on the day he was fired from the TBI and inside Emory's apartment the other day.

"I started this after he broke into your apartment. It should help us get to his identity and motives."

"Impressive. I didn't know you could be so organized."

"I'm organized." Jeff tapped his temple. "Up here. Oh, speaking of which, I've come up with an idea for your curse problem."

"Why are your bringing that up?"

"Because I know you believe in it, and I'm trying to help." Jeff headed back to his desk. "What do you call it when you hold a trial for someone but the accused isn't actually there?"

"Trial in absentia."

"Really? That doesn't sound right. Maybe what I'm thinking is more of an effigy thing." Jeff typed on his computer.

"What are you talking about?"

"Give me your phone."

"Why?"

"Just do it."

Emory handed Jeff his cell phone. "What are you doing?"

"Found it!" Jeff turned the monitor around for Emory to see.

Emory leaned forward to read the banner on the webpage. "Transference spell?"

"I got the idea from Warcraft, but this is a little different. We make a personal object – your phone – an effigy of you using a transference spell, like a voodoo doll. Then we destroy, or kill, the object." Jeff put air quotes around the second verb. "Voila! The curse is broken."

Emory laughed. "First off, that's a ridiculous idea."

"More ridiculous than believing in curses? It's obviously distracting you, and I'm just trying to help get it out of your head."

"Second, doesn't what happens to a voodoo doll also happen to the person it represents?"

"Maybe that was a bad analogy. We'll make sure it doesn't."

"Third, you're not destroying my phone."

When Emory retrieved his phone, Jeff winced at the slight twisting of his wrist. "Damn it." He cupped his wound to ease the pain. "You know this never would've happened if you had been at work on time. We could've taken him together."

"I didn't know my parents were going to show up. Did you?"

"Why would I have known?"

"I just thought since you and my mom are buddies now. Besides, I left a voicemail for Virginia. She didn't tell you?"

"She wasn't here either."

"She wasn't? Where is she?"

Jeff threw up his hands. "I don't know. Everyone's abandoning me."

"When did you last speak to her?"

"Yesterday afternoon. I asked her to join me for a drink. She stood me up."

Jeff checked his phone. "Oh yeah, I forgot about that. She left me a voicemail about Becky getting $750,000 from Corey's life insurance."

"Whoa! That's a lot of motive."

"I know. Although she couldn't have killed Corey herself."

"With that money, she could've easily hired someone to do it for her."

Jeff threw up his hands. "Wait a second. I just remembered I asked Virginia to follow up a lead on why the TVA switched properties. She was supposed to track down the report for the original tract from the survey company."

Emory followed Jeff as he hurried to Virginia's desk. "The one that did the physical survey of the land?"

"Yeah, but Frank said he never received anything from them.

I thought there might be something in that report. I asked her to take care of it yesterday, but it was kind of late. Maybe she waited until this morning."

"Okay." Emory saw some pages in the printer tray, and he picked them up to read through them.

Jeff looked at the clock. "It's past noon."

"Hey, look at this." Emory handed him the papers one at a time as he finished reading them. "Last week Frank Belcher deposited $9,000 cash into his checking account."

"Where would he get that kind of money and in a lump sum?"

"And what did he have to do for it?" Emory headed for the door. "I'll just go ask him."

Jeff laughed. "Good luck. You think he's going to tell you?"

"When confronted with indisputable proof, people usually—"

"You try it your way. I'll try it mine."

"What does that mean?"

Jeff headed for the door while shaking his head and raising his index finger. "You're going back to the TBI. You'll need plausible deniability."

Emory shook his head as they both left the office. "I hate when you say that."

CHAPTER 29

FRANK BELCHER RETURNED to his office with a file folder, which he came close to dropping when he saw Emory seated in front of his desk. "Excuse me, what are you doing in my office unannounced?"

Emory turned toward him, and Frank could see he was on a cell phone. "Thank you." He hung up and pointed to Frank's desk phone. "I just left you a voicemail announcing myself." *God, I think Jeff is rubbing off on me.*

Frank scrunched his brows together and slapped the file to his desk. "I'm very busy today. I don't have time—"

"How are you liking your new job?" Emory held his trump card as he tried to feel him out.

Frank descended into his chair. "Fine. Why do you ask?"

"It's just that Corey's death has been pretty beneficial to you."

The diminutive man scoffed at the notion. "A ten-percent raise and an even greater increase in responsibility hardly makes up for Corey no longer being here. I miss him."

Emory placed the information Virginia had printed onto his desk. "I'm sure the $9,000 you deposited into your checking account three days before your former boss was murdered helps temper your nostalgia."

Frank studied the papers and uttered, "I don't understand."

"Your current boss told us that the TVA is losing money, so I'm assuming this money isn't a bonus. That leaves me with one question. What did you do to earn it?"

Frank became very still. "I swear, I didn't know about this money. It has to be a mistake."

"Go ahead, check your account."

"I don't have the password."

"To your computer?"

Frank's face reddened as he admitted, "To the bank account. My wife handles the finances."

"Really?" Emory scooted back in his chair. "Okay. Where does your wife work?"

"Edmund's. It's a hardware store. One of those twenty-four-hour places. She works the early morning shift."

"So not a job that would pay her a $9,000 bonus. Do you know where your wife would've received such a large sum?"

"Probably from... her brother." Like a turtle emerging from its shell, Frank found his footing and went with it. "That's what it is! No mystery. Her brother does really well, and he gives her money sometimes."

This guy is full of crap, but I can't prove it right now. "Very well."

"Listen, I have an offsite meeting I have to get to." Frank grabbed the file folder from his desk and placed it in his briefcase. "If you have any other questions, please call."

Jeff waited until he spotted someone – who didn't matter. *Here comes someone now.* He jumped out of his rental car and retrieved a cardboard box from the trunk. He hurried along the walkway to catch up with the older man approaching the door of the apartment building. "Could you hold the door for me?"

The man unlocked the secured door and held it open for him. "Are you moving in?"

"Thank you." *Great. Now I have to make small talk. I should've picked the lock myself. If only it had been dark and there weren't so many eyes on this street.* "Yes, I just moved here from Nashville."

"How nice. Are you familiar with our fair city?" The man pushed the elevator call button.

"I've been here a few times."

A chime announced the elevator's arrival, and the two men stepped inside. "You have to try The Belfry. It's a wonderful British restaurant. I know the Brits aren't renowned for their culinary prowess, but trust me on this place. What floor?"

"Huh? Oh, eleventh."

"Perfect! I'm am too." He pushed the floor button.

Great!

The man extended a hand but dropped it when he realized Jeff wouldn't be able to shake. "I'm Sherman, by the way."

Jeff blurted out the first name to come to mind. "Blake."

"Nice meeting you, Blake. So which apartment is it? I don't recall one for rent."

"I'm subleasing it."

"Oh. Which one is it?"

"You know, I still haven't memorized my address. I'll know it when I see it." The elevator doors opened into the middle of a hallway, and Jeff nodded to Sherman. "Go ahead. I don't want to hold you up."

"Don't worry about me. You're the one with the heavy load." Sherman waved him toward the door.

Damn! Jeff stepped into the hallway and turned around to Sherman.

"Don't you remember where your apartment is?"

"No, I do. I just wanted to say thanks for welcoming me."

"No problem at all."

Why is he not moving? "Where's your apartment?"

Sherman pointed to his left. "I'm right down there. Apartment 1114."

Jeff nodded in the opposite direction. "I'm down this way. I'll see you around."

The two men went their separate ways. Jeff passed a trash chute in the wall, and he looked to make sure Sherman was no longer in view before dumping the empty box inside. He checked the notes on his phone to find Frank Belcher's apartment number. "Damn! Apartment 1112?"

Jeff walked back the other way until he found the apartment. Sure enough, it was right beside Sherman's. From his coat he retrieved his lock-picking kit but waited to use it. *I should make sure his wife isn't home.* He knocked, but no one answered. *All clear.*

The door to apartment 1114 opened. *Spoke too soon!*

Sherman poked his head out the door. "Sorry, it sounded like my door... Blake?"

Jeff stuffed the kit into his back pocket and pointed to him. "There you are! I thought you said you were in apartment 1112."

"You were looking for me?"

"Yes. Yes, I was. Would you happen to have a lightbulb? My bathroom light is out, and I don't have any supplies yet."

"Of course. What kind do you need? Seventy-five?"

"No, a one-fifty."

Sherman sucked in air. "Oh, I know I don't have anything that high."

"That's okay then. Thanks anyway." Jeff began to walk away.

"Sorry," Sherman closed the door.

As soon as Sherman's door closed, Jeff got to work on Frank Belcher's lock, and within a few seconds, he was inside. "Ooh, it's warm in here." He was tempted to take off his coat but told himself it wouldn't be wise. *I won't be here long.*

The two-bedroom apartment was tacky but immaculate

– every figurine equidistant from the other, every glass shelf dust-free and every gold-plated fixture polished to a garish sheen. From the entryway, he could see a sliding door leading to a balcony on the opposite end of the living room. Jeff forewent that room in favor of the nearest bedroom, which looked to be a combination guest bedroom/office. He wormed around the twin bed with the pink-rose comforter to the pressed-wood desk and searched the drawers but found nothing of interest. He slid open the closet door and found something curious.

Hanging in the closet were several maid uniforms, all the same size but varying in design. "This can't be his wife's. She's as tall as I am and girthier. She couldn't fit in these small outfits. They have a maid? Is she a live-in?" Jeff closed the closet door and wiped away the sweat accumulating on his forehead as he headed to the dresser. Sure enough, he found women's underwear and lingerie in the top drawer. "Damn it! I better hurry. Who knows when she'll be back."

He headed into the master bedroom, where another sliding door led to the balcony. He had just peered into the closet when he heard keys jingling at the apartment door.

"Shit!" Jeff shouted under his breath. He darted for the sliding door, but as soon as he stepped onto the balcony, he came face-to-face with something that made him almost jump back inside. Two inches from his forehead hovered a shoebox-sized drone.

CHAPTER 30

WHEN HE SAW the drone flying in front of his face, Jeff yelled, "What the hell?!" He covered his mouth, hoping whoever had just walked in the front door of the apartment didn't hear his voice from the balcony.

The lens of the attached camera peered at him as the drone ascended. Jeff glanced up at the blinking red light on its belly before the drone scudded away.

The sound of jingling keys jerked him back to his current danger. He closed the sliding door behind him and looked for a place to hide. The two wicker chairs on either side of a glass-topped, gold-plated table offered no cover, so he suctioned his back to the wall between the living room and bedroom sliders.

After a moment, he scooched to his right so he could peek into the living room. *Frank's wife!*

Lettie Belcher trod into the apartment wearing a pant suit and a look of exhaustion. She threw her purse on the entryway table and kicked off her heels as she walked, leaving them where they fell. She fanned her face and adjusted the wall thermostat before heading toward the sliding door.

Jeff jerked his head back and shuffled to the other door. He pulled the bedroom slider open as Lettie did the same to the living room slider. He jumped into the bedroom and waited for her to go on the balcony. *Now's my chance! I'll run to the front door.*

Lettie, however, didn't step onto the balcony. Instead she slid closed the screen door, leaving the glass door open. "Get some fresh air in here."

Jeff heard her walking through the living room now. He hurried back onto the balcony, closing the bedroom slider behind him. He returned to his position against the wall. *Maybe she'll take a shower or a nap.*

She didn't do either. Instead she sat on the couch and was about to turn on the TV when the apartment door opened again.

Jeff gritted his teeth. *Seriously? Now who's here?*

He heard Lettie's voice. "What are you doing home?"

"I took off for lunch. I need to talk to you."

That's Frank. Great. I'm going to be stuck out here all night!

"You just got a promotion. You should eat lunch at your desk."

"It's important. Did you deposit $9,000 into our account?"

Jeff's ears perked up. *The money!* He turned to face the wall and craned his neck to peek through the screen door.

Lettie jumped up from the couch and met her husband in the entryway. "What are you doing snooping around the account for?"

"I didn't. One of those PIs asked me about it."

Lettie took a menacing step forward as she glared down at her husband. "What do you mean? How did he find out?"

"I think he has connections with the TBI. I don't know. Does it have anything to do with the windfarm? Is that why you wanted me to move it?"

Lettie hauled off and slapped Frank, slamming him to the floor!

Holy shit! Jeff had to cover his mouth to keep from screaming the words.

"What did I tell you about questioning me?!"

Cowering on the floor, Frank raised a defensive hand. "Lettie, I'm sorry. But he wanted to know where it came from."

Lettie kicked her husband in the stomach. "What did you tell him?"

"I told him you got it from your brother. I said he makes a lot of money, and he gives you some sometimes."

"Did he believe it?"

"I don't know. Maybe."

"Why is he looking into our affairs? Did you say something to them to make them suspicious?"

"I wouldn't know anything *to* say." Frank lowered his hand and pushed himself into a seated position on the floor. "Suspicious of what?"

"Nothing." Lettie walked back into the living room.

Frank stood up but didn't move from his spot. "Lettie, just so I know how to answer if I'm asked again – or how not to answer – should you just tell me what's going on?"

Lettie clenched her fists and lunged at her husband, backing him against the wall. She clutched his slender neck and started choking him. With his back still pressed against the wall, she lifted him by the neck so that his feet dangled two inches above the floor. "There you go questioning me again!"

Red-faced and gagging, Frank grabbed his wife's wrists, but he couldn't break her grip.

Oh my god! She's going to kill him! Jeff reached for the screen door.

Lettie threw her husband to the floor. Without another look at him, she walked back to the couch. "I'm not happy about this."

Jeff moved away from the screen just in time not to be seen. He returned his back to the wall and listened.

In between coughs, Frank sputtered out, "I'm sorry."

Lettie turned on the TV. "Sorry isn't going to cut it. You know what to do."

Jeff waited for a response but heard nothing. *What? What does he have to do?* The next sound he heard was of the sliding door opening. He jerked his eyes toward the bedroom slider. *Still shut. Where was that...* Jeff looked back the other way and saw Sherman stepping onto the balcony of the apartment next door. *Shit! Don't let him see me! Don't let him see me!*

Sherman lit a cigarette and was about to sit down when he snapped his fingers. He left the cigarette in an ashtray and returned indoors.

Jeff released a sigh of momentary relief. He heard a thwacking sound from inside the Belchers' living room, followed by a cry of pain. He peeked through the screen door again and gasped.

Lettie was holding a riding crop, ready to strike again at Frank's ass. As if that weren't enough to shock the peeping PI, Frank was also now wearing one of the maid uniforms.

Holy shit!

"Blake, is that you?"

Stunned, Jeff turned his attention to the other balcony to see Sherman smiling at him.

"I thought that was you." Sherman pointed to the balcony. "This is your apartment?"

Jeff whispered. "Yes. I got turned around."

"Why are you whispering?"

"I don't want to disturb the neighbors."

"You don't have to worry about that." Sherman did his best Tarzan yell while beating his chest.

Jeff waved his hands toward the ground, trying to get him to be quiet. "Shh!"

Sherman laughed. "It's fine. No one cares how loud you are during the day."

Jeff heard a scream from inside the Belchers' apartment – only this time, it didn't come from Frank. He turned toward the screen door and saw a horrified Lettie pointing at him. *Shit!*

"Burglar! Frank, get him! I'll call the police!"

Frank Belcher, in his little maid uniform, ran toward the screen door as ordered. Jeff bolted through the other sliding door and into the bedroom, but before he could get to the bedroom door, Lettie blocked it. She hit him with the riding crop again and again.

Jeff shielded himself, but each blow stung his forearms, even through his coat sleeves. "Stop it! I'm not a burglar!" As he backed away from her, he tripped onto the bed, and Lettie came flying on top of him. Jeff struggled to push the weight off.

"I got the handcuffs, honey!"

Lettie took the cuffs from her husband and slapped them around Jeff's wrists.

Frank got his first good look at the intruder. "Jeff Woodard?"

Emory sat at his desk, researching Lettie Belcher's family on his laptop, when his cell phone rang. He checked the ID but didn't recognize the number. "Hello?"

"Emory, it's Jeff."

"Hey Jeff. So Frank told me his wife's brother gave her the money."

"It was a lie."

"I know. How do you know?"

"I'll tell you about it when I see you. Is Virginia there? I just tried calling her cell again."

Emory glanced at her desk. "She's still not back."

"By the way, it's possible Corey wasn't being paranoid when he talked of drones watching him. I saw one hovering over Frank Belcher's balcony."

"How did you happen to see that?"

"That is something I wanted to talk to you about. I need you to do me a favor."

"What is it?"

"I need you to bail me out."

CHAPTER 31

EMORY KNOCKED ON the apartment door, and a moment later, Lettie Belcher was standing before him. "Yeah? Who are you?"

"I saw you at Corey Melton's funeral, but we haven't officially met. I'm Emory Rome, Mourning Dove Investigations. Is Frank here? I went by his office, and they said he had a family emergency."

"You work with that guy who broke into our apartment?"

"Yes."

"We have nothing to say to you."

As Lettie started to close the door, Emory blocked it with a rigid arm. "That's fine. I'll do all the talking."

"Talking about what?"

"Dropping the charges against my partner."

Lettie jabbed a fist into her hip. "Why would we do that?"

"Because you'll be in the cell next to him if you don't."

Lettie glared at him for a second and stepped aside to allow him entry. "Come on in."

"Where's your husband?"

"He's in the other room cleaning. Frank, we have company!" Lettie waved him to the couch. "Have a seat. What do you have to say?"

"We should wait for your husband."

"Frank!"

Frank appeared a moment later in the clothes he had worn that day at work. "Mr. Rome, what are you doing here?"

Emory got right to the point. "You're going to drop the breaking and entering charges against Jeff."

Frank looked at him as if he had just spilled red wine on his overstuffed, leopard-pattern couch. "What? He broke into our home! He saw... He invaded our privacy!"

"All true. You know what else is true? Your wife's brother is a cashier at a convenience store, so I don't imagine he has a lot of loaning money lying around." He turned to Lettie. "You received $9,000 from someone. Who was it, and what could you possibly have done to earn it?"

Lettie sat in the chair across from Emory. "It's none of your business."

"Is that your final word on the matter?"

"Yes."

"Okay." Emory stood and headed for the door. "Then my next stop is to see Frank's boss."

Frank blocked his path. "Darren? Why?"

"Just to let him know about the deposit and then wonder aloud what project could've possibly been altered in return for that much money."

Lettie didn't budge. "Go ahead. You can't prove anything."

Emory looked down at Frank. "How long do you think you'll be able to hold onto your new title with the suspicion of bribery in the air?"

Frank stepped out of Emory's path to plead with his wife. "Lettie, if I lose my job..."

Her arms crossed, Lettie glowered at the TV.

"Lettie."

"Okay!" Lettie jumped out of her chair "We'll drop the damn charges!"

"Great. You can ride with me, or I can follow you to the police station."

Jeff followed Emory from the police station and took a deep breath at the top of the steps. "Man, time crawls in lockup."

"You were in there for two hours, max."

Jeff was all grins. "Oh, you are not going to believe what I saw!"

Emory's lips curled in the opposite direction. "Is that all you have to say?"

"No, I'm about to tell you. Just trying to build a little suspense."

"I don't care what you saw! I'm talking about the fact that you got arrested for breaking and entering!"

"I had a feeling you'd dwell on that."

"Dwell on it? I haven't even started." Emory plopped into the driver seat. "You realize you could've lost your license over this. Then where would you be? B & E is one of those lines we discussed that shouldn't be crossed."

Jeff slid into the passenger seat and slammed the door. "Sometimes it's the only way to get the information you need to solve a case. I'm not a TBI agent. I can't just snap my fingers and get a warrant."

Emory started the car and drove from the station. "Then to paraphrase you, you have to come up with more creative means to fish out the information."

"That's what I did."

"Within the law!"

"Within the law, huh? How did you get the Belchers to drop the charges against me?"

Emory fidgeted in his seat. "I just appealed to them and promised you wouldn't do it again."

"No way. I know how angry they were, and Lettie was quite literally out for my blood. They wouldn't have just rolled over out of the goodness of their hearts." Emory fell silent and continued focusing on the road. "You threatened them."

"No, I—"

"Yes, you did. Admit it."

Emory sighed. "I tried to think of what you would do if our situations were reversed."

"So you threatened to go to Frank's boss about the money they received and suggest that it was a work-related bribe?"

"I just applied a little pressure."

Jeff poked him in the shoulder. "That pressure's called coercion or blackmail, both of which are against the law. Here you're talking all high and mighty."

"Fine. I'm no better. You happy?"

"I am, but not because of that." Jeff placed a hand on Emory's. "You did it for me."

Emory interlocked his fingers with Jeff's.

CHAPTER 32

EMORY COULD SEE the growing anguish on Jeff's face. They had just come from Virginia's apartment, which showed no signs of foul play.

From the passenger seat, Jeff banged his fist on the dashboard of Emory's car. "I should've started looking for her sooner."

"It hasn't even been twenty-four hours since you spoke to her last, and you've been working the case. Stop beating yourself up." Emory parked the car outside the Rutherford Geophysical Survey Company. "We're going to find her, and she's going to be fine."

Jeff leapt from the car to the sidewalk. "It's getting late. I hope they're still open."

Once inside, they asked the first person they encountered who handled surveys for the TVA, and they were directed to the office of Fred Leakey.

The bearish man at the desk looked up through his shrubby eyebrows to see who entered his office. "What can I do for you?"

Emory shook his hand. "Hello, Mr. Leakey. We're here looking for a friend of ours."

"Does he work here?"

"No, *she* was supposed to call here to inquire about the survey report for the TVA windfarm property in Brume Wood."

"No one called. A woman came by here yesterday asking about it."

Jeff showed him a picture of Virginia on his phone. "Is this her?"

"She's the one."

"Did she get the report on the TVA windfarm property from you?" Jeff returned his phone to his pocket.

"I told her Clayton Barnes hadn't submitted the report yet."

Emory typed the name into his phone. "What else did you tell her?"

"I said he works out in the field most days, so he usually just checks in when he's done with a job. She insisted on speaking with him, so I called his cell and left a message." Fred looked at his desk phone. "No messages, so I'm guessing he hasn't called me back yet."

Emory waited a second for anything else. "Is that it?"

"Yep. She left after that."

Jeff thought about the argument he had with Virginia outside Becky's home. "Maybe she went to find him. Does Clayton have a home number or a family member we can call?"

"Family? He moved here from Idaho a couple of years ago. I don't think he has any family here."

Jeff was growing impatient. "Can you just give us his number and address?"

"The number I can give you. The address wouldn't be appropriate." Fred wrote the number down for them.

Emory shook his hand again. "Thank you for your time."

As the PIs exited the building, Emory pulled out his phone. "I'll call Clayton to—" His phone rang before he could finish. "It's my dad. I need to take this."

Jeff took the number from him. "I'll call Clayton."

Separating from his partner, Emory answered the phone. "Hi Dad."

From the sheriff's station in Barter Ridge, Sheriff Rome greeted his son. "I had the picture and envelope you gave me tested. Everything was clean, except for one thumbprint on the picture."

Emory raised a celebratory fist. "You got a print? That's excellent! Were you able to identify it?"

"I was." The sheriff sighed before spitting it out. "Emory, the fingerprint belonged to your father. It was Carl Grant's."

"Wow. Well, okay. That's to be expected. He had to be the one to take the picture from Granny's house, so that makes sense. Whoever took it from him must've kept it in a safe place and only touched it with gloves before delivering it to me."

"It's possible, but…"

Jeff came back to him and mouthed, "No answer."

Emory nodded that he understood. "What is it, Dad?"

"The picture, front and back, was totally clean except for that one clear print right smack dab in the middle of the picture. It was like someone wanted you to find it."

The weight of the sheriff's words piled onto Emory's heart, leaving him without enough breath to speak.

"And you'd think after eight years, the print might've been smudged a little or a bit worn, but it was like it was touched yesterday."

Emory inhaled enough to say, "But he's dead. We saw it."

"I know. I know, Son."

"His fingerprint is on file. Someone must've gotten ahold of it and fashioned a way to transfer it. Latex or something."

"There's something else." Sheriff Rome cleared his throat. "The envelope. It looked familiar to me. Then it hit me. It was your mother's."

"He kept a memento from her?"

"Not your birth mother. Lula Mae. It's the same as the envelopes in the stationery set she keeps in her desk at home."

Emory tried to picture the postcard-sized envelope. A thin red line bordered the entire edge of the white paper, and a curious red tornado garnished the flap. "It looked pretty ordinary to me, apart from the little whirlwind."

"That's actually a vortex. Lula Mae bought the stationery when we went to Sedona for our twenty-fifth. Some little bo-tique shop."

Emory shook his head. "That letter was slid under my door a month ago. That would mean your house was broken into twice."

"Emory, I don't think the TBI is behind the break-in at your place or mine. Something else is going on here."

Emory nodded. "But what?"

"But she's missing! Do you not get that?"

From behind the wheel, Emory listened as Jeff argued with a representative from Virginia's car recovery service and waited for him to hang up. "Can't they track her car?"

"They can." Jeff added a mocking tone to his voice. "But I'm not authorized to receive that information. Between them and the police just telling me they'll 'look into it,' no one is taking her disappearance seriously."

Emory looked at the clock and the street for their current location. "I have an idea." He spun the car into a U-turn. "He's going to be getting off work soon, so we have to hurry."

"Who?"

Emory ignored him and pushed his Bluetooth button. "Call Wayne Buckwald, office."

"Wayne? Why the hell are you calling him? He's not going to care. He's just going to tell us to call the police."

As Wayne answered the phone, Emory held up a finger to silence his partner. "Hello Wayne. It's Emory."

"Emory? Why the hell are you calling me?"

Jeff put his palms before him as if to say, "See!"

"I'm calling because I need your help."

Wayne snorted. "Why on Earth would I help you?"

"We're working on the Corey Melton case—"

"That case is closed, you idiot. Haven't you heard?"

"I know you've arrested Peter West, but surely you're smart enough to realize by now he didn't kill Corey."

"You're wrong, once again."

Jeff cupped his mouth to silence a laugh, and Emory gave him the "Shh" sign.

"Virginia Kennon's car is missing."

"Who's that?"

"One of my new partners."

"So file a report with the police. What are you bothering me for?"

"Out of respect for you and your reputation, I wanted to help you avoid embarrassment when proof surfaces revealing the real killer is not the one you've arrested."

"What the hell are you talking about?"

"Virginia was chasing down a lead and was given evidence explaining the real motive behind Corey's murder and implicating the murderer, but before she could look at it, her car disappeared. The car is registered with a recovery service, but they won't tell me where it is because I'm not the owner. They would, of course, assist law enforcement in finding it."

"Why doesn't this Virginia just call them and get her car back?"

Unsure how to answer, Emory shrugged at Jeff, who then imitated Emory's voice. "She's out of the country. She was on her way to the airport when she came into possession of the evidence."

"So her car was stolen with this so-called evidence inside?"

Emory didn't answer Wayne's question. "My fear is that if the police find the car first, they'll see the evidence and then realize the TBI – you, really – got it wrong. I'd like to work with you to get it before that happens. Then we could share the information, and you could announce the new suspect. If you're the one who found the real killer, people would overlook the fact that you initially charged someone else by mistake. Will you help me track down the car?" Wayne was silent, so Emory added, "For old times' sake?"

"What's her name again, and what's the name and number of the recovery service?"

Emory gave him the information. "So you'll call me back once you have the location."

"Yeah. Just wait for my call."

As soon as the line disconnected, Jeff made a prediction. "He's not going to call you back."

"I know that." Emory parked his car across the street from the Knoxville Consolidated Facility of the Tennessee Bureau of Investigation. "That's why we're here."

A few minutes later, they saw Wayne exit the building and get into his car. As he pulled out of the parking lot, Emory waited until he had driven far enough ahead before following him.

CHAPTER 33

"YOU'RE GETTING TOO close."

Emory shook his head at Jeff's comment. "Wayne never notices his surroundings. During one drug bust he walked into a dealer's home and called, 'Clear.' I came in after him and noticed someone hiding behind the curtains."

"Oh my god! I thought that only happened in Shakespeare. That actually worked?"

"It did on Wayne. And the guy was armed. After that, I always insisted on being the first in. I think he used to be a good agent. He just grew lazy."

When Wayne turned onto another road, Emory spotted a barn he had seen before. "Do you realize where he's going?"

Jeff looked ahead but didn't recognize anything. "No. Where?"

"Brume Wood. The windfarm tract, the original one, is about ten miles ahead."

"Well what are you waiting for? Gun it."

"I can't pass him now. He'll see me."

"I don't care! We need to find Virginia!" Jeff stomped onto Emory's right foot, accelerating them toward Wayne's car.

"What are you doing? Get off me!"

Keeping his foot planted on Emory's, Jeff pointed at Wayne's car. "Pass, or you're going to hit him!"

Emory swerved, causing his car to fishtail and straddle the line between the pavement and the shoulder. The rear passenger-side corner snapped one of the wooden legs of a sign welcoming people to Brume Wood. Emory regained control and held a hand to the side of his face as he passed Wayne and zoomed ahead. "Now get off me!" Jeff relented, and Emory tried to get his breathing back under control. "Damn it, you could've killed us!"

"Do you need a pill?"

Emory hated to admit it, but he did. "I'm out, and I haven't had a chance to get a refill."

"Oh." Jeff pursed his lips and looked at the windshield. "Hey, keep up the pace. The more of a head start we have, the better."

Emory did, slowing down only once they had reached the original windfarm tract. "We should've stayed behind Wayne. There are thirteen different properties within the tract. We have no idea which one it is."

"Just keep driving around until we spot her car. It's not a four-wheeler. It has to be on the road or in a driveway."

They passed property after property, each of varying size and each with a posted auction sign. "There!" Jeff yelled at last.

Emory's eyes followed his pointing finger. "I don't see it."

"It's behind that house."

Emory backed up and pulled onto the dirt driveway of the dilapidated white house. The driveway continued to the back of the house, where two vehicles were parked – Virginia's black hybrid and a brown truck with more dents and scratches than square inches of untouched paint.

Jeff bolted from the passenger seat to inspect Virginia's car. Once Emory joined him, he concluded, "Nothing's amiss here." Turning his attention to the truck, he saw the last hints of sunlight glinting from the silver frame around the Idaho license plate. "Damn Idahoans!"

Emory was a bit taken aback by the out-of-nowhere statement

but not enough to ask about it at the moment. "This must be the surveyor's. Clayton." He opened the truck door. "There's nothing in here. No papers, no devices."

Jeff headed for the house and tried the back door. "Locked. Do you have a crowbar?"

"Hang on a second before you go breaking in."

"Don't start on the breaking and entering."

"I wasn't going to, but look at the dirt on the step. Yours are the only footprints."

"Maybe they went in the front door."

"Or maybe they didn't go into the house at all." Emory pointed to the trees at the other end of the property. "I think Mary Belle Hinter's old property is on the other side of those woods." He retrieved two flashlights from the trunk of his car, and the two searched the property in the dimming light.

"I wish there was fresh snowfall. I can't see any tracks." Jeff's shoe kicked a metal box.

"What was that?"

"It looks kind of like a battery."

Emory inspected the dashboard on top of the device. "I think this is an underground metal detector."

"I guess we're on the right track then." They both aimed their beams down and crisscrossed the ground before them.

"Is that a sinkhole?" Emory fixed his light on a hole about six feet in diameter a few yards ahead of them.

"Look!" Jeff aimed his light at a rope tied around the base of the nearest tree, and he swept the beam along the length to the other end. "It stops at the hole." The light continued to a fallen tripod next to the hole. "There's some more equipment." He started toward the hole.

"Be careful! There's no telling how stable the surrounding ground is."

Jeff stopped for a second before cat-stepping forward. "It's got to be the surveyor's rope. A couple of months ago, we were working on a lost dog case."

"You look for lost dogs?"

"When the client pays me $5,000 to find her beloved Australian shepherd, I do. Anyway, we found him stuck on the side of a ravine at the foothills. Virginia wanted to rappel down to get him, but she didn't have a rope in her car. We ended up calling the fire department." Jeff reached where the rope touched the rim of the hole and pulled up its sliced end. He turned a worried face toward Emory. "It's cut."

"Crap. How deep does it look?"

"Virginia!" Jeff yelled into the black opening. He lowered himself onto his stomach, held the rocky rim and poked his head over the hole. "What's the surveyor's name?"

"Clayton."

"Clayton!" Jeff waited for an answer before scooting away. "If someone's down there…" He turned his ear back to the hole.

"Do you hear something?"

Jeff motioned him to be quiet, but there was no need. They both heard it this time – Virginia's voice. "Down here!"

"Virginia! Are you hurt?!"

"Sore and weak, but okay! There's someone else here! He's not good!"

"It must be Clayton. I'll call for help." Emory walked a few feet away to make the call.

"Virginia, how far down are you?!"

"I can't tell for sure! Fifty feet maybe!"

"Okay, just hang on! We're going to get you out!"

Emory tried to call 911 but to no avail. "I'm not getting a signal. Can you try?"

Jeff looked at his phone. "Nothing."

"What the hell is going on here?!"

Emory and Jeff jerked around to see who asked the question,

and they saw a man with a flashlight approaching. Emory raised his flashlight to Wayne's angry face, and the TBI agent shielded his eyes. "Get that damn light out of my face!"

Emory lowered the beam. "Wayne. Thank you for calling me back."

"I don't owe you a phone call. What are you doing here, interfering with my investigation? I thought you didn't know where her car was."

Jeff answered for Emory. "I had a hunch, and it led me here."

"Stop with the damn lies, and tell me what's going on!"

CHAPTER 34

"JEFF, HURRY! IT'S freezing down here!"

Wayne cursed under his breath. "Who the hell is down there?"

Emory responded with a question of his own. "Do you have rope?"

A few minutes later, Wayne tied his rope around the same tree as the previous rope, while Jeff placed a tarp over the edge of the hole to keep the rocks from cutting this one.

Emory shined a light into the hole again. "Jeff, are you sure you want to do this?"

"Would you rather do it?"

"God no. I was horrible at climbing the rope in gym. What I meant was Wayne called for help on his satellite phone, so they should be here soon."

Jeff turned on the flashlight he had clipped to his belt. "I'm not going to make Virginia wait one minute longer than she has to." He looped the rope around one leg and backed himself up to the rim of the hole. He nodded toward Wayne while asking Emory, "Can you make sure that knot doesn't come undone? I don't trust him."

Emory cracked a grin. "I'll hold it myself." When Jeff took another step back, Emory told him, "Wait!" and kissed him.

Emory could hear Wayne behind him groan, "Good god."

"Be careful."

Jeff nodded, took a deep breath and stepped onto the edge. Before he lowered himself into darkness, he saw Emory plop onto the ground and dig his heels in as he gripped the rope.

Jeff began his descent. "Virginia! I'm coming."

"I see your light!"

With his powerful forearms, Jeff had no problem supporting his own weight, and his feet touched the ground thirty seconds after entering the hole.

Virginia threw her arms around him. "What the hell took you so long?"

"I'm sorry." Jeff released the rope and hugged her back. "You're freezing." He removed his coat and wrapped it around her shoulders. "How long have you been down here?"

"Since about six last night. I was hoping it would get warmer when the sun came up this morning, but the light never made it down here."

"That explains the unmelted snow." Jeff placed his flashlight on the snow-covered ground, casting light on the broken skeleton. The PI jumped back and fell on his butt. "Whoa! What the hell is that?"

"Someone must've fallen down here long ago and was never found." Her eyes began to well. "I thought that would be us."

Jeff focused on the man lying on the ground with Virginia's coat covering most of his torso. "Is he—"

"He's still breathing, but he stopped talking a few hours ago."

"There's a bottle of water in my coat pocket, if you're thirsty." Jeff stooped to check his condition. "Clayton." He slapped the man's face a few times. "Clayton!" The man didn't stir, but Jeff could hear him breathing. "We'll have to leave him for the professionals. He could have a broken back."

After a glance at his shivering friend, he stood and grabbed the rope. "Let's get you out of here." He tied it around her legs and waist and yelled for Emory to pull her up.

Seconds after Virginia climbed over the rim, the rope was thrown back down the hole, and he heard Emory ask, "Jeff, do you want me to pull you up?"

"I'll manage!" Jeff took a breath and began his journey up, which took about twice as long as his descent. As soon as he touched the rim, he could feel Emory's hands clasp around his wrists, and his partner helped him crawl to the ground.

"Are you okay?"

Jeff nodded. "Where's Virginia?" He plopped his butt on the ground and gave the front of his green pullover a few tugs to peel the sweaty cotton from his torso.

Staring at his partner's torso, Emory answered, "She went to her car to warm up. You know, I could've pulled you up."

"Nah, I like climbing rope." Jeff pushed the sleeves up to show off the blood-filled veins in his forearms. "It's a great workout." He glanced at Wayne, who had dropped the end of the rope and was now making a beeline for Virginia. "We need to stop him."

By the time Jeff and Emory caught up to Wayne, he was already questioning Virginia through the open car window. "What's his name?"

From behind the steering wheel of her car, Virginia answered, "He said his name was Clayton."

"Is he the killer?"

"What? I don't think so."

Jeff sidled up to Wayne and cracked open the door between the inquisitor and his presumed informant. "Virginia, scoot over. I'm driving you to the hospital to be checked out."

Wayne pushed the door shut. "An ambulance is on the way, and she's not going anywhere until she answers my questions." He pointed an angry finger at Virginia. "If I arrested the wrong man, you need to tell me right now!"

Virginia shrugged. "Why are you asking me?"

Jeff and Emory turned toward the shrill of a siren, and lights from the approaching fire engine strobed their faces. Emory slapped the roof of the car and nodded toward the road. "Wayne, the rescue team is here. You should greet them."

"She doesn't know anything, does she?" Wayne sneered at his former partner. "You lied to me."

"Yes, and I'm still waiting for you to call me back."

Wayne growled, "Asshole," as he walked away.

Virginia stepped out of the car. "Guys, what was that all about?"

Emory shook his head. "Nothing important." He pointed to the ambulance pulling into the driveway behind the fire engine. "We should get you checked out."

A few moments later, while Wayne and the firemen worked on bringing Clayton safely to the surface, Virginia sat at the back of the ambulance for an assessment from the EMT.

As the clean-cut, silver-haired EMT took her pulse and blood pressure, Jeff questioned her. "We know you went looking for the survey report, and the man at that office gave you the name of the surveyor. What happened after that?"

"I thought he might still be at one of the properties for the windfarm tract since he hadn't filed a report yet, so I drove out here and spotted what I figured was his truck. I walked around looking for him, and I heard moaning."

Jeff noticed Emory turn to look at the edge of the woods, just beyond the hole. "What is it?"

"Oh my god. The moaning I heard in the woods yesterday, that was him!"

"You heard moaning and didn't investigate?"

Emory cupped his cheek in his palm. "I didn't know it was a person."

"What did you think it was?" When Emory didn't answer, Jeff rephrased his question. "Did you think it was a ghost?"

"No. Of course not."

"Oh my god, you did!" Jeff laughed. "For such a devout follower of reason, you sure get led astray by the oddest superstitions."

Ignoring Jeff, Emory crossed his arms and focused on Virginia, who said, "Jeff, don't laugh. I think I saw a UFO."

The male PIs asked in unison, "What?"

The EMT removed the blood pressure cuff as Virginia explained. "Let me back up a minute to where I left off. When I saw the hole, I called down, and I heard a faint voice. I tried calling 911, but I couldn't get a signal."

Jeff sat next to her. "Okay, but how did you end up in the hole with him?"

"I got the rope from my car and rap—"

"You had rope?"

The EMT held a pin light to Virginia's eyes to check her pupils just as she nodded to Emory. "I need you to keep your head still, ma'am."

"Sorry. Yes. We could've really used a rope for a situation a couple of months ago, but we didn't have it readily available. I bought it to have on hand."

"I heard the story."

Jeff elbowed her. "You rappelled?"

With the light removed from eyes, Virginia blinked several times. "What? I did it when I was in the Marines. Anyway, that's when I saw it."

"The UFO?" asked Emory.

Virginia nodded. "It was getting dark. I was holding the rope, and I was trying to pep myself up to go down the hole. Then I heard something. I looked up, and there it was. This red light floating in the sky. I couldn't make out the shape of the craft. All I could see was the light – like that little red one in Close Encounters."

The EMT chuckled as he handed her a cup with two pills and a tiny bottle of water. "Take this."

Virginia frowned at the handsome man and insisted, "I'm telling the truth."

The EMT responded, "You're very lucky. No broken bones or

apparent internal injuries, but you might have a slight concussion. That could explain why you were seeing things."

"It was *before* I fell."

"Regardless, I recommend we take you to the hospital for a thorough examination."

Virginia downed the pills. "I'm fine."

"It's your call, but if you start feeling dizzy or have a persistent headache, you need to get the emergency room. Understood?"

"Understood."

One of the firemen yelled from the hole, "We got him!"

As the investigators turned to see Clayton being lifted from the hole, the EMT grabbed his case and hurried to tend to him.

A light went off in Jeff's head. "Wait a second. A red light. Virginia, could it have been a drone?"

"A drone? You mean like a military drone? No way—"

"No, like a commercial one."

"I hadn't thought about that, but I guess so."

Emory pointed to Jeff. "You think it's the same one you saw on the Belchers' balcony?"

"And maybe the same one Corey saw."

"Our killer's been keeping tabs." Emory shook his head. "Crap, why didn't I think of that before?!"

"What?" asked Jeff.

"When we went to see Randy Graham that first time, remember I heard something after we got out of the car and I saw something just before it flew over the trees. It had to have been a drone. That's how the killer knew where we were, and then he tampered with your tire while we were inside."

Virginia threw up her hands. "Well great. Thanks for ruining that for me. I really wanted it to be a UFO. I spent god knows how many hours in a damn hole in a ground, and you couldn't give me that?"

Emory snapped his fingers. "I just thought of something else. Drones have to be registered with the FAA."

"That's right! Virginia, you could see if anyone on our suspect list has a registered drone?"

Emory glanced at his frazzled partner, and grabbed Jeff's arm. "Perhaps it could wait for her to rest a bit."

"Thank you, Emory." Virginia shot Jeff a see-he's-watching-out-for-me glare.

Jeff huffed. "That's what I meant. Virginia, you still haven't told us how you ended up trapped down there."

"I was about halfway down when the rope snapped, and I must've passed out."

Jeff bit his tongue but not enough to keep from sniping at her carelessness. "You could've been killed."

"I was trying to help him. Look, I sit at a desk all day. You guys are always out in the field, getting your hands dirty. I thought this was one tiny bit of action I could do on my own. Anyway, when I came to, the first thing I saw was that skeleton."

"Skeleton?" Emory's ears perked up. "There's a skeleton down there?"

Virginia nodded, and Jeff corroborated. "I saw it too. Someone must've fallen down there years ago."

"I think I know who."

CHAPTER 35

WALKING FROM HIS car on a chillier-than-expected Saturday morning, Emory gripped a folded twenty dollar bill in his gloved hand. He stopped before reaching the office to check both sides of the street in each direction, but he didn't see Phineas anywhere, so he pocketed the money and unlocked the door to Mourning Dove Investigations. He placed his satchel on the floor next to a leg of his tiny desk and was about to sit down when he heard noise coming from Jeff's office.

Emory opened the bookshelf door and found his partner standing within an arc of stacked books.

"Emory? What are you doing here? It's the weekend."

"I don't take a day off when I'm working on a case. What are you doing?"

Jeff heaved a great sigh. "I'm turning all my paintings and books upside down for a while."

"Why on Earth are you doing that?"

"It gives you a fresh perspective. Helps unblock your mind and open it to more critical and creative thinking." Jeff nodded toward Emory's clothes. "You should try it in your closet. Your new clothes can't possibly still be at the dry cleaners."

"I haven't had a chance to pick them up." Emory waved his palms over the stacks of books. "I'm still not clear on the *why* here."

Jeff returned to his work. "Trying to focus on the case. We have too many suspects, and we need to start weeding them down. Get this damn thing solved so we can both move on."

Emory was in no mood to discuss his potential move to the TBI. He went to the bookshelf beside the one Jeff was working on and started helping him turn the books upside down. "All right then. Let's talk this out and start narrowing down the list. The way I see it, we have two primary motives for Corey's murder – money and—"

"Vengeance," said Jeff, to which Emory nodded. "Under money, we have the grieving, soon-to-be-moderately-rich widow, Becky Melton. She doesn't have the strength, but she could've hired someone with the life insurance money."

"Hitmen don't usually take IOUs. It would've had to be someone she knows well enough to trust they'd actually get paid."

"Someone like pseudo-therapist Randy Graham." Jeff grinned and clenched his fist. "God, I so want it to be him."

Emory held up a cautious finger. "We have other suspects to go through. The museum curator and her husband also go in the *money* category. From what Virginia told us, Claire and Monty Beckett will have a sizeable supplement to their annual income now that Corey's out of the picture. Monty could've easily thrown Corey from the building."

Jeff nodded. "True. Last under *money*, we have Corey's replacement at the TVA, Frank Belcher. He couldn't have done the actual deed, but I don't think his wife Lettie would've had a problem with it, the way she manhandled her husband."

"Not to mention the mysterious $9,000 deposit." Emory shook his head. "I still can't believe what you told me about them."

Jeff raised his hand as if taking an oath. "I swear I didn't embellish a thing. I didn't need to."

"Okay. So that's three potentials for the actual act in that category. Now for *vengeance*, we have everyone who lost their property to the windfarm."

Jeff said, "But only two would've been angry enough to kill – our favorite department store clerk, Peter West, and your little old witch."

"Well, she couldn't have thrown him."

Grinning, Jeff pinched his own nose and moved it side to side. "Maybe with a twitch of her nose. What about her nephew?"

Emory answered, "He's physically able, but he wasn't close enough to his aunt to murder for her, and she had no money to pay for it. Still, they are the only family they each have."

"So we're done! We have five people with varying degrees of motive who could've thrown Corey off the roof the needed distance. Six if you count witchcraft." Jeff snickered before stoning his face. "Seriously though. Thank you for going through that with me."

"All right, come on."

"Where are we going?"

"The auction's today."

CHAPTER 36

BY THE TIME Emory and Jeff arrived at the outdoor auction in Brume Wood, the auctioneer had already started going over the process for purchasing the properties. Even with the dryness of the information, the slight, elderly man with the big voice delivered the words with the rhythmic rat-a-tat of a rapper. The square speakers propped on the front corners of the makeshift wooden stage magnified his prose, ensuring it crackled through the crisp mountain air.

Each of the thirteen properties that had been taken by the TVA through eminent domain, including seven with homes, would be sold with their original boundaries intact. The auction for all thirteen properties (or lots, as the auctioneer referred to them) would be held at a single location, here at Lot One – which was one the PIs had not visited before. Poster-sized collages with a map and pictures of each lot were displayed on easels, all in a row and in sequential order, near the auctioneer's stage. All sales would be final and require payment in full before leaving that day, and final deeds would be ready at the Knoxville TVA office on Monday. To avoid any misinterpretation of gestures or vocalizations, bidding would require a raised hand from the bidder. With the rules explained, the auctioneer began the bidding for Lot One.

Plodding through the muddy ground from the car to the

center of the action, Jeff and Emory greeted the local sheriff, a fortyish man with a kind face but inquisitive eyes. Walking away, Emory whispered to Jeff, "That must be the sheriff who physically removed Ms. Mary Belle from her property."

"I'm sure that wasn't a pretty sight." Jeff nodded toward a small table near the posters. "There's Corey Melton's old boss sitting at that table."

Clutching his jacket closed at the chest, Emory's eyes followed Jeff's to Darren Gleeson. "He's probably handling the paperwork for the TVA. Who's that woman he's talking to?"

"Maybe it's his wife."

"No, I saw her at the funeral. This woman's younger."

Jeff pointed to the posters on easels. "We should see how the lots are numbered."

Emory and Jeff snaked through the robust crowd toward the posters so they could see which property corresponded to which lot number. Darren Gleeson came to greet them. "Gentlemen, are you here to bid on some land?"

"Thinking about it." Jeff winked at Emory.

Darren laughed. "Good. We need the money. Actually, I'm thinking of bidding on one of them myself. Beautiful views up here. Good luck to you." With a nod, he returned to the table and his female companion.

Jeff pointed to the first collage. "Lot One is a tiny piece of land."

Emory stepped in front of the second one. "Lot Two is the one with the sinkhole." He continued down the line. "And Ms. Mary Belle's is Lot Twelve."

Jeff passed his partner to the last collage, which included a photo of a double-wide trailer. "This must be Peter West's property. Lot Thirteen. I wonder if his wife is here to bid on it." He scanned the crowd.

"Do you know what she looks like?"

"I know what their kids look like."

Emory turned his attention to the hands being raised for Lot One. He took a few steps back so that Jeff stood between him and the crowd, and he pulled out his phone, telling his partner, "Pose."

Jeff arced his eyebrows. "I'm not going to take my shirt off here."

"No, I mean just pose for a regular picture, tourist style." He whispered, "I'm trying to nonchalantly take pictures of the people bidding."

"Ah." Jeff crossed his arms and posed for the camera.

After taking one picture of a nearby bidder, Emory spotted someone behind Jeff that made him say, "Oh my god."

Jeff followed his gaze. "Peter? How did you get out?"

Peter West grinned at the PIs. "They dropped the charges. Said they didn't have enough evidence."

Emory shot a knowing glance in Jeff's direction. "Wayne."

"Wow. He actually listened to you. We're happy for you, Peter."

"Sold!"

Emory jumped when he heard the auctioneer's announcement. "Crap, who bought it?"

Jeff looked too but didn't see anyone moving toward the table where Darren was seated. "I don't know."

"Now on to Lot Two." The auctioneer described the property up for sale.

As soon as the bidding started, Peter West raised his hand.

"Mr. West, you're bidding on Lot Two? I thought Lot Thirteen was yours."

"Have you seen where I lived? This property has an actual house. I know it's run down, but I can fix it up." He raised his hand again following someone's else bid.

Jeff elbowed him. "Where's your family?"

"I left them at the motel. I have enough to deal with today." Peter threw his hand up again. "Who keeps bidding against me?"

Jeff and Emory both turned their attention toward the middle of the crowd, where a hairless arm dropped to the side of a long-haired man wearing a sleeveless, quilted vest. The PIs faced each other. "Randy Graham."

Emory led Jeff through the crowd to the holistic counselor. "Mr. Graham."

With a slight jump at the sound of his name, Randy frowned when he saw its caller. "Are you following me now? I'm all out of helpful information."

"We're surprised to see you here," said Jeff.

Randy raised his hand after Peter upped the bid. "When I heard you talking on the phone about the auction, I asked Becky about the property, and I decided to check it out."

"Actually, I'm glad you're here. You told me Corey had become paranoid, that he was being watched. Did he mention when it all started?"

Randy thought for a moment before answering. "He had said something about someone threatening him at work, but he wouldn't elaborate. I pushed him on it, but anything work-related, he treated it like it was confidential – even to me."

Jeff gave a knowing look to Emory. "That's okay. I think I know what the threat was."

"By the way. If you're here to bid on anything, you might as well leave now." Randy smirked at them. "I'm going to buy them all."

Emory asked, "Why?"

"I want to create a holistic retreat, a place where people can come and stay for a week or two and truly get in touch with their inner beings." He raised his hand again. "I'm going to build cabins, sweat lodges, vegan restaurants—"

Jeff cut him off. "We get the picture. So I guess that noble stance against your parents' money has taken a back seat to your ambition."

Randy sneered and raised his hand again. "I have my own money."

Seeing the confusion on Emory's face, Jeff clarified. "His parents are loaded. Tobacco money."

Emory led Jeff out of Randy's hearing range. "But he said it's his own money."

"He's lying again."

"Or maybe Becky is giving him some of Corey's life insurance money as payment for killing him."

"They are sleeping together."

"Sold!" declared the auctioneer.

While Randy clenched his fist in victory, Peter could be heard shouting a profanity. Over scattered laughter, the auctioneer continued. "Moving on. Lot Three."

As Randy raised his hand, Emory said, "Okay, this is bad. If he's planning on buying everything and has the money to back it up, Ms. Mary Belle will never get her property back."

"What can we do about it?"

Emory rubbed the back of his neck. "I don't know."

"Well, we have nine lots to figure it out."

CHAPTER 37

EMORY STOOD ON his toes to look over the heads of the auction attendees. "We need to find Luke."

Jeff followed Emory as he searched for Ms. Mary Belle's nephew. "What does he look like?"

"Tall. Blond. About our age..." Emory stopped with the descriptors as soon as he spotted the subject. "There he is." The PI approached him and shook his hand. "Luke, it's good to see you."

"You too."

Emory nodded toward Jeff. "This is my partner, Jeff Woodard."

When Jeff faced him for the first time, he couldn't hide his surprise. "You're Luke?"

"Yeah. Why?"

"After meeting your aunt, you're just not what I expected."

Luke laughed. "She definitely has her own way about her. Thank god, it's not hereditary."

Jeff told him, "It's nice of you to try getting her property back for her."

Luke shrugged. "That's assuming she's well enough to leave the hospital."

"She's in the hospital?" Emory asked.

"They called me as I was leaving to come here. Said she had another attack."

Emory gasped. "Oh no!"

"I'm going to stop by after I'm done here. Hopefully, I'll have some good news for her."

Emory frowned at him. "I'm afraid we have more bad news."

"What is it?"

"Someone's here to bid on all the properties, and apparently he's got the money to outbid everyone."

"Shit!" snarled Luke. "Dude, I only have a little bit more money than the TVA paid her to begin with. Who is it? Do you know him?"

Emory said that he did. "His name is Randy Graham. He owns a holistic center, and he wants to build a retreat area here."

Luke's face reddened, and he clenched his fists. "This sucks!"

Jeff placed a hand on his shoulder. "We'll get him out of the running before it gets to her property."

"How?"

"We don't know yet, but we'll figure something out." Jeff grabbed Emory's arm to lead him away, telling Luke, "As a matter of fact, I just came up with an idea. Hang in there. We'll be back."

Emory waited until they were out of Luke's earshot before inquiring about his plan. "What's your idea?"

"I don't know. I just said that to make him feel better."

"That's just going to make matters worse when he finds out we have nothing."

"Maybe we can get Randy disqualified."

"It's not a pageant. As long as he has the money, he can bid."

"Let's verify that." Jeff led his partner through the crowd until they reached the TVA's director of generation resources.

"Sold!" the auctioneer once again declared.

Darren had lost his companion and was now focused on the auction. Jeff caught his attention, saying, "There's someone here intent on buying all the properties."

"So I've noticed," grumbled Darren through grim lips.

"Well, is there a limit to how many one person can purchase?"

"No. If he can afford it, he can buy as many as he wants."

Emory followed Jeff's lead. "Aren't you taking a big chance letting one person scoop them all up? How can you know that he actually has the finances to afford it?"

Darren shook his head. "If he doesn't have the money, he's still liable for the cost. One way or another, we'll get paid."

Jeff stepped away with his partner. "We have to think of something else."

Emory sighed. "I have an idea, but Wayne might throw me in jail if I do it."

"What is it?"

"I could finger Randy as the killer."

"Oh, that's evil. Let's do it!"

"It would just be temporary. After the auction, I'll tell him I was mistaken, and he'll let him go."

"Sold!"

Jeff glanced at the auctioneer. "We have to hurry."

Emory walked away from the noise so he could call Wayne. When he returned, he found Jeff lurking behind Randy Graham. Realizing they didn't have a shot, many of the potential bidders had left, so the crowd had dwindled to more of a small gathering. Luke lingered, but his expression had morphed from one of hope to one of dejection. Peter West stomped the ground in a pace as he realized his chances for reclaiming his home were drifting into fantasy.

Jeff spotted his partner returning. "That didn't take long. What did he say?"

"He didn't buy it. What number are we on?"

"Lot Seven."

Emory let a rare expletive slip out. "Shit!"

"Hardly anyone is bidding now." Jeff spotted a black object in Randy's vest pocket. "I have an idea!" He stepped in front of Randy to snap a quick photo with his phone. "Smile."

Randy covered his face too late. "What are you doing?"

Jeff pointed over his shoulder. "I think someone's outbidding you."

"Going once…" The auctioneer eyed Randy to see if he would increase the bid.

Randy raised his hand, while Jeff returned to Emory and cropped the picture around the face so the location could not be discerned.

"What was that all about?"

"No time to explain. Just trust me. What's your dad's number?"

Emory gave him the number, and Jeff walked away. He reached the outskirts of the crowd and was about to make a phone call when he noticed the sheriff a few feet away, talking to an elderly woman.

The sheriff removed his hat to talk to her. "Yes ma'am, it's been a hectic first week for me. Makes me thankful for quiet days like today."

"I was so sorry to hear about your predecessor. Do they know what killed him?"

"Heart attack."

"Such a tragedy." The woman bowed her head in respect.

Jeff continued walking until he was behind the posters before he made his call. He returned to Emory's side just as the auctioneer declared, "Sold!" on Lot Eleven.

Emory waited a few seconds for an explanation. "Well?"

Jeff looked at the sheriff, who was now on the phone. "Watch."

The sheriff moved the phone from his face to look at it, and he scanned those still in attendance. He said something more on the phone before pocketing it. The sheriff gripped the handle of his pistol without drawing it and made a beeline for his target. "Randy Graham?"

Randy turned a puzzled face to the sheriff. "Yes."

"You're under arrest for suspected burglary in Barter Ridge. The sheriff there has asked that you be remanded into his custody."

"This is ridiculous! I don't even know where Barter Ridge is!"

Emory whispered to Jeff, "How on Earth did you get Dad to agree to this?"

"I just told him the truth, basically. That if we couldn't stop this guy, a little old lady was going to be kicked out of her home and that we were out of options."

"Place your hands behind your back."

"But I'm not done here."

Darren came over to investigate the commotion. "What's going on here?"

"This man is under arrest for robbery, and I'm taking him in."

Darren stepped in front of Randy. "So you don't have the money to purchase the lots you've bid on?"

"I do! I swear it! I'm rich! This is a mistake!"

Darren wasn't convinced, but he fought to keep the sales. "Sheriff, you have to let him sign for the lots he's purchased. Please."

The sheriff hesitated. "Fine. Mr. Graham, you can put your hands in front so you can use a pen."

Randy held his hands in front for the sheriff to handcuff him. "And let me bid on the remaining two properties."

"Don't push it." The sheriff led him to the table to sign, and the auction continued.

"Lot Twelve," the auctioneer called.

Luke Hinter raised his hand to bid. One other person bid against him, but once the gavel dropped, Luke was victorious. He jumped with a celebratory fist. "Thank you guys so much for your help."

Jeff shook his hand. "We're glad it worked out."

Luke shook Emory's hand. "I have to take care of all the paperwork, and then I really need to catch up on some work. Would you mind checking on Aunt Mary Belle?"

"Not at all. We'll let you know how she's doing."

"Thanks man." Luke headed for the table. "I really appreciate all you've done."

The auctioneer held up the last property description. "The final lot!"

Peter West appeared relieved that his competition had been taken out, and he threw his hand up as soon as the bidding on his former home had begun. However, he would not be unopposed. Darren left the table to join in.

Back and forth the two went until Peter had bid five thousand more than he had been paid for the property. Darren hesitated before he lifted his hand once more. Peter dropped his head as the auctioneer asked for any other bids.

"Sold!" the man on the stage shouted. "Ladies and gentlemen, that does it for today's sale. Thank you all for participating."

Peter West tramped over to Darren Gleeson and punched him in the face.

CHAPTER 38

WHEN THE PIS stepped out of the hospital elevator, Jeff nodded to a directional sign. "What's her room number again?"

Emory checked his phone. "Five forty-three."

Jeff pointed to the right. "This way."

As they walked down the white hallway, Emory saw a familiar face loitering outside one of the rooms. "Isn't that Fred Leakey?"

"Who?"

"The guy from the surveying company who gave us the information on—"

"Oh yeah, yeah. That's him."

Emory waved to him. "Mr Leakey. Do you remember us?"

Fred looked up from his phone and took a second to recall them. "You're the guys who came into the office asking about Clayton."

Perhaps seeking some nominal compensation, Jeff added a clarification. "And we're the ones who found him."

"Has he said anything about what happened to him?"

"He's been in a coma since he was brought in."

"Is he going to be okay?"

"The doctor said he has a concussion, two broken ribs and a fractured ankle. He doesn't think there's any brain damage, so he could make a full recovery."

Jeff patted him on the shoulder. "That's good to hear."

"Mr. Leakey, about the survey report Clayton was going to file, did you find it?"

As his phone rang, Fred rushed his response, "We haven't recovered his laptop. It wasn't in his truck. Excuse me." He answered the phone and walked a few feet away.

Emory turned to Jeff. "Do you think someone pushed him into that hole so they could take the laptop?"

"Maybe. But why?"

"I really want to know what's in that report."

Jeff nodded toward Fred Leakey. "I don't think he's going anywhere for a while. Let's go see the old lady."

Emory nodded. "But don't tell her about the auction. That's Luke's news to share."

The two headed toward Ms. Mary Belle's room, and they found her looking well in spite of being laid up with an IV in her arm. Emory called to her. "Ms. Mary Belle."

She turned her attention from the TV to the young men and greeted them with a relieved smile. "Sweet sassafras, wasn't 'spectin' ta see y'all. Come ta sprin' me?"

"No, we just came to check on you."

"Ain't no need for that. I'm fine. Just wanna go home. Did m' nephew get back m' prop'ty?"

Jeff answered for Emory. "We don't know. Luke just left us a message asking us to check on you until he could get here himself."

She pointed at his chest. "Where's that charm I give you?"

Jeff reached into the neck of his shirt and pulled out the rock that hung by a thin leather strap. "I have it right here."

Emory shot Jeff a curious look, to which he responded with a shrug.

"It workin' yet?"

Jeff chuckled. "Too soon to tell."

"Give it time."

Jeff's phone rang. "It's Virginia." He exited the room, leaving his partner alone with the witch.

"Ms. Mary Belle, I need to tell you something." Emory took a deep breath, unsure how to proceed. "We found something on your neighbor's property, where your Specter used to live."

"What was it?"

"In the ground holler, we found... remains."

"Remains of what?"

"A body." Emory waited for a response, but the words didn't seem to register with her. "The medical examiner confirmed it was a teenage woman and estimated she died fifty to sixty years ago. Ms. Mary Belle, I think we found your Specter."

Sudden understanding swept across her face, releasing a squall of emotions from within the withered woman. She wailed as tears deluged her face like a summer flood. Emory sat on the edge of the bed, and for what seemed like several minutes, he held her hand as she mourned the loss of her life's only love. "I knowed it. I knowed he kilt her."

"I'm so sorry."

Ms. Mary Belle pulled her sheet up to wipe her eyes. "Maybe she can rest now." She patted Emory's hand. "I need ta rest."

Is she saying she doesn't want to live anymore? "What do you mean?"

"I'm tired. I need ta sleep."

"Okay." Emory got up from the bed. "If you need anything, just give me a call."

The old woman closed her eyes without another word.

Out in the hallway, Jeff was glued to his phone. "That's it!" He looked up when he heard Emory step out of Ms. Mary Belle's room. "What was all that commotion in there?"

"I told her about the body we found."

"Are you sure you should've done that?"

"She had a right to know." Emory touched the charm hanging from Jeff's neck. "You didn't tell me she gave you this."

Jeff frowned at him. "She didn't give it to me. She charged me ten bucks."

"You paid ten bucks for a piece of gravel?"

"I know. I'm a softie."

"What did Virginia want?"

"She said she can't get into the FAA's database to search for drone registries, and they're closed on Saturdays so she can't call to make an inquiry."

"So we have to wait until Monday."

"Actually, she thinks she might be able to track purchases if I can find exactly the model I saw, which I just did." He held up his phone so Emory could see the picture on the website.

"Huh. It doesn't even look like it could fly."

Jeff scrolled down the page to show him another picture. "And it comes with this cool carrying case."

Emory glanced at the image of the silver metallic case on wheels. "That looks like a suitcase." He tilted his head. "I think I've seen something like this before."

"Where?"

"I don't remember."

"Before I forget," Jeff said as he pulled another cell phone from his pants pocket. "You left your phone in the office this morning."

"I did?" Taking possession, Emory told him, "We need to catch Fred Leakey before he leaves." They headed back toward Clayton's room and found Fred sitting in a chair by the bed. Although Clayton was in a coma, Emory whispered, "Mr. Leakey, I'm sorry to bother you again, but could we ask you one more question?"

"Sure," Fred answered in a normal voice. "By the way, you don't have to whisper. We actually want him to wake up."

"Right. We were thinking that maybe Clayton had the laptop

with him when he fell into the sinkhole. Has anyone looked down there?"

Fred shook his head. "No, and it's little late now. As of today's auction, that property no longer belongs to the TVA, so we'd need the new owner's permission. And, by the way, it's not really a sinkhole. It's an abandoned zinc mine from a vein that dried up about a hundred years ago."

"Zinc?"

"You mean like in vitamins?" Jeff asked.

"Technically. But more like the zinc used in galvanizing iron or steel and in manufacturing things like batteries, pennies—"

Jeff interrupted him. "Ah, boring stuff."

Fred laughed. "I guess if you consider money boring. Zinc mines all over the world are drying up. They mined about a half million metric tons out of that old vein before it dried up. At the current rate, that would've fetched about $1.5 billion."

Jeff cupped one of his ears. "Did I hear that right? Billion?"

Fred pointed to his charm. "You have some hanging from your neck there."

"This?" Jeff grabbed the rock to inspect it.

Emory gasped. "Oh my god. There's a second vein!"

CHAPTER 39

MONDAY, JUST BEFORE noon, Emory stood in Frank Belcher's office, chatting with him about the auction, when Randy Graham walked in. He all but ignored Emory as he focused on Frank. "I'm here to pick up my deeds."

"Oh yes." Frank glanced at the wall clock above Emory's head. "It's about that time. My boss is finishing them up and will be here in a minute. Please have a seat."

Randy complied and eyed Emory. "I know you had something to do with that fiasco on Saturday."

Emory's eyes widened. "I assure you I didn't. What happened after you left?"

"The damn sheriff had just pulled onto the interstate when the sheriff who made the complaint called him to say it was a mistake. Damn idiots!"

"You only missed out on two properties. Don't you have enough land for your retreat?"

"It just won't be as big as I wanted."

Luke Hinter knocked on the office door and entered. "Today's the big day."

Frank acknowledged him with a slight tip of his head. "Good to see you again, Mr. Hinter."

Emory pointed to them both. "You two have met before?"

"When I found I had to take care of my aunt, I came to see him to ask if there was any way to get her house back."

Frank chimed in, "Actually, he had come to see Corey, but he hadn't started work yet that morning. I told him not to get mad at me. I would've chosen a different site. Mr. Hinter, I'm glad it worked out for you and your aunt."

All eyes turned to the door as Darren entered holding twelve manila envelopes, a clipboard and several sets of house keys. "Hi gentlemen. I have your deeds, notarized and recorded, and I have keys for the properties with homes." He split the deeds and keys between the two buyers. "Eleven deeds and four keys for Mr. Randy Graham, and one of each for Ms. Mary Belle Hinter and Mr. Luke Hinter."

"The deed's in both your names?" asked Emory.

Frank answered his ringing office phone, while Luke answered Emory. "My lawyer suggested it. I'm her only living relative, so it'll keep me from having to pay inheritance tax when she dies."

"Smart thinking. I just need you guys to sign another document, and you can be on your way." Darren pulled some papers from his clipboard and set them on the desk for Randy and Luke to sign.

Frank pulled the phone from his ear. "Emory, it's your partner. He says your phone is going straight to voicemail."

Emory pulled out his cell phone and checked it. "Damn, I forgot to charge it last night. It's dead." With everyone crowded around the desk, he asked Frank to put the call on speakerphone.

From outside somewhere, Jeff's voice came through the speaker. "Emory, I just talked to Becky, and she made me realize there's something the police and TBI overlooked."

Emory spoke loud enough for everyone in the room to hear him. "What could that be?"

"Corey's cell phone. It was never found. Becky said that Corey was in the habit of recording himself as he meditated and then he would play it back before going to sleep. She found an audio file from that day on their shared cloud, but it didn't fully upload, so she couldn't play it."

"You think he recorded his murder?"

"Only one way to find out. Find the phone."

Emory stepped closer to the phone so he didn't have to raise his voice. "It's got to be on the roof of this building."

"That's what I was thinking."

"Can you go look?"

"Not right now."

"But you're in the building."

"I'm already late for my meeting with the TBI."

Jeff whispered over the phone, although everyone in the room with Emory could hear. "Whatever you do, don't tell the TBI about the phone. I want us to find it. I'm heading over there now to look for it."

"Talk to you later." Emory nodded to Frank. "You can hang up. Thank you for your time." With that, he left the office and headed to the roof to await Corey Melton's killer.

CHAPTER 40

KILLING TIME, EMORY counted the seconds it took each of his visible breaths to dissipate as he waited on the roof of the Godfrey Tower for the murderer to arrive. Anticipation stilled the air, although he could almost hear the blood pulsing from his anxious heart. A sudden gust of wind preceded clanging. He looked up to see the flagpole had been repaired, and the Stars and Stripes now waved at him from forty feet above. Behind it along one edge of the roof rose the billboard, still emblazoned with the advertisement for Mourning Dove Investigations.

He heard the door to the roof creak open. He watched as the killer soft-shoed it to the flagpole – the place where Corey had been thrown from the roof.

Emory stepped from behind the ventilation system and held up a cell phone. "Is this what you're looking for?"

The killer jumped when he heard his voice. "Emory. I was just coming up for some fresh air."

"We know it was you, Luke."

Luke Hinter squinted and smiled at him. "What are you talking about?"

"When the sheriff called you to pick up your aunt, you said it was the first time you stepped foot in Brume Wood since you were a toddler. You must've seen her collection of charms." Emory was now wearing the charm necklace Ms. Mary Belle had given Jeff, and he held up the rock for Luke to see.

"What about it? It's gravel."

Emory let the rock drop back to his chest. "But you know it's not just gravel. You told me yourself you started out as a geology major before your parents made you switch to finance."

Luke laughed. "I took a few classes like five years ago. I don't remember any of that."

"I might've believed you didn't recognize them as zinc ore if I hadn't seen you toting the shiny new silver case behind you that day. You said it was your aunt's, but I've seen her belongings. She doesn't own anything from the past three decades."

"I bought her that suitcase to put her stuff in."

"But it wasn't a suitcase. It was a carrying case for your drone."

Luke pulled a knife from his pocket. "I'm going to need that phone."

"A switchblade?" Jeff appeared above them, standing on the ventilation system and aiming his blue-barreled PD10 handgun at the knife-wielder. "Seriously? Who carries around a switchblade?"

Luke pointed the knife at Jeff, although the roof of the ventilation system was seven feet above where he stood. "Always be prepared."

"So Boy Scouts." Jeff nodded at Emory, who pocketed the phone and pulled out his pistol. "Actually, I owe you a beatdown for loosening the lug nuts on my tires." He holstered his gun and headed for the ladder attached to the wall of the ventilation system.

Emory said, "He also loosened Becky's tire when he was trying to convince Corey to change his mind about which property to take."

"He should've heeded the warning. Luckily for his replacement, his wife's a greedy bitch."

Jeff stepped onto the ventilation system's ladder. "So you did pay Lettie to make her husband switch properties."

Luke threw his knife into the shoulder of Emory's gun-toting arm.

"Ahhh!" Emory dropped the gun and threw his other hand to his shoulder, clenching it around the knife's hilt.

Luke grabbed Emory's gun as soon as it hit the ground.

"Emory!" Jeff jumped from the ladder and rushed to his partner's aid.

Luke aimed the gun at Jeff, stopping him a few feet from Emory. "Back up! Now!"

Jeff complied, while Emory pulled the knife from his shoulder and let it clunk to the floor.

"Take your gun out. Slowly. And slide it to me."

Again Jeff complied.

Luke picked up Jeff's gun and pushed it inside his belt. "No one was supposed to investigate Corey's death. It should've looked like a suicide. He was so light. I couldn't believe how far out he flew. I didn't see the rope from the flagpole he'd wrapped around his wrist. I knew that was going to be a problem." Luke pulled a chicken-bone doll from his jacket and leaned it against the flagpole.

Emory told him, "I know you wanted to give credence to your aunt's curses, but those are actually for good luck."

Luke shrugged. "No matter. They fed the fear."

Jeff glanced at the blood coursing down Emory's right sleeve before setting his eyes on Luke. "What do you plan to do now? You can't make this look like an accident."

"I don't intend to. I have both your guns. You two came up here to investigate the case, and you got into a spat. Things elevated, and you shot each other."

Jeff laughed. "No one's going to believe that!"

Luke responded, "I saw you two together the other night." He nodded to Emory. "You were wearing a cowboy hat."

"That was in my apartment. How did you see that?" Right

after Emory asked the question, the answer hit him. "You were watching us with the drone."

"Domestic disputes are always the deadliest." Luke pointed Emory's gun at its owner. "Now give me the phone."

Emory retrieved the phone from his pocket as Luke extended his free hand to receive it. Instead, Emory tossed it to Jeff.

As soon as Luke turned his eyes to Jeff, Emory lunged for him, pushing him back against the railing along the edge of the roof. The PI banged his wrist against the railing until the gun fell to the sidewalk thirty-two stories below.

Jeff ran to tackle Luke just as the killer punched Emory in his injured shoulder. Emory grabbed at the pain, allowing Luke to jump away from the railing. Jeff hit the railing full force, almost falling over it.

Luke kicked Emory in the mouth, causing his back to slam into the flagpole. He grabbed the lapels of Emory's jacket and flung him toward the edge.

Emory reached for the flagpole to try regaining his balance, but it wasn't enough. His fingers could only lock around the flagpole rope as momentum carried him to the very edge and over.

"No!!" Jeff screamed.

The flagpole rope was in one continuous loop all the way to the top of the flagpole and down, with several feet of slack at the bottom. Now clinging to the bottom loop of the rope with both hands, Emory looked up to see Jeff's head and right arm protruding from the edge of the rooftop.

"Emory! Grab my hand!"

Emory stretched for his partner's hand. Their fingers touched just before the rope slipped and the dangling PI fell beyond reach.

"Emory!" Jeff looked over his shoulder and saw Luke cutting the rope at the flagpole with his bloody switchblade. The frayed section of the rope had snapped, changing the loop into one long line of rope. The snaphooks that secured the flag caught in the metal pulley at the top of the flagpole, anchoring one end of the rope, but the other end was now loose, and Emory was sliding down to meet it.

Emory's hand had been locked into the bottom of the rope loop, but with the loop now broken, he had only his grip on the rope to keep him from plunging to the sidewalk below. His hold on the thin line, however, was not enough to keep him in place. The rope burned the palms of his hands as he continued to slide down the extra forty feet of rope that had snaked over the edge of the roof.

With ten feet remaining before he would slide to the end of the rope, Emory stopped his downward slide. It took every ounce of strength in his hands and forearms to maintain his grip, but he knew holding on would not be good enough. He would have to climb.

Watching from above, Jeff sighed a bit of relief when he saw Emory holding steady. He pushed back from the railing to see Luke about to cut the rest of the rope. Jeff held the phone up. "Luke! Back away, and I'll give you the phone."

Luke released the rope and took two steps back. Instead of handing him the phone, Jeff threw it up to the billboard. It hit Emory's picture before coming to rest on the narrow catwalk in front of the sign.

Luke pocketed the knife and bolted for the catwalk ladder, which ran up alongside the middle post of the billboard.

Emory started climbing the rope to get back on the roof. When he lifted the soles of his shoes to glass, however, he realized it wasn't glass at all. It was plywood. *This is where Corey Melton crashed through the window and died. They haven't replaced the glass!*

Sure enough, there was glass all around except for the square of wood on which his feet now rested. *I might be able to break through the wood!*

Emory held the rope with one hand so he could wrap it around his other wrist to provide some stability. He jumped off the wood, sending his body swinging out two feet from the building like a narrow pendulum. When he started swinging back to the building, he put his feet together to concentrate the force. The wood shuddered when he hit it, but it didn't break.

This isn't going to work unless I hit it with more force. Emory kicked off the wood with greater strength, but the wood still didn't break when he swung back.

Emory was sweating nonstop now, including his palms. He tightened his aching hands. *I've got to go for it!*

He kicked off with all his strength, and he flew almost ten feet from the building. When he swung back, he clenched his entire body to make himself the stiffest projectile possible. His feet rammed through the wood, splintering a big enough hole for him to fly through. His body slammed to the office floor, just shy of where Corey had landed a week earlier.

The office employees flocked around him. Some screamed while others asked, "Is he dead?"

Jeff rushed to rescue his partner, but no one was hanging from the rope. "Emory! Where are you?!" Even though he couldn't see a body on the sidewalk below, he knew Emory must've fallen.

As tears blurred his eyes, he clenched his fists and screamed at Luke, who was now scurrying along the catwalk in front of the billboard, "I'm going to kill you!"

Jeff darted for the ladder to the billboard catwalk and grabbed the bottom rung with a single leap. As he climbed, he looked above and below and realized one end of the billboard protruded over the side of the building. He crawled onto the catwalk just as Luke picked up the cell phone and pocketed it.

Jeff ran and punched him, sending him flying backwards onto the catwalk. He jumped onto Luke's torso and punched him over and over again.

Luke reached into his pocket to retrieve his switchblade, and he sliced Jeff's forearm.

Jeff retreated a few steps as Luke climbed back to his feet. "You're wasting your time, Luke. That's Emory's cell phone. There was no recording."

"I don't believe you." Luke tossed the phone over the side of the catwalk and didn't watch as it plummeted to the sidewalk. He plodded toward Jeff, slicing the air with each step.

Jeff backed up until he couldn't back up anymore. He glanced down. Between the grates of the metal catwalk, he could see the sidewalk thirty-two stories below.

Luke grinned at his cornered prey. He held the knife over his head and lunged for Jeff.

Jeff ducked, and the blade stabbed the billboard – right into Emory's torso in the picture. Luke lost his footing and slipped off the catwalk. His grip on the knife's hilt was the only thing keeping him from falling to his death.

Jeff hesitated before reaching for him. "Give me your hand!"

Luke held up his free hand. The knife in his other hand slipped and continued cutting a path down the billboard. The knife's downward slicing stopped for a second when it hit the metal frame until the blade dislodged altogether.

Helpless, Jeff watched while Luke flailed at the air before thudding against the sidewalk.

Emory had slammed open the door to the roof just in time to see Luke's plunge.

CHAPTER 41

HALF AN HOUR after Luke's death, EMTs bandaged Emory's hands and shoulder and Jeff's forearms while the PIs talked to Virginia on the roof of the Godfrey Tower. Police cataloged the scene – there and on the street below. Virginia put a consoling arm around her shivering friend. "Jeff, are you sure you're all right? It's okay not to be."

Jeff stared at the roof. "I tried to keep him from falling."

"I believe you." Emory winced when the EMT applied an ointment to his left hand. "I know whatever you did was in self-defense."

"Did you see it?"

Emory shook his head. "I opened the door just in time to see him fall."

Chin trembling, Jeff caressed Emory's cheek. "I thought he killed you."

"I thought he did too."

"You know, just once I'd love to solve a case without putting any of our lives in danger." He glanced up at the ruined ad. "Looks like he did kill your picture. Hey, your phone."

"What about it?"

"Luke dropped it before he fell. There's no way it survived a fall from thirty-two stories."

Emory frowned at him. "I don't care about the damn phone right now."

"No, it was your effigy. Remember Saturday, when I handed you your phone."

"Because I left it in the office."

"I actually lifted it from you and took it to Miss Luann, that clairvoyant down the street. She did the transference spell for me. The phone is destroyed, so now your curse is broken."

Emory grinned. "I appreciate the effort, but I had actually stopped worrying about that."

"What changed your mind?"

"It was that sheriff at the auction. The Crick Witch cursed him, and he's fine."

Jeff flashed to the conversation he overheard at the auction between the new sheriff and the elderly woman. *I'm not going to tell him that sheriff she cursed actually did die.*

With his partner at his side, Wayne arrived at the scene. "I'm glad you find a man's death so funny, Emory."

The PI dropped the grin from his face. "I wasn't smiling about that."

"I don't care. Just tell me what happened."

The PIs recounted the events that led to Luke Hinter's death, and Jeff ended with his blow-by-blow of the fight.

At the end, Steve Linders spoke up. "What made you suspect Luke killed Mr. Melton?"

"We knew the killer was using a drone to gather information on Corey and his other victims – the Belchers, me, Emory, Virginia, that surveyor."

Virginia clutched her chest. "Me?"

Jeff answered for him. "We're pretty sure he cut your rope when you discovered the surveyor. Anyway, I saw the drone first-hand, and when I found the same model online, I saw that it came with a metal carrying case." Jeff nodded in deference to his partner.

"Jeff showed me the case, and I realized I had seen it before. When I first met Luke, he was rolling a case that looked just like it."

Wayne scoffed at the connection. "That's not proof."

"I agree, but the clencher was when Fred Leakey from the survey company identified the charm Ms. Mary Belle Hinter gave to Jeff." Emory removed it from around his neck and held it up for a second before handing it back to Jeff. "He said it was zinc ore. Ms. Mary Belle Hinter's property is full of these rocks. She was sitting on a billion dollar vein of the stuff, and Luke was her only heir."

"Whoa!" Steve's eyes widened. "Billion with a 'B'?"

Jeff nodded. "That's right, and the TVA took it away from her without even knowing its value. That's why he was so determined to get it back."

Wayne waved toward the damaged billboard. "So why didn't you inform the TBI once you knew? Why the ruse?"

Emory shrugged. "We had to be sure."

When the Mourning Dove staff left the Godfrey Tower that afternoon, Emory noticed a familiar blue SUV with tinted windows parked in front. "Hey guys, I'm parked down here. I'll catch up with you tomorrow."

Virginia waved goodbye to him, but Jeff had a question to ask. "Does that mean you're coming into the office?"

"Actually, I was thinking of driving to Brume Wood in the morning to take Ms. Mary Belle home."

"I'll go with you. Swing by to pick me up?"

Emory said he would and waited for them to turn the corner before entering the back of the SUV. He greeted the head of the TBI. "Mr. Alexander."

Anderson Alexander shook his hand. "I heard what happened. Good work, Mr. Rome."

"Thank you, and I'm glad you're here. There's something I've been meaning to talk to you about."

"My job offer?"

"That too, but…" From his pocket, Emory pulled the listening device that had been planted in his apartment. "Do you have any idea why I'm being bugged?"

Anderson examined the device. "It's the brand the TBI uses, but if you believe I had you bugged, you're mistaken." He handed it back to Emory. "Ah, now I've spotted the rabbit hole of logic in which your foot is stuck. You surmised my offer was a stalling tactic while we searched for something salacious to assail your character, which would then force dismissal of the lawsuit."

Emory nodded. "In a nutshell."

Anderson placed a hand on the young man's shoulder. "Emory, my word travels the well-paved road of veracity, free from the potholes of deceit. My offer is sincere, and I do hope you accept it."

Emory could see the sincerity in his grey eyes. "I believe you, Sir."

"Good. Now do you have any idea who would want to spy on you?"

"I can't think of anyone."

"Have you considered your new partner?"

The suggestion shocked Emory. "Wha… What? No. He's a good person, which brings me to the next topic."

"You're turning me down, aren't you?"

"I am. Please, don't think me ungrateful. Your offer was exceedingly generous, and I'm probably a fool for not taking it. It's just, if I can be honest, I've been so focused in my life."

"That's what makes you a good special agent."

"I appreciate that, but it goes deeper than that." Emory's eyes dropped to his hands. "This past month has been extremely difficult for me. After I was fired, I fell to a place I hadn't been to since... I was younger."

"Son, I know what happened eight years ago."

"I figured you did." Emory nodded without looking up. "Last night I slept for seven hours. That hasn't happened since I don't know when."

Anderson raised his hands. "I'm... happy for you?"

Emory laughed. "The point is, I feel like I'm just beginning to experience who I think I would've been if that whole thing had never happened, and I don't want to stop. I want to see where it leads." He looked up, a little flushed. "I'm sorry. I didn't mean to be so... open."

"Perfectly all right, Son." Anderson patted him on the shoulder. "So do you like being a private investigator?"

"I don't know yet. Being a PI might be temporary or it might not, but it doesn't matter."

"I wish you the best in this new venture."

"Thank you, Sir. I appreciate that."

"I hate to be crass, but what about the lawsuit?"

Emory smiled at him. "I told my lawyer this morning to drop it."

"I am relieved to hear that. The TBI is a wonderful organization, and I would hate for the actions of your former boss to diminish its standing in the public eye."

"I agree."

"If you would allow me, I'd like to impart a word of advice."

"I'd welcome anything you have to say."

Anderson stared him right in the eyes. "Reconsider any plans to align yourself with Jeff Woodard. Strike out on your own. You do not want your future entwined with his."

"Why do you say that?"

Anderson produced a manila envelope. "I have information on him. He's not being completely honest with you. Read the file before making a decision you'll likely regret."

"I think I know him pretty well now. I doubt there's anything in there that could change my mind."

"Just take it home." Anderson pushed the envelope into Emory's hands. "Read it or don't. And I know I gave you a deadline, but let's just say there's an extended grace period. If you read it and change your mind, let me know."

Pinching his lips, Emory looked at the envelope in his hands.

CHAPTER 42

WITHIN MINUTES OF arriving at Willow Springs Retirement Home the next morning, Emory and Jeff delivered the news to Ms. Mary Belle of her nephew's accidental fall. (They omitted the details of Luke's crimes to preserve her memory of him.) The PIs consoled her and waited for her to come to terms with his passing before bringing up the fact that he had been successful in getting her property back.

With the help of her new friends, Ms. Mary Belle needed little time to pack her things and leave. On the way to her once and future home, she was as gabby and giddy as a schoolgirl, giving Jeff and Emory scant time to comment before she began each new story. Once the car came to a stop in front of her old house, she hopped out and told the men, "Get m' stuff inna m' house. I'm gonna see m' woods."

"Ms. Mary Belle!" Emory called. "Wait! I have something to show you."

Copper cane in hand, she didn't wait. By the time they caught up to her, she was standing in front of a gravestone just inside the woods.

Emory wrapped an arm around the woman's shoulder. "I wanted to tell you. I had your Specter buried here." He saw tears pooling in her eyes before the flood started. "Is that okay?"

Ms. Mary Belle dropped her cane and threw her arms around his waist, squeezing with all her might. "Thank you," she exhaled in between shudders of quiet wailing. When she broke from him, she wiped away her tears and knelt at the gravestone. "I got lots ta catch you up on, Specter."

Jeff picked up her cane and handed it to her, and she walked – or pranced – into the woods, talking to her Specter.

"You didn't tell her about the zinc?"

"I will. I'm just letting her get settled in." Emory gestured toward her. "I really don't think she's going to care about the money. She loves the land too much to destroy it with a mine."

"What's going to happen when she dies?"

"I doubt she has a will, so the state will get it. Hopefully, a good portion of the money will stay local. These mountain communities could use it."

Jeff sighed and kicked at the ground. "So I guess this is it."

"What do you mean?"

"The case is over. You'll be going back to the TBI."

"And here I thought you were a detective. You really do need my help."

"What are you saying?"

Emory grabbed Jeff's collar and drew him in for a kiss. When they parted, Ms. Mary Belle was standing there, staring at them. She pointed to Jeff. "I made that love charm too po'erful. You're attractin' men. Gimme it, and I'll dampen it for you."

Jeff laughed. "Don't worry about it. It's working fine."

Emory told him, "I just thought of something. We still don't know the identity of the ski mask man."

"That kiss made you think of him. You've got some hidden issues."

"No, I just don't like loose ends."

Jeff put his arm around him as he led him back to the car. "Maybe that will be our next case. Partner."

Jeff and Virginia walked down the sidewalk, leading a blindfolded Emory. "Guys, is this really necessary?"

Virginia answered him. "It's called a surprise for a reason."

Jeff positioned Emory in front of a window. "And we're here."

Emory removed the blindfold and realized they were standing outside the building attached to theirs. "Am I facing the wrong way?"

Virginia laughed, and Jeff explained it to him. "This is the surprise. We're buying this little store so you can have your own office."

Virginia patted her chest. "So I can get mine back to myself."

Jeff clutched Emory with one hand and used the other to paint an imaginary canvas. "We're going to break a hole into the wall and put a door to connect your office to Virginia's, across from the door that leads to mine."

"Plus, it has a basement," said Virginia. "We can also knock down the wall between it and the one in our building to increase our storage space."

Jeff dropped his arms. "I didn't see a basement."

"If you had taken the time to tour the place with the real estate agent—"

"I didn't need to. I trust your judgement."

Virginia turned her attention back to Emory. "Well what do you think?"

Emory was stunned and didn't know what to say at first. "I love it. I really love it."

"Excellent!" Jeff gave him a bear hug. "We'll fix it up nice like mine."

"Like yours? It's my office. I should decorate it the way I want."

Jeff dismissed the idea. "Oh no, I've seen your anti-style."

Emory suggested, "Let's put it to a vote."

"Vote? Virginia agrees with me."

They both waited for her response. "I'm going to have to side with Emory on this. It's his office."

"What?" Jeff followed the other two back to the office. "Is that how it's going to be now, the two of you ganging up on me. Virginia, you're supposed to be *my* friend."

CHAPTER 43

EMORY WALKED INTO his living room with a glass of wine in one hand and the unopened manila envelope in the other. He placed the glass on the end table, sat on the couch and opened the file. He pulled out a thin stack of documents and began reading. He had only skimmed to the middle of the first page when he gasped, "Oh my god!"

After the last business closed for the night in the Old City district of Knoxville, a rental truck pulled in front of Mourning Dove Investigations and parked. Wearing gloves, Jeff Woodard jumped from the driver seat and retrieved an empty dolly from the back.

Rolling the dolly inside Mourning Dove, he made sure the front door locked behind him before pushing it into his office. He pulled on *The Secret in the Old Attic* to open the passage behind the bookshelf near his desk. Instead of taking the spiral staircase to his second-floor apartment, he carried the dolly down the stairs that led to the basement. After the last step, he reached his free hand up to yank the pull chain of the ceiling lightbulb.

To his right, beyond a few antique chairs and tables, he saw the old leather bar from the building's speakeasy past. Behind it, on a melting wall of mirror, a sign in faded red paint proclaimed, "The Prohibition Perdition." The setting always sparked a Gatsby-esque daydream of *What if I had been born 100 years earlier?*

His eyes veered left, over the plastic bins of office records and memories from his past to the red brick wall opposite him. *That's the common wall with the new space.*

Leaving the dolly at the foot of the stairs, Jeff looked for something he could use as a shovel. He grabbed a three-hole punch from the metal office supply shelf at his left and proceeded to the wall. Each step he took puffed dust into the air, as the untended hardwood floor had long since disintegrated into the earth it had once covered. The dust trail stopped in front of several bins stacked against the wall. One at a time, he moved the bins a few feet away before dropping to his knees.

Jeff raked the dirt with the edge of the three-hole punch over and over again until it scraped against a solid wooden surface that had been buried beneath. He dug a trench to outline the wood – a rectangle about six-and-a-half feet by two feet. He dropped the three-hole punch and dusted the midsection of the wood with his palms, exposing text painted in cerulean blue:

The mourning dove flies

On the broken heart's wings.

The mourning dove cries

While the thoughtless bird sings.

And the mourning dove dies

In the fervor hate brings.

Jeff wrapped his fingers around one of the long edges of the wood and pulled open the pine coffin. He glanced at the decomposing body inside, lowered his face and sighed.

Epilogue

CURLED UP ON his couch with Bobbie nestled beside him, Jeff finished typing his case report into his laptop. When he was done, he closed the file and looked at the name of the document, which as usual, he left as a sequential case number until it was finished. He right-clicked on the file and changed the name to "Case of Death Opens a Window" before moving it to the folder named…

Case Closed

Made in the USA
Las Vegas, NV
01 August 2021

27370006R00166